Merry Christm̶a̶s̶

Love,
Aunt Gerry
1972

YOUNG YEARS

BEST LOVED STORIES AND

YOUNG

Editor
AUGUSTA BAKER
Story Telling Specialist
THE NEW YORK PUBLIC LIBRARY

Research Editors
EUGENIA GARSON
DAVID LEGERMAN

POEMS FOR LITTLE CHILDREN

YEARS

Art Editor
GEORGE GEYGAN

Executive Editor
BRADFORD CHAMBERS

Original Illustrations By

GEORGE GEYGAN
OSCAR LIEBMAN
KURT WERTH

BERNARD LIPPMAN
NICHOLAS AMOROSI
WILLIAM FRACCIO

Published by
PARENTS' MAGAZINE
PRESS
A division of
Parents' Magazine Enterprises, Inc.
New York, N. Y.

1971 Edition

Library of Congress Catalog Card No. 60–6299

Standard Book Number: 8193-0356-9

Manufactured in the United States of America

CONTENTS

NURSERY RHYMES

NURSERY STORIES

FABLES

FAIRY TALES

POETRY

Preface for Parents

All parents want to give their children the best of themselves, and their hopes for their children are the highest. They want them to grow fully and to have a rich, abundant life, and a good part of this stems from the family's relationships. There is a desire to do things together, and family reading is one way of satisfying this desire.

Accordingly, a family shares books at the earliest age of the first child. Parents who love books and who have shared their reading with each other will find themselves unconsciously speaking poetry and nursery rhymes, singing nursery songs to the small person who lies in his crib and listens. The child who has heard the songs from Walter Crane's *The Baby's Opera* is well prepared later for his pictures and for those of Kate Greenaway and Randolph Caldecott. The foundation is being made for this child's lifetime reading habits and tastes, and so it goes without saying that only the best is good enough for him.

Good taste can be developed, and so the standards for children's books must be high. A story or book must wear well artistically, and it is better to have a few of these outstanding books than many of the more modern yet mediocre titles conceived for the child. Give him the book that has been written with skill and a respect for words and style. All children read some books of doubtful merit, but the child with a good literary background can shed the ordinary and absorb the outstanding.

Sharing books should be a spontaneous, joyous activity and should be fun for both parents and children. It should not be a solemn duty motivated by a grim determination to make the child a little literary genius. There should be the contagion of real enthusiasm for reading so that the smallest child catches it from the lilt in the voice, and the reading child listens for the words, "This looks like a good book to read," or "Why don't you read this book and tell me whether or not you like it?" Bedtime is

always a good time for the "reading period," but other times can be just as suitable. Mary Ellen Chase writes about the "reading periods" of her childhood held in the kitchen of the old Maine farmhouse. It had a large, sunny kitchen with red geraniums on its windows and a large black wood stove known as "The Rising Sun," the name in raised iron letters across the oven door. In *Recipe for a Magic Childhood*, Miss Chase writes, "My mother usually somehow managed, at eleven, to sit down for half an hour in the red rocking-chair by the window. She called this half hour her "respite," a word which early charmed me; and on days when no drafts were blowing across the floor (for even The Rising Sun was not always victorious over the worst of Maine weather) she would help us down from our Parnassus [the old secretary] and allow us to sit upon our red stools while, our cookies and milk consumed, she herself would read aloud to us. Here was the very doorsill to complete enchantment, for she was seemingly as lost as we in whatever she was reading. . . . There was always the excitement of our father's coming home at noon. . . . He was always interested, as he lifted us down from the secretary, in what we had been reading; and . . . he would sometimes promise to go on that evening with an especial book, reading to us himself by the living-room fire while my mother, as avid a listener as we, would darn the countless socks and patch the red flannel underwear."

The exposure of a child to fine art and beauty cannot begin too early. It need not be presented stuffily as a lesson in art appreciation, but it can come about naturally through the child's handling of good picture books. These are the pictures that show both the familiar and the unfamiliar with beauty, humor, and vitality so that a child's sense of visual beauty is cultivated. Great care and thought have gone into the choice of illustrations for *Young Years*, so that Randolph Caldecott, Walter Crane, Leslie Brooke, Kate Greenaway, Beatrix Potter, Gustave Doré, Edward

Lear, Sir John Tenniel, and other more modern artists have been brought together in this one volume for sampling by the children. No small child should be deprived of his association with these great artists, and he will visit them many times as he handles the book himself. There are words to go along with the pictures, and they require a freshness and rhythm which makes their reading a listening delight. Parents should make every effort to read beautifully and to sing as sweetly as possible, for there is no better way of teaching the child who is learning to speak that words are musical. The child who is read to quickly understands the meaning and use of unfamiliar words. He shows a lively interest in these new words, enjoying the "feel" and sound of them as he repeats them over and over again. This is the beginning of interest and pleasure in language, and it leads to a discriminating and accurate use of it.

In the beginning, one reads and recites the familiar—the rhymes and jingles of Mother Goose, old nursery rhymes and songs, for they are the natural heritage of the young. With every reading these old verses gain new vitality, and there is no need to change one word. For over two hundred years small children have chanted:

> "Baa, Baa, black sheep,
> Have you any wool?
> Yes, sir, yes, sir,
> Three bags full;
> One for the master,
> And one for the dame,
> And one for the little boy
> Who lives down the lane."

No one really knows who Mother Goose was or where the legend about her originated. The first book expressly made for children which contained traditional rhymes appeared in England in the early eighteenth century, and was called *A Little Book for Little Children.* Then followed *Tom Thumb's Pretty Song Book,* in two

volumes, and *Mother Goose's Melody or Sonnets for the Cradle*.
John Newbery is credited with being the publisher of the latter
book and the first to use the name Mother Goose in connection
with rhymes. Boston children hear about Dame Goose, and legend
has it that she sang nursery rhymes to her grandchildren, and her
son-in-law, Thomas Fleet, published them (1719) in a little book,
Songs for the Nursery; or Mother Goose's Melodies. Unfortunately, no copy of this edition has ever been found to prove the
truth of this legend. There is such a variety of subject matter and
mood that the child is captivated by the fresh ideas. The rhythm
and rhyme make him say, "Sing it again." He rocks his body, claps
his hands, and taps his feet as Mother says,

> *"Hey! diddle, diddle,*
> *The cat and the fiddle,*
> *The cow jumped over the moon."*

The two-year-old develops his vocabulary as he repeats the rhymes,
for they are simple to learn. Still another quality of these verses is
their action. Mother Goose rides on her gander, Little Boy Blue
blows his horn, and Humpty Dumpty falls down. The gay good
humor of these verses sows the seed for the child's future sense
of humor, a quality which the world truly needs.

The child moves from nursery rhymes to simple stories, but
the quality of writing should still be high. In the eighteenth century, children read Isaac Watts' *Divine and Moral Songs for Children*. It was his intention to give children pleasure while making
them aware of moral truths. This little guide to good moral con-
duct and other similar books were the main reading fare for English children; and then, one day, they received the first translation
of the folk tales written by Charles Perrault. They were called
Histoires ou Contes du temps passé, or, more familiarly, *Contes
de ma Mère l'Oye* (Tales of Mother Goose). English children met
Sleeping Beauty, Little Red Riding-Hood, and Cinderella. Today

these are still favorite characters, but other simple stories have joined them in the nursery. Peter Rabbit and Jemima Puddleduck are characters in Beatrix Potter's miniature stories in which the animals are dressed in old-world costumes even while they retain all of the characteristics of small animals. Her stories and pictures are perfect in every detail. These simple nursery tales have a true theme which is developed through action and a recognizable plot and a combination of the familiar and imaginative, which gives the child a sense of extension beyond his own limited environment.

Folk and Fairy tales have been included in *Young Years*. These tales are man's heritage, and they must be kept alive. Like the nursery rhymes, they are part of that great body of literature, anonymously created, known as folklore. It reveals man's efforts to explain and deal with the strange phenomena of nature, to understand and interpret the behavior of human beings and to express deep universal emotions. The Brothers Grimm collected the German tales; Peter Asbjörnsen and Jörgen Moe, as well as Sir George Dasent, collected the Norse tales. Andrew Lang and Joseph Jacobs were also well-known folklorists. Though these stories were not originally intended for children, they soon were claimed by them and adapted and retold for young readers. Though the youngest read the nursery tales and the simple folk tales, such as "Three Billy Goats Gruff," children reach their peak of interest in fairy tales when they are around eight and nine years old. The distinction between the old folk tale and the modern fairy tale is primarily one of authorship. The former came from the people, while the latter is the creative work of one imaginative mind. Hans Christian Andersen is usually credited with the first fairy tale. He began with skillful adaptations of traditional tales, but so creative was his genius that he turned them into literary gems and removed them entirely from the body of folk literature. Such stories as "Ugly Duckling" and "Real Princess" belong to Hans Christian Andersen and not the folk. Perrault's stories, embellished though they were by a skilled writer, remained genuine folk tales. At times, the reading of these stories by children has been attacked by well-meaning adults who say it is "untruthful rubbish, contrary to what I am teaching my child is right." The truth of the matter is that people in folk tales behave pretty much as people do in real life. Annis Duff says, "Fairy tales do not 'condone' behavior that is contrary to ethical principle. They simply recognize the fact that it occurs. The mother who was so flustered about the possible detriment to her children of reading fairy tales overlooked the fact that she herself had read them and still retained a well-developed sense of right and wrong.

Children also enjoy the fables though they are better understood by the older children because of their intellectual quality as compared with the simple folk tales. They make abstract ideas objective enough to be understood with their maxims, adages, and brief moralizings. One rarely sympathizes with the fable creature, for he is an impersonal exemplification of virtue or folly. Younger children will enjoy the few fables which have strong story appeal or obvious humor, such as "The Town Mouse and the Country Mouse," "The Hare and The Tortoise," or "Dog in the Manger." The English-speaking child is familiar with Aesop's fables while French children associate fables with Jean de la Fontaine. Aesop is said to have lived between 620 and 560 B.C. and to have been a Greek slave from Ethiopia. La Fontaine (1621–1695) was a poet, a member of the Royal Academy, and a contemporary of Perrault. He drew upon many sources for his fables, including Aesop and the Indian fables of Bidpai. The oldest and largest body of fables is the collection of Jatakas, which formed a part of ancient Buddhist literature. Since the maxims of these great fablers and fabulists have passed into our thinking and our language, every child should be introduced to them. The fables selected for this anthology are the ones most popular with the children, and even the youngest child knows what it means when he is likened to "the dog in the manger," or when he is told that he is like "the fox and the sour grapes."

It is never too soon to speak poetry to a child. Mother Goose should keep company with Shakespeare, William Blake, and Christina Rossetti. Nonsense makers, such as Edward Lear and Lewis Carroll, should be included, for a good laugh is priceless. Starting

with Mother Goose, the family moves from the little verse, used to point up an occasion or provoke laughter, to the real poem which touches upon the why and how of being. Poetry is essential to the full development of the child, and, if he stores up beauty and magnificence, there is less room for the ugly and mediocre. Poetry should be shared by the family and, if possible, recited from memory rather than read. If it is not recited, it should be read with affection and feeling. Reading a poem aloud catches elements which are missed when it is read silently. The melody and movement of oral interpretation suggest action and establish mood. Use poetry with children for their enjoyment, for stimulation and relaxation, for quiet reassurance. Be not concerned with the meaning of a poem or its difficulty because of the child's limited experience, for a great poem speaks to the emotions rather than to the intellect. A child may learn a poem for its beautiful words and imagery only to realize its deeper meaning years later. The child who is introduced to poetry in his infancy will love and appreciate it throughout his entire life. The selections in *Young Years* are an introduction, a taste of the great body of poetry, and it is hoped that this taste will lead to a long and exciting relationship between the child and the poem.

The selections for *Young Years* were made by people who have devoted many years to books and children. The editors of this book hope that these carefully made selections will serve as a springboard to further exploration of children's literature. Here is a starting point for the parents who are a little unsure of their own knowledge and judgment. The public library is a reliable source of information, and there are many fine books on children's reading, the most important of which have been listed in this book's bibliography.

A. B.

Special Acknowledgements

Thanks are due to the librarians and staff of the Central Children's Room and Picture Section of the New York Public Library, with particular gratitude to Miss Helen Masten, Librarian in charge, Miss Maria Cimino, Associate Librarian in charge, and Miss Romona Javitz, Superintendent of the Picture Collection, for making available hundreds of rare old children's books and illustrations which were consulted in the course of preparing *Young Years*.

D. L.

Publisher's Note

Young Years is published to fill the need — long expressed by parents — for a profusely illustrated anthology of the literary classics appealing to very young children. The immortal nursery rhymes, nursery stories, fables, fairy tales, and poems included in this volume have been edited to meet the high standards of contemporary children's literature. Passages of the selections considered not suitable or too lengthy for children of the age for which *Young Years* is intended have been purposely omitted. The editors have retained, as far as possible, the selections in their original versions, a fact that explains the minor inconsistencies the reader will occasionally come across in style, usage and punctuation.

The guiding motive in the choice of illustrations has been to keep the best of the old, while substituting new art works for variety and liveliness, or where the traditional works did not meet the publisher's standards of excellence. The artists who designed *Young Years* have endeavored to infuse vivid, harmonious colors throughout the volume, and the child can find exciting and brilliantly colored pictures on every double page spread. To the traditional illustrations, therefore, color has often been added where none originally existed. On the other hand, some of the details in these older illustrations that young children find too confusing have been retouched or slightly altered to enhance their appearance.

B.C.

Old prints from the following classic illustrators of children's stories are included in this volume:

John D. Batten
Percy Billinghurst
Reginald Birch
Charles E. Brock
Leslie Brooke
Gelett Burgess
Randolph Caldecott
Walter Crane

George Cruikshank
Gustave Dorè
Fontenier
Henry J. Ford
Arthur B. Frost
Kate Greenaway
George P. Hood
Edward Lear

Frank T. Merrill
Thomas Nast
Frederick Opper
Beatrix Potter
Howard Pyle
Charles Robinson
Thomas H. Robinson
H. L. Stephens

John Tenniel   Hugh Thomson

NURSERY

RHYMES

OLD MOTHER HUBBARD

Old Mother Hubbard
      Went to the cupboard,
To get her poor dog a bone,
      But when she got there
The cupboard was bare,
      And so the poor dog had none.

She went to the baker's
    To buy him some bread,
But when she came back
    The poor dog was dead.

She went to the joiner's
    To buy him a coffin,
But when she came back
    The poor dog was laughing.

She went to the fishmonger's
    To buy him some fish,
And when she came back
    He was licking the dish.

She went to the ale-house
    To get him some beer,
But when she came back
    The dog sat in a chair.

She took a clean dish
    To get him some tripe,
But when she came back
    He was smoking his pipe.

She went to the barber's
    To buy him a wig,
But when she came back
    He was dancing a jig.

She went to the tavern
    For white wine and red,
But when she came back
    The dog stood on his head.

She went to the hatter's
    To buy him a hat,
But when she came back
    He was feeding the cat.

She went to the tailor's
    To buy him a coat,
But when she came back
    He was riding a goat.

She went to the fruiterer's
    To buy him some fruit,
But when she came back
    He was playing the flute.

She went to the cobbler's
    To buy him some shoes,
But when she came back
    He was reading the news.

She went to the seamstress
    To buy him some linen,
But when she came back
    The dog was spinning.

She went to the hosier's
    To buy him some hose,
But when she came back
    He was dressed in his clothes.

The dame made a curtsy,
    The dog made a bow,
The dame said, "Your servant,"
    The dog said, "Bow, wow."

THE MAN IN

THE MOON

The man in the moon,
Came down too soon,
To inquire his way
    to Norwich:
He went by the south,
And burnt his mouth
With eating cold
    plum-porridge.

LITTLE BO-PEEP

Little Bo-peep has lost her sheep,
    And can't tell where to find them;
Leave them alone, and they'll come home,
    And bring their tails behind them.

24

Little Bo-peep fell fast asleep,
    And dreamt she heard them bleating;
And when she awoke, she found it a joke,
    For they still were all fleeting.

Then up she took her little crook,
    Determin'd for to find them;
She found them indeed, but it made her heart bleed,
    For they'd left all their tails behind 'em.

HUSH-A-BYE,
BABY

Hush-a-bye, baby,
          on the tree top,
When the wind blows,
          the cradle will rock;
When the bough breaks,
          the cradle will fall
Down will come baby,
          bough, cradle, and all.

LITTLE
MISS
MUFFETT

Little Miss Muffett
    She sat on a tuffett,
Eating of curds and whey;

There came a black spider,
    And sat down beside her,
Which frightened Miss Muffett away.

THERE WAS AN OLD WOMAN WHO LIVED IN A SHOE

There was an old woman
    who lived in a shoe;
She had so many children
    she didn't know what to do.

She gave them some broth
    without any bread;
She whipped them all soundly,
    and put them to bed.

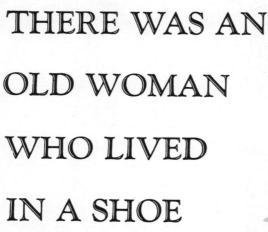

BYE, BABY

BUNTING

Bye, Baby bunting,
　　　Daddy's gone a-hunting,
To get a little
　　　rabbit skin
To wrap a baby
　　　bunting in.

SING A SONG OF SIXPENCE

Sing a song of sixpence,
    A pocket full of rye;
Four and twenty blackbirds
    Baked in a pie.

    When the pie was opened,
        The birds began to sing;
    Was not that a dainty dish,
        To set before the king?

The king was in his counting-house
      Counting out his money;
The queen was in the parlor
      Eating bread and honey.

The maid was in the garden
      Hanging out the clothes,
There came a little blackbird,
      And snapped off her nose.

HOW MANY MILES

TO BABYLON?

How many miles is it to Babylon?
      Threescore miles and ten.
Can I get there by candle-light?
      Yes, and back again!
If your heels are nimble and light,
      You may get there by candle-light.

MISTRESS MARY,

QUITE CONTRARY

Mistress Mary,
    quite contrary,
How does your
    garden grow?
With cockle-shells,
    and silver bells,
And pretty maids
    all in a row.

JACK
AND
JILL

Jack and Jill
        went up the hill,
To fetch
        a pail of water;

Jack fell down
      and broke his crown
And Jill came
      tumbling after.

Up Jack got
      and home did trot
As fast as
      he could caper;
To Old Dame Dob
      Who patched his knob
With vinegar
      and brown paper.

HEY! DIDDLE, DIDDLE

Hey! diddle, diddle!
    The cat and the fiddle.
The cow jumped over the moon;

    The little dog laughed
    To see such sport,
And the dish ran away with the spoon.

SIMPLE SIMON

Simple Simon met a pieman,
        Going to the fair;
Says Simple Simon to the pieman,
        "Let me taste your ware."

Says the pieman to Simple Simon,
     "Show me first your penny."
Says Simple Simon to the pieman,
     "Indeed I have not any."

Simple Simon went a-fishing
     For to catch a whale;
All the water he could find
     Was in his mother's pail!

Simple Simon went to look
     If plums grew on a thistle;
He pricked his fingers very much,
     Which made poor Simon whistle.

He went to catch a dicky bird,
     And thought he could not fail,
Because he had a little salt,
     To put upon its tail.

He went for water with a sieve,
     But soon it all ran through;
And now poor Simple Simon
     Bids you all adieu.

AS I WAS GOING TO ST. IVES

As I was going to St. Ives,
I met a man with seven wives,
Every wife had seven sacks,
Every sack had seven cats,
Every cat had seven kits:
Kits, cats, sacks, and wives,
How many were there going to St. Ives?

HICKETY, PICKETY,
MY BLACK HEN

Hickety, pickety, my black hen,
     She lays eggs for gentlemen;
Gentlemen come every day,
     To see what my black hen doth lay.

JACK SPRAT

Jack Sprat could eat no fat,
      His wife could eat no lean,
And so between them both, you see,
      They licked the platter clean.

RIDE A COCK-HORSE

Ride a cock-horse
      to Banbury Cross,
To see an old lady
      upon a white horse,
Rings on her fingers,
      and bells on her toes,
She shall have music
      wherever she goes.

PUSSY-CAT, PUSSY-CAT, WHERE HAVE YOU BEEN?

"Pussy-cat, Pussy-cat,
    where have you been?"
"I've been to London, to see the Queen!"
    "Pussy-cat, Pussy-cat,
    what did you there?"
"I frightened a little mouse under the chair!"

WEE WILLIE WINKIE

Wee Willie Winkie runs
      through the town,
Upstairs and downstairs,
      in his nightgown,
Rapping at the window,
      crying through the lock,
"Are the children in their beds?
      now it's eight o'clock."

THE QUEEN OF HEARTS

The queen of hearts,
     She made some tarts,
All on a summer's day;

The knave of hearts,
　　　　　He stole those tarts,
And with them ran away:

The king of hearts
　　　　　Called for those tarts,
And beat the knave full sore;

The knave of hearts
　　　　　Brought back those tarts,
And said he'd ne'er steal more.

TOM, TOM,

THE PIPER'S SON

Tom, Tom, the piper's son,
Stole a pig and away he run;
The pig was eat,
And Tom was beat,
And Tom went howling
down the street.

SEE-SAW,

MARGERY DAW

See-Saw, Margery Daw,
Jenny shall have
        a new master;
And she shall have
        but a penny a day,
Because she can't
        work any faster.

OLD KING COLE

Old King Cole
Was a merry old soul,
And a merry old soul was he;

He called for his pipe,
        And he called for his bowl,
And he called for his fiddlers three.

And every fiddler he had a fine fiddle,
	And a very fine fiddle had he;
"Twee tweedle dee, tweedle dee,"
	went the fiddlers.
Oh, there's none so rare,
	As can compare
With King Cole and his fiddlers three.

PETER, PETER,
PUMPKIN-EATER

Peter, Peter, pumpkin-eater,
      Had a wife, and couldn't keep her;
He put her in a pumpkin-shell,
      And there he kept her very well.

LITTLE JACK HORNER

Little Jack Horner
      sat in the corner,
        Eating a Christmas pie;
He put in his thumb,
      and he took out a plum,
        And said, "What a good boy am I!"

THREE LITTLE KITTENS

Three little kittens
    lost their mittens,
And they began to cry,
    "O mother dear,
    We very much fear
That we have lost
    our mittens."

"Lost your mittens!
    You naughty kittens!
Then you shall have no pie."
    "Mee-ow, mee-ow, mee-ow."
"No, you shall have no pie."
"Mee-ow,
        mee-ow,
           mee-ow."

The three little kittens
    found their
    mittens,
And they began to cry,
    "O mother dear,
    See here, see here
See! we have found
    our mittens."

"Put on your mittens,
    You silly kittens,
And you may have some pie."
    "Purr-r, purr-r, purr-r,
Oh, let us have the pie.
    Purr-r, purr-r, purr-r."

The three little kittens
    put on their mittens,
And soon ate up the pie;
  "O mother dear,
  We greatly fear
That we have soil'd
    our mittens."

"Soiled your mittens!
  You naughty kittens!"
Then they began to sigh,
  "Mee-ow, mee-ow,
       mee-ow."
Then they began to sigh,
"Mee-ow,
    mee-ow,
      mee-ow."

The three little kittens
  washed their
    mittens,
And hung them out
  to dry;
  "O mother dear,
  Do you not hear,
That we have washed
    our mittens?"

"Washed your mittens!
  Oh, you're good kittens.
But I smell a rat close by!"
  "Hush, hush! mee-ow, mee-ow!
We smell a rat close by!
Mee-ow,
    mee-ow,
      mee-ow!"

Eliza Lee Follen

HERE WE GO ROUND

THE MULBERRY BUSH

Here we go round the mulberry bush,
      The mulberry bush, the mulberry bush;
Here we go round the mulberry bush,
      On a cold and frosty morning!

This is the way we wash our clothes,
      Wash our clothes, wash our clothes;
This is the way we wash our clothes,
      On a cold and frosty morning!

This is the way we dry our clothes,
      Dry our clothes, dry our clothes;
This is the way we dry our clothes,
      On a cold and frosty morning!

This is the way we mend our shoes,
      Mend our shoes, mend our shoes;
This is the way we mend our shoes,
      On a cold and frosty morning!

This is the way the ladies walk,
      Ladies walk, ladies walk;
This is the way the ladies walk,
      On a cold and frosty morning!

This is the way the gentlemen walk,
      Gentlemen walk, gentlemen walk;
This is the way the gentlemen walk,
      On a cold and frosty morning!

LITTLE BOY BLUE

Little boy blue, come blow your horn,
            The sheep's in the meadow,
                the cow's in the corn.
Where's the boy that looks after
                the sheep?
            He's under the haycock,
                fast asleep.

Will you wake him? No, not I;
            For if I do, he'll be sure to cry.

GEORGIE PORGIE

Georgie Porgie, pudding and pie,
    Kissed the girls and made them cry.
When the boys came out to play,
    Georgie Porgie ran away.

GOOSEY,
GOOSEY,
GANDER

Goosey, goosey, gander,
      Who stands yonder?
Little Betsey Baker;
      Take her up, and shake her.

Goosey, goosey, gander,
      Where shall I wander?
Upstairs, downstairs,
      And in my lady's chamber.

There I met an old man
    That would not say his prayers
I took him by the left leg,
    And threw him downstairs.

BAA, BAA,

BLACK SHEEP

Baa, baa, black sheep,
   Have you any wool?
Yes, sir, yes, sir,
   Three bags full.

One for my master,
    And one for my dame,
And one for the little boy
    Who lives in the lane.

DING, DONG, BELL

Ding, dong, bell,
Pussy's in the well!
Who put her in?
Little Tommy Lin.
Who pulled her out?
Little
　　　Johnny
　　　　　Stout.

What a naughty boy
　　　　was that
To drown the poor,
　　　　poor pussy-cat
Who never did him
　　　　any harm,
But killed the mice
　　　in his father's barn.

64

HICKORY,
DICKORY,
DOCK

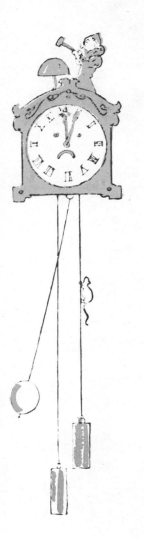

Hickory,
   dickory,
      dock,
The mouse ran up
   the clock;
The clock struck
   one,
And down he run,
Hickory,
   dickory,
      dock.

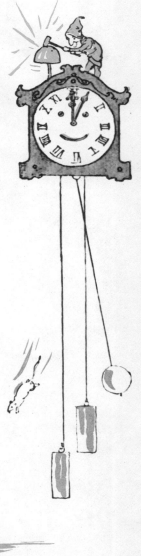

A

WAS AN APPLE PIE

B

BIT IT

C

CUT IT

D

DEALT IT

E

EAT IT

F

FOUGHT FOR IT

G

GOT IT

H

HAD IT

I & J

JUMPED FOR IT

K

KNELT FOR IT

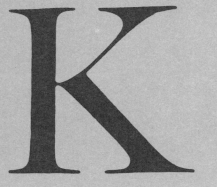

L

LONGED FOR IT

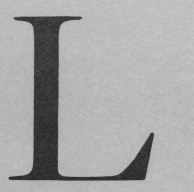

M

MOURNED FOR IT

N

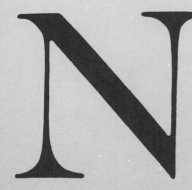

O

P

Q

NODDED AT IT

OPENED IT

PEEPED IN IT

QUARTERED IT

69

R

RAN FOR IT

S

SANG FOR IT

T

TOOK IT

ALL HAD A LARGE SLICE
AND WENT OFF TO
BED

U V W
X Y Z

ONE, TWO, BUCKLE
MY SHOE

One, two,
Buckle my shoe;

Three, four,
Shut the door;

Five, six,
Pick up sticks;

Seven, eight,
Lay them straight;

Nine, ten,
A good fat hen;

Eleven, twelve,
Who will delve?

Thirteen, fourteen
Maids a-courting;

Fifteen, sixteen,
Maids a-kissing;

Seventeen, eighteen,
Maids a-waiting;

Nineteen, twenty,
My stomach's empty
Pray, dame, give me some supper.

THIS LITTLE PIG
WENT TO MARKET

This little pig
  went to market;

This little pig
  stayed at home;

This little pig
      had roast beef;

This little pig
      had none;

74

This little pig
said, "Wee, wee!
I can't find my way

home."

I SAW A
SHIP A-SAILING

I saw a ship a-sailing,
    A-sailing on the sea;
And, oh! it was all laden
    With pretty things for thee!

There were comfits in the cabin,
    And apples in the hold;
The sails were made of silk,
    And the masts were made of gold.

The four-and-twenty sailors
    That stood between the decks
Were four-and-twenty white mice,
    With chains about their necks.

The captain was a duck,
    With a packet on his back;
And when the ship began to move,
    The captain said, "Quack! quack!"

JACK

BE NIMBLE

Jack be nimble,
    And Jack be quick;
And Jack jump over
    The candlestick.

HUMPTY DUMPTY

Humpty Dumpty sat on a wall,
      Humpty Dumpty had a great fall;
All the King's horses and all the King's men
      Couldn't put Humpty Dumpty together
      again.

I HAD A
LITTLE NUT TREE

I had a little nut-tree;
      nothing would it bear
But a silver nutmeg
      and a golden pear;
The King of Spain's daughter
      came to visit me
And all was because of my
      little nut-tree.

I skipped over water,
      I danced over sea,
And all the birds in the air
      couldn't catch me.

COCK A DOODLE DOO

Cock a doodle doo!
      My dame has lost her shoe;
My master's lost his fiddling stick,
      And don't know what to do.

Cock a doodle doo!
      What is my dame to do?
Till master finds his fiddling stick,
      She'll dance without her shoe.

Cock a doodle doo!
      My dame has found her shoe,
And master's found his fiddling stick,
      Sing doodle doodle do!

Cock a doodle doo!
      My dame will dance with you,
While master fiddles his fiddling stick,
      For dame and doodle doo.

LITTLE NANCY

ETTICOAT

Little Nancy Etticoat,
   In a white petticoat,
And a red nose;
   The longer she stands,
The shorter she grows.

A FROG HE WOULD
A-WOOING GO

A FROG he would a-wooing go,
    Heighho, says Rowley!
Whether his Mother would let him or no.
    With a rowley-powley, gammon and spinach,
    Heighho, says Anthony Rowley!

So off he set with his opera hat,
    Heighho, says Rowley!
And on his way he met with a Rat.
    With a rowley-powley, gammon and spinach,
    Heighho, says Anthony Rowley!

"Pray, Mister Rat, will you go with me?"
    Heighho, says Rowley!
"Pretty Miss Mousey for to see?"
    With a rowley-powley, gammon and spinach,
    Heighho, says Anthony Rowley!

Now they soon arrived at Mousey's Hall,
    Heighho, says Rowley!
And gave a loud knock, and gave a loud call.
    With a rowley-powley, gammon and spinach,
    Heighho, says Anthony Rowley!

"Pray, Miss Mousey, are you within?"
    Heighho, says Rowley!
"Oh yes, kind Sirs, I'm sitting to spin."
    With a rowley-powley, gammon and spinach,
    Heighho, says Anthony Rowley!

"Pray, Miss Mousey, will you give us some beer?"
    Heighho, says Rowley!
"For Froggy and I are fond of good cheer."
    With a rowley-powley, gammon and spinach,
    Heighho, says Anthony Rowley!

"Pray Mister Frog, will you give us a song?"
    Heighho, says Rowley!
"But let it be something that's not very long."
    With a rowley-powley, gammon and spinach,
    Heighho, says Anthony Rowley!

"Indeed Miss Mouse," replied Mister Frog,
    Heighho, says Rowley!
"A cold has made me as hoarse as a Hog."
    With a rowley-powley, gammon and spinach,
    Heighho, says Anthony Rowley!

84

"Since you have caught cold," Miss Mousey said,
    Heighho, says Rowley!
"I'll sing you a song that I have just made."
    With a rowley-powley, gammon and spinach,
    Heighho, says Anthony Rowley!

But while they were all thus a merry-making,
    Heighho, says Rowley!
A cat and her kittens came tumbling in.
    With a rowley-powley, gammon and spinach,
    Heighho, says Anthony Rowley!

The Cat she seized the Rat by the crown;
    Heighho, says Rowley!
The kittens they pulled the little Mouse down.
    With a rowley-powley, gammon and spinach,
    Heighho, says Anthony Rowley!

This put Mister Frog in a terrible fright;
    Heighho, says Rowley!
He took up his hat, and he wished them good night.
    With a rowley-powley, gammon and spinach,
    Heighho, says Anthony Rowley!

But as Froggy was crossing over a silvery brook,
    Heighho, says Rowley!
A lily-white duck came and gobbled him up.
    With a rowley-powley, gammon and spinach,
    Heighho, says Anthony Rowley!

So there was an end of one, two and three,
    Heighho, says Rowley!
The Rat, the Mouse, and the little Frog-ee
    With a rowley-powley, gammon and spinach,
    Heighho, says Anthony Rowley!

Nursery Stories

Johnny-Cake

ONCE upon a time there was an old man and an old woman, and a little boy. One morning the old woman made a Johnny-cake, and put it in the oven to bake. "You watch the Johnny-cake while your father and I go out to work in the garden." So the old man and the old woman went out and began to hoe potatoes, and left the little boy to tend the oven. But he didn't watch it all the time, and all of a sudden he heard a noise, and he looked up and the oven door popped open, and out of the oven jumped Johnny-cake, and went rolling along end over end, towards the open door of the house. The little boy ran to shut the door, but Johnny-cake was too quick for him and rolled through the door, down the steps, and out into the road long before the little boy could catch him. The little boy ran after him as fast as he could clip it, crying out to his father and mother, who heard the uproar, and threw down their hoes and gave chase too. But Johnny-cake outran all three a long way, and was soon out of sight, while they had to sit down, all out of breath, on a bank to rest.

On went Johnny-cake, and by-and-by he came to two well-diggers who looked up from their work and called out: "Where ye going, Johnny-cake?"

He said: "I've outrun an old man, and an old woman, and a little boy, and I can outrun you too-o-o!"

"Ye can, can ye? we'll see about that!" said they; and they threw down their picks and ran after him, but couldn't catch up with him, and soon they had to sit down by the road-side to rest.

On ran Johnny-cake, and by-and-by he came to two ditch-diggers who were digging a ditch. "Where ye going, Johnny-cake?" said they. He said: "I've outrun an old man, and an old woman, and a little boy, and two well diggers, and I can outrun you too-o-o!"

"Ye can, can ye? we'll see about that!" said they; and they threw down their spades and ran after him too. But Johnny-cake soon outstripped them also, and seeing they could never catch him, they gave up the chase and sat down to rest.

On went Johnny-cake, and by-and-by he came to a bear. The bear said: "Where are ye going, Johnny-cake?"

He said: "I've outrun an old man, and an old woman, and a little boy, and two well diggers, and two ditch-diggers, and I can outrun you too-o-o!"

"Ye can, can ye?" growled the bear, "we'll see about that!" and trotted as fast as his legs could carry him after Johnny-cake, who never stopped to look behind him. Before long the bear was left so far behind that he saw he might as well give up the hunt first as last, so he stretched himself out by the roadside to rest.

On went Johnny-cake, and by-and-by he came to a wolf. The wolf said: "Where ye going, Johnny-cake?"

He said: "I've outrun an old man, and an old woman, and a little boy, and two well-diggers, and two ditch-diggers, and a bear, and I can outrun you too-o-o!"

"Ye can, can ye?" snarled the wolf, "we'll see about that!" And he set into a gallop after Johnny-cake, who went on and on so fast that the wolf saw there was no hope of overtaking him, and he too lay down to rest.

On went Johnny-cake, and by-and-by he came to a fox that lay quietly in a corner of the fence. The fox called out in a sharp voice, but without getting up: "Where ye going, Johnny-cake?"

He said: "I've outrun an old man, and and an old woman, and a little boy, and two well-diggers, and two ditch-diggers, a bear, and a wolf, and I can outrun you too-o-o!"

The fox said: "I can't quite hear you, Johnny-cake won't you come a little closer?" turning his head a little to one side.

Johnny-cake stopped his race for the first time, and went a little closer, and called out in a very loud voice: *"I've outrun an old man, and an old woman, and a little boy, and two well-diggers, and two ditch-diggers, and a bear, and a wolf, and I can outrun you too-o-o!"*

"Can't quite hear you; won't you come a little closer?" said the fox in a feeble voice, as he stretched out his neck toward Johnny-cake, and put one paw behind his ear.

Johnny-cake came up close, and leaning towards the fox screamed out: "I'VE OUTRUN AN OLD MAN, AND AN OLD WOMAN, AND A LITTLE BOY, AND TWO WELL-DIGGERS, AND TWO DITCH-DIGGERS, AND A BEAR, AND A WOLF, AND I CAN OUTRUN YOU TOO-O-O!"

"You can, can you?" yelped the fox, and he snapped up the Johnny-cake in his sharp teeth in the twinkling of an eye.

The Three
Billy Goats Gruff

ONCE upon a time there were three Billy Goats who wanted to go up to the hillside to make themselves fat, and the name of all the three was "Gruff."

On the way up, they had to cross a bridge over a brook; and under the bridge lived a great ugly Troll, with eyes as big as saucers and a nose as long as a poker.

First of all came the youngest Billy Goat Gruff to cross the bridge.

93

"Trip, Trap! Trip, Trap!" went the bridge.

"WHO'S THAT tripping over my bridge?" roared the Troll.

"Oh! It is only I, the tiniest Billy Goat Gruff, and I'm going up to the hillside to make myself fat," said the Billy Goat in such a small voice.

"Now, I'm coming to gobble you up," said the Troll.

"Oh, no! Pray don't take me, I'm too little, that I am," said the Billy Goat. "Wait a bit till the second Billy Goat Gruff comes; he's much bigger."

"Well! Be off with you," said the Troll.

A little while after, came the second Billy Goat Gruff to cross the bridge.

"Trip, Trap! Trip, Trap! Trip, Trap!" went the bridge.

"WHO'S THAT tripping over my bridge?" roared the Troll.

"Oh! It's the second Billy Goat Gruff, and I'm going up to the hillside to make myself fat," said the Billy Goat, who hadn't such a small voice.

"Now, I'm coming to gobble you up," said the Troll.

"Oh, no! Don't take me. Wait a bit till the big Billy Goat Gruff comes; he's much bigger."

"Very well! Be off with you," said the Troll.

Just then up came the big Billy Goat Gruff.

TRIP, TRAP! TRIP, TRAP!
TRIP! TRAP! TRIP, TRAP!" went
the bridge, for the big Billy Goat was
so heavy that the bridge creaked and
groaned under him.

"WHO'S THAT tramping over my
bridge?" roared the Troll.

"It's I! THE BIG BILLY GOAT
GRUFF!" said the Billy Goat, who had

an ugly hoarse voice of his own.

"Now, I'm coming to gobble you up," roared the Troll.

Then the Big Billy Goat Gruff said:

"Well, come along! I've got two spears,
And I'll poke your eyeballs out at your ears;
I've got besides two curling-stones,
And I'll crush you to bits, body and bones."

That was what the big Billy Goat said. And so he flew at the Troll and poked his eyes out with his horns, and crushed him to bits, body and bones, and tossed him into the brook. After that he went up to the hillside. There the Billy Goats got so fat they were hardly able to walk home again; and if the fat hasn't fallen off them, why they're still fat; and so—

Snip, snap, snout
This tale's told out.

The Cock, The Mouse and the Little Red Hen

ONCE upon a time there was a hill, and on the hill there was a pretty little house.

It had one little green door, and four little windows with green shutters, and in it there lived

A COCK, and A MOUSE, and A LITTLE RED HEN.

On another hill close by there was another little house. It was very ugly. It had a door that wouldn't shut, and two broken windows, and all the paint was off the shutters. And in this house there lived

A BOLD BAD FOX and FOUR BAD LITTLE FOXES.

One morning these four bad little foxes came to the big bad fox, and said:— "Oh, father, we're so hungry!"

"We had nothing to eat yesterday," said one.

"And scarcely anything the day before," said another.

"And only half a chicken the day before that," said the third.

"And only two little ducks the day before that," said the fourth.

The big bad fox shook his head for a long time, for he was thinking. At last he said in a big gruff voice:—

"On the hill over there I see a house. And in that house there lives a cock."

"And a mouse," screamed two of the little foxes.

"And a little red hen," screamed the other two.

"And they are nice and fat," went on the big bad fox. "This very day, I'll take my great sack, and I will go up that hill, and in at that door, and into my sack I will put the Cock, and the Mouse, and the little Red Hen."

"I'll make a fire to roast the cock," said one little fox.

"I'll put on the saucepan to boil the hen," said the second.

"And I'll get the frying pan to fry the mouse," said the third.

"And I'll have the biggest helping when they are all cooked," said the fourth, who was the greediest of all.

So the four little foxes jumped for joy, and the big bad fox went to get his sack ready to start upon his journey.

But what was happening to the cock and the mouse, and the little red hen, all this time?

Well, sad to say, the cock and the mouse had both got out of bed on the wrong side that morning. The cock said the day was too hot, and the mouse grumbled because it was too cold.

They came grumbling down to the kitchen, where the good little red hen, looking as bright as a sunbeam, was bustling about.

"Who'll get some sticks to light the fire with?" she asked.

"*I* shan't," said the cock.

"*I* shan't," said the mouse.

"Then I'll do it myself," said the little red hen.

So off she ran to get the sticks.

"And now, who'll fill the kettle from the spring?" she asked.

"*I* shan't," said the cock.

"*I* shan't," said the mouse.

"Then I'll do it myself," said the little red hen.

And off she ran to fill the kettle.

"And who'll get the breakfast ready?" she asked as she put the kettle on to boil.

"*I* shan't," said the cock.

"*I* shan't," said the mouse.

"I'll do it myself," said the little red hen.

All breakfast time the cock and the mouse quarrelled and grumbled. The cock upset the milk jug, and the mouse scattered crumbs upon the floor.

"Who'll clear away the breakfast?" asked the poor little red hen, hoping they would soon leave off being cross.

"*I* shan't," said the cock.

"*I* shan't," said the mouse.

"Then I'll do it myself," said the little red hen.

So she cleared everything away, swept up the crumbs and brushed up the fireplace.

"And now, who'll help me to make the beds?"

"*I* shan't," said the cock.

"*I* shan't," said the mouse.

"Then I'll do it myself," said the little red hen.

And she tripped away upstairs.

But the lazy cock and mouse each sat down in a comfortable arm-chair by the fire, and soon fell fast asleep.

Now the bad fox had crept up the hill, and into the garden, and if the cock and mouse hadn't been asleep, they would have seen his sharp eyes peeping in at the window. "Rat tat tat, rat tat tat," the fox knocked at the door.

"Who can that be?" said the mouse, half opening his eyes.

"Go and look for yourself, if you want to know," said the rude cock.

"It's the postman perhaps," thought the mouse to himself, "and he may have a letter for me." So without waiting to see who it was, he lifted the latch and opened the door.

As soon as he opened it, in jumped the big fox, with a cruel smile upon his face!

"Oh! oh! oh!" squeaked the mouse, as he

tried to run up the chimney.

"Doodle doodle do!" screamed the cock, as he jumped on the back of the biggest arm-chair.

But the fox only laughed, and without more ado he took the little mouse by the tail and popped him into the sack, and seized the cock by the neck and popped him in too.

Then the poor little red hen came running downstairs to see what all the noise was about, and the fox caught her and put her into the sack with the others. Then he took a long piece of string out of his pocket, wound it round and round and round the mouth of the sack, and tied it very tight indeed. After that he threw the sack over his back, and off he set down the hill.

"Oh! I wish I hadn't been so cross," said the cock as they went bumping about.

"Oh! I wish I hadn't been so lazy," said the mouse, wiping his eyes with the tip of his tail.

"It's never too late to mend," said the little red hen.

"And don't be too sad. See, here I have my little work-bag, and in it there is a pair of scissors, and a little thimble, and a needle and thread. Very soon you will see what I am going to do."

Now the sun was very hot, and soon Mr. Fox began to feel his sack was heavy, and at last he thought he would lie down under a tree and go to sleep for a little while. So he threw the sack down with a big bump, and very soon fell fast asleep.

Snore, snore, snore, went the fox. As soon as the little red hen heard this, she took out her scissors, and began to snip a hole in the sack, just large enough for the mouse to creep through.

"Quick," she whispered to the mouse, run as fast as you can and bring back a stone just as large as yourself."

Out scampered the mouse, and soon came back, dragging the stone after him.

"Push it in here," said the little red hen, and he pushed it in in a twinkling.

Then the little red hen snipped away at the hole, till it was large enough for the Cock to get through.

"Quick," she said, "run and get a stone as big as yourself."

Out flew the cock, and soon came back quite out of breath, with a big stone, which he pushed into the sack too.

Then the little Red Hen popped out, got a stone as big as herself, and pushed it in. Next she put on her thimble, took out her needle and thread, and sewed up the hole as quickly as ever she could.

When it was done, the cock and the mouse and the little red hen ran home very fast, shut the door after them, drew the bolts, shut the blinds and felt quite safe.

The bad fox lay fast asleep under the tree for some time, but at last he woke up.

"Dear, dear," he said, rubbing his eyes and then looking at the long shadows on the grass,

"how late it is getting. I must hurry home."

So the bad fox went grumbling and groaning down the hill, till he came to the stream. Splash! In went one foot. Splash! In went the other, but the stones in the sack were so heavy that at the very next step down tumbled Mr. Fox into a deep pool. And then the fishes carried him off to their fairy caves and kept him a prisoner there, so he was never seen again. And the four greedy little foxes had to go to bed without any supper.

But the cock and the mouse never grumbled again. They lit the fire, filled the kettle, laid the breakfast, and did all the work, while the good little red hen had a holiday, and sat resting in the big armchair.

No foxes ever troubled them again, and for all I know they are still living happily in the little house with the green door and green shutters, which stands on the hill.

Henny-Penny

O NE day Henny-Penny was picking up corn in the cornyard when—whack! —something hit her upon the head. "Goodness gracious me!" said Henny-Penny, "the sky's a-going to fall: I must go and tell the king."

So she went along, and she went along, and she went along, till she met Cocky-Locky. "Where are you going, Henny-Penny?" says Cocky-Locky. "Oh! I'm going to tell the king the sky's a-falling," says Henny-Penny. "May I come with you?" says Cocky-Locky. "Certainly," says Henny-Penny. So Henny-Penny and Cocky-Locky went to tell the king the sky was falling.

They went along, and they went along, and they went along, till they met Ducky-Daddles. "Where are you going to, Henny-Penny and Cocky-Locky?" says Ducky-Daddles. "Oh! we're going to tell the king the sky's a-falling," said Henny-Penny and Cocky-Locky. "May I come with you?" says Ducky-Daddles. "Certainly," said Henny-Penny and Cocky-Locky.

So Henny-Penny, Cocky-Locky, and Ducky-Daddles went to tell the king the sky was a-falling.

So they went along, and they went along, and they went along, till they met Goosey-Poosey. "Where are you going to, Henny-Penny, Cocky-Locky and Ducky-Daddles?" said Goosey-Poosey. "Oh! we're going to tell the king the sky's a-falling," said Henny-Penny and Cocky-Locky and Ducky-Daddles. "May I come with you?" said Goosey-Poosey. "Certainly," said Henny-Penny, Cocky-Locky, and Ducky-Daddles. So Henny-Penny, Cocky-Locky, and Ducky-Daddles, and Goosey-Poosey went to tell the king the sky was a-falling.

So they went along, and they went along, and they went along, till they met Turkey-Lurkey. "Where are you going, Henny-Penny, Cocky-Locky, Ducky-Daddles, and Goosey-Poosey?" says Turkey-Lurkey. "Oh! we're going to tell the king the sky's a-falling," said Henny-Penny, Cocky-Locky, Ducky-Daddles, and Goosey-Poosey. "May I come with you, Henny-Penny, Cocky-Locky, Ducky-Daddles, and Goosey-Poosey?" said Turkey-Lurkey. "Oh, certainly, Turkey-

Lurkey," said Henny-Penny, Cocky-Locky, Ducky-Daddles, and Goosey-Poosey. So Henny-Penny, Cocky-Locky, Ducky-Daddles, Goosey-Poosey, and Turkey-Lurkey all went to tell the king the sky was a-falling.

So they went along, and they went along, and they went along, till they met Foxy-Woxy, and Foxy-Woxy said to Henny-Penny, Cocky-Locky, Ducky-Daddles, Goosey-Poosey, and Turkey-Lurkey: "Where are you going, Henny-Penny, Cocky-Locky, Ducky-Daddles, Goosey-Poosey, and Turkey-Lurkey?" And Henny-Penny, Cocky-Locky, Ducky-Daddles, Goosey-Poosey, and Turkey-Lurkey said to Foxy-Woxy: "We're going to tell the king the sky's a-falling." "Oh! but this is not the way to the king, Henny-Penny, Cocky-Locky, Ducky-Daddles, Goosey-Poosey, and Turkey-Lurkey," says Foxy-Woxy; "I know the proper way; shall I show it you?" "Oh, certainly, Foxy-Woxy," said Henny-Penny, Cocky-Locky, Ducky-Daddles, Goosey-Poosey, and Turkey-Lurkey. So Henny-Penny,

Cocky-Locky, Ducky-Daddles, Goosey-Poosey, Turkey-Lurkey, and Foxy-Woxy all went to tell the king the sky was a-falling. So they went along, and they went along, and they went along, till they came to a narrow and dark hole. Now this was the door of Foxy-Woxy's cave. But Foxy-Woxy said to Henny-Penny, Cocky-Locky, Ducky-Daddles, Goosey-Poosey, and Turkey-Lurkey: "This is the short way to the king's palace: you'll soon get there if you follow me. I will go first and you come after, Henny-Penny, Cocky-Locky, Ducky-Daddles, Goosey-Poosey, and Turkey-Lurkey." "Why of course, certainly, without doubt, why not?" said Henny-Penny, Cocky-Locky, Ducky-Daddles, Goosey-Poosey, and Turkey-Lurkey.

So Foxy-Woxy went into his cave, and he didn't go very far, but turned round to wait for Henny-Penny, Cocky-Locky, Ducky-Daddles, Goosey-Poosey, and Turkey-Lurkey. So at last Turkey-Lurkey went through the narrow dark hole into the cave. He hadn't got far when "Hrumph," Foxy-Woxy snapped off Turkey-Lurkey's head and threw his body over his left shoulder. Then Goosey-Poosey went in, and "Hrumph," off went her head and Goosey-Poosey was thrown beside Turkey-Lurkey. Then Ducky-Daddles waddled down, and "Hrumph," snapped Foxy-Woxy, and Ducky-Daddles' head was off and Ducky-Daddles was thrown alongside Turkey-Lurkey and Goosey-Poosey. Then Cocky-Locky strutted down into the cave, and he hadn't gone far when "Snap, Hrumph!" went Foxy-Woxy and Cocky-Locky was thrown alongside of Turkey-Lurkey, Goosey-Poosey, and Ducky-Daddles.

But Foxy-Woxy had made two bites at Cocky-Locky, and when the first snap only hurt Cocky-Locky, but didn't kill him, he called out to Henny-Penny. But she turned tail and off she ran home, so she never told the king the sky was a-falling.

THE OLD WOMAN
AND HER PIG

AN OLD woman was sweeping her house, and she found a little crooked sixpence. "What," said she, "shall I do with this little sixpence? I will go to market, and buy a little pig."

As she was coming home, she came to a stile: but the piggy wouldn't go over the stile.

She went a little further, and she met a dog. So she said to him: "Dog! dog! bite pig; piggy won't go over the stile; and I shan't get home tonight." But the dog wouldn't.

She went a little further, and she met a stick. So she said: Stick! stick! beat dog; dog won't bite pig; piggy won't get over the stile; and I shan't get home tonight." But the stick wouldn't.

She went a little further, and she met a fire. So she said: "Fire! fire! burn stick; stick won't beat dog; dog won't bite pig; piggy won't get over the stile; and I shan't get home tonight." But the fire wouldn't.

She went a little further, and she met some water. So she said: "Water! water! quench fire; fire won't burn stick; stick won't beat dog; dog won't bite pig; piggy won't get over the stile; and I shan't get home tonight." But the water wouldn't.

She went a little further, and she met an ox. So she said: "Ox! ox! drink water; water won't quench fire; fire won't burn stick; stick won't beat dog; dog won't bite pig; piggy won't get over the stile; and I shan't get home tonight." But the ox wouldn't.

She went a little further, and she met a butcher. So she said: "Butcher! butcher! kill ox; ox won't drink water; water won't quench fire; fire won't burn stick; stick won't beat dog; dog won't bite pig; piggy won't get over the stile; and I shan't get home tonight." But the butcher wouldn't.

She went a little further, and she met a rope. So she said:

"Rope! rope! hang butcher; butcher won't kill ox; ox won't drink water; water won't quench fire; fire won't burn stick; stick won't beat dog; dog won't bite pig; piggy won't get over stile; and I shan't get home tonight." But the rope wouldn't.

She went a little further, and she met a rat. So she said: "Rat! rat! gnaw rope; rope won't hang butcher; butcher won't kill ox; ox won't drink water; water won't quench fire; fire won't burn stick; stick won't beat dog; dog won't bite pig; piggy won't get over the stile; and I shan't get home tonight." But the rat wouldn't.

She went a little further; and she met a cat. So she said: "Cat! cat! kill rat; rat won't gnaw rope; rope won't hang

butcher; butcher won't kill ox; ox won't drink water; water won't quench fire; fire won't burn stick; stick won't beat dog; dog won't bite pig; piggy won't get over the stile; and I shan't get home tonight." But the cat said to her, "If you will go to

yonder cow, and fetch me a saucer of milk, I will kill the rat."
So away went the old woman to the cow.

But the cow said to her: "If you will go to yonder hay-stack, and fetch me a handful of hay, I'll give you the milk." So away went the old woman to the hay-stack; and she brought the hay to the cow.

As soon as the cow had eaten the hay, she gave the old woman the milk; and away she went with it in a saucer to the cat.

As soon as the cat had lapped up the milk, the cat began to kill the rat; the rat began to gnaw the rope; the rope began to hang the butcher; the butcher began to kill the ox; the ox began to drink the water; the water began to quench the fire; the fire began to burn the stick; the stick began to beat the dog; the dog began to bite the pig; the little pig in a fright jumped over the stile; and so the old woman got home that night.

LITTLE RED RIDING-HOOD

ONCE upon a time there lived in a certain village a little country girl, the prettiest creature that ever was seen. Her mother was very fond of her, and her grandmother loved her still more. This good woman made for her a little red riding-hood, which became the girl so well that everybody called her Little Red Riding-Hood.

One day her mother, having made some custards, said to her:—

"Go, my dear, and see how your grandmother does, for I hear she has been very ill; carry her a custard, some cakes and this little pot of butter."

Little Red Riding-Hood set out immediately to go to her grandmother's, who lived in another village.

As she was going through the wood, she met Mr. Wolf, who had a very great mind to eat her up; but he dared not, because of some woodcutters hard by in the forest. He asked her whither she was going. The poor child, who did not know that it was dangerous to stay and hear a wolf talk, said to him:—

"I am going to see my grandmother, and carry her a custard, some cakes and a little pot of butter from my mamma."

"Does she live far off?" said the Wolf.

"Oh, yes," answered Little Red Riding-Hood; "it is beyond that mill you see there, the first house you come to in the village."

"Well," said the Wolf, "and I'll go and see her, too. I'll go this way, and you go that, and we shall see who will be there first."

The Wolf began to run as fast as he could, taking the shortest way, and the little girl went by the longest way, amusing herself by gathering nuts, running after butterflies, and making nosegays of such little flowers as she met with.

The Wolf was not long before he reached the old woman's house. He knocked at the door—tap, tap, tap.

"Who's there?" called the grandmother.

"Your grandchild, Little Red Riding-Hood," replied the Wolf, imitating her voice, "who has brought a custard, some cakes and a little pot of butter sent to you by mamma."

The good grandmother, who was in bed because she was somewhat ill, cried out:—

"Pull the bobbin, and the latch will go up."

The Wolf pulled the bobbin, and the door opened. He fell upon the good woman and swallowed her whole for he had not eaten anything for more than three days. He then shut the door, went into the grandmother's bed, and waited for Little Red Riding-Hood, who came sometime afterward and knocked at the door—tap, tap, tap.

"Who's there?" called the Wolf.

Little Red Riding-Hood, hearing the big voice of the Wolf, was at first afraid; but thinking her grandmother had a cold, answered:—

" 'Tis your grandchild, Little Red Riding-Hood, who has brought you a custard, some cakes and a little pot of butter sent to you by mamma."

The Wolf cried out to her, softening his voice a little:—

"Pull the bobbin, and the latch will go up."

Little Red Riding-Hood pulled the bobbin, and the

door opened.

The Wolf, seeing her come in, said to her, hiding himself under the bedclothes:—

"Put the custard, the cakes and the little pot of butter upon the stool."

Little Red Riding-Hood was much surprised to see how her grandmother looked in her nightclothes.

She said to her:—

"Grandmamma, what great arms you have got!"

"That is the better to hug thee, my dear."

"Grandmamma, what great legs you have got!"

"That is to run the better, my child."

"Grandmamma, what great ears you have got!"

"That is to hear the better, my child."

"Grandmamma, what great eyes you have got!"

"It is to see the better, my child."

"Grandmamma, what great teeth you have got!"

"That is to eat thee up."

And, saying these words, the wicked Wolf sprang at the little girl but Little Red Riding-Hood quickly ran out of the house screaming, "Help! Help!" A woodcutter who was passing by heard her cry and lifted up his axe and with one blow killed the Wolf. He quickly cut open the Wolf and out stepped grandmother, alive and well. She and Little Red Riding-Hood rushed into each other's arms, hugging and kissing. Then they invited the woodcutter to join them in eating the goodies which Little Red Riding-Hood had brought and they all had a jolly time together.

THE THREE LITTLE PIGS

Once upon a time
    when pigs spoke rhyme
And monkeys chewed tobacco,
And hens took snuff
    to make them tough,
And ducks went quack,
    quack, quack, O!

THERE was an old sow with three little pigs, and as she had not enough to keep them, she sent them out to seek their fortune. The first that went off met a man with a bundle of straw, and said to him:

"Please, man, give me that straw to build me a house."

Which the man did, and the little pig built a house with it. Presently came along a wolf, and knocked at the door, and said:

"Little pig, little pig, let me come in."

To which the pig answered:

"No, no, by the hair of my chinny chin chin."

The wolf then answered to that:

"Then I'll huff, and I'll puff, and I'll blow your house in."

So he huffed, and he puffed, and he blew his house in, and ate up the little pig.

The second little pig met a man with a bundle of furze and said:

"Please, man, give me that furze to build a house."

Which the man did, and the pig built his house. Then along came the wolf, and said:

"Little pig, little pig, let me come in."
"No, no, by the hair of my chinny chin chin."
"Then I'll puff, and I'll huff, and I'll blow your house in."

So he huffed, and he puffed, and he puffed, and he huffed, and at last he blew the house down, and he ate up the little pig.

The third little pig met a man with a load of bricks, and said:

"Please, man, give me those bricks to build a house with."

So the man gave him the bricks, and he built his house with them. So the wolf came, as he did to the other little pigs, and said:

"Little pig, little pig, let me come in."

"No, no, by the hair on my chinny chin chin."

"Then I'll huff, and I'll puff, and I'll blow your house in."

Well, he huffed, and he puffed, and he huffed and he puffed, and he puffed and huffed; but he could *not* get the house down. When he found that he could not, with all his huffing and puffing, blow the house down, he said:

"Little pig, I know where there is a nice field of turnips."

"Where?" said the little pig.

"Oh, in Mr. Smith's farm, and if you will be ready tomorrow morning I will call for you, and we will go together, and get some for dinner."

"Very well," said the little pig, "I will be ready. What time do you mean to go?"

"Oh, at six o'clock."

Well, the little pig got up at five, and got the turnips before the wolf came (which he did about six), who said:

"Little pig, are you ready?"

The little pig said: "Ready! I have been and come back again, and got a nice potful for dinner."

The wolf felt very angry at this, but thought that he would be up to the little pig somehow or other, so he said:

"Little pig, I know where there is a nice apple tree."

"Where?" said the pig.

"Down at Merry-garden," replied the wolf, "and if you will not deceive me I will come for you at five o'clock tomorrow and get some apples."

Well, the little pig bustled up the next morning at four o'clock, and went off for the apples, hoping to get back before the wolf came; but he had further to go, and had to climb the tree, so that just as he was coming down from it, he saw the wolf coming which, as you may suppose, frightened him very much. When the wolf came up he said:

"Little pig, what! are you here before me? Are they nice apples?"

"Yes, very," said the little pig. "I will throw you down one."

And he threw it so far, that, while the wolf was gone to pick it up, the little pig jumped down and ran home. The next day the wolf came again, and said to the little pig:

"Little pig, there is a fair at Shanklin this afternoon, will you go?"

"Oh yes," said the pig, "I will go; what time shall you be ready?"

"At three," said the wolf. So the little pig went off before time as usual, and got to the fair, and bought a butter churn, which he was going home with, when he saw the wolf coming.

Then he could not tell what to do. So he got into the churn to hide, and by so doing turned it round, and it rolled down the hill with the pig in it, which frightened the wolf so much, that he ran home without going to the fair. He went to the little pig's house, and told him how frightened he had been by a great round thing which came down the hill past him. Then the little pig said:

"Hah, I frightened you, then. I had been to the fair and bought a butter churn, and when I saw you, I got into it, and rolled down the hill."

Then the wolf was very angry indeed, and declared he would eat up the little pig, and that he would get down the chimney after him. When the little pig saw what he was about, he hung on the pot full of water, and made up a blazing fire, and, just as the wolf was coming down, took off the cover, and in fell the wolf; so the little pig put on the cover again in an instant, boiled him up, and ate him for supper, and lived happy ever afterwards.

The Three Bears

A LONG time ago, there were three bears who lived together in a house of their own in a wood: one, a great huge bear which was the father; one, a middle-sized bear which was the mother; and a little wee bear which was the son.

They each had a bowl for their porridge: a great huge bowl for the great huge bear, a middle-sized bowl for the middle-sized bear, and a little wee bowl for the little wee bear.

And they had each a chair to sit on: a great huge chair for the great huge bear, a middle-sized chair for the middle-sized bear, and a little wee chair for the little wee bear.

And they also had each a bed to sleep in: a great huge bed for the great huge bear, a middle-sized bed for the middle-sized bear, and a little wee bed for the little wee bear.

One morning, after they had boiled the porridge for their breakfast, and poured it into their bowls, they went into the wood to take a walk while the porridge was cooling.

A few minutes after they had gone, a little girl named Goldilocks came to the house and looked in at the window; then she peeped in at the keyhole and not seeing anybody in the house, she lifted the latch. The door was not fastened because the bears were good and honest bears who did nobody any harm and never thought that anybody would harm them. So little Goldilocks opened the door and went in. She was well pleased when she saw the porridge in the bowls. If she had been a good child, she would not have touched it, but would have waited until the bears came home, when perhaps they would have asked her to take some with them, for they were good kind-hearted bears.

But little Goldilocks did not wait. She first tasted the porridge of the great huge bear, and that was too hot for her; then she tasted the porridge of the middle-sized bear, and that was too cold for her; and then she tasted the porridge of the little wee

bear, and that was neither too hot nor too cold, but just what she liked.

She took the bowl in her hand and sat in a chair which was the chair of the great huge bear, but that was too hard for her; then she sat down in the next chair which was the chair of the middle-sized bear, and that was too soft for her; so she thought she would try the other which was the chair of the little wee bear, and that was neither too hard nor too soft, but just what she liked.

Then she sat down to eat the bowl of porridge which she held in her hand; but before she had quite finished the porridge the chair broke and let her fall, basin and all.

After this, little Goldilocks went upstairs into the bears' sleeping room where she saw three beds.

First she lay down upon the bed of the great huge bear, but that was too high at the head for her; then she lay down upon the bed of the middle-sized bear, and that was too high at the foot for her; and then she lay down upon the bed of the little wee bear, and that was neither too high at the head nor too high at the foot, but just what she liked; so she got snugly into it and fell fast asleep just as the three bears came home, thinking their porridge would be quite cool enough.

Now little Goldilocks had left the spoon of the great huge bear standing in his porridge.

"SOMEBODY HAS BEEN AT MY PORRIDGE," said the great huge bear in his great huge voice.

"SOMEBODY HAS BEEN AT MY PORRIDGE," said the middle-sized bear in a middle voice; and then the little wee bear looked for his bowl and saw it on the floor.

"Somebody has been at my porridge, and has eaten it all up," said the little wee bear in his little wee voice.

Now the three bears knew that some one must have come into their house while they were absent, and they began to look about them. Little Goldilocks had not put the cushion straight when she rose from the chair of the great huge bear.

"SOMEBODY HAS BEEN SITTING IN MY CHAIR," said the great huge bear in his great huge voice like thunder. And little Goldilocks had crushed the soft cushion of the mid-

dle-sized bear.

"SOMEBODY HAS BEEN SIT-
TING IN MY CHAIR," said the middle-sized bear in a middle voice.

"Somebody has been
sitting in my chair, and has
broken it down," said the
little wee bear in his little wee voice.

The three bears now
felt sure there was some
one in the house, and
they went upstairs to
their sleeping room to
search further.

"SOMEBODY
HAS BEEN LYING ON MY BED,"
said the great huge bear; for little
Goldilocks had tumbled the bed and
put the pillow out of its place.

"SOMEBODY HAS BEEN LYING ON
MY BED," said the middle-sized bear;
for little Goldilocks had also tumbled
this bed very much.

"Somebody has been
lying on my bed, and here
she is," said the little
wee bear with his little
wee voice. Goldilocks
had not been roused
from her sleep by the

loud voices of the great huge bear and the middle-sized bear, but the little wee voice of the little wee bear was so sharp and shrill that it awoke little Goldilocks at once.

When she saw the three

bears in the room and close to the side of the bed in which she was sleeping, she was very much frightened. She started up and ran to the window which was open, and jumped out. The three bears went to the window

to look after her, and saw her running into the woods.

But she never came back to their house, and they never saw her again.

TALE OF PETER RABBIT

By Beatrix Potter

ONCE upon a time there were four little Rabbits, and their names were—

Flopsy,
Mopsy,
Cotton-tail,
and Peter.

They lived with their Mother in a sand-bank, underneath the root of a very big fir-tree.

"Now my dears," said old Mrs. Rabbit one morning, "you may go into the fields or down the lane, but don't go into Mr. McGregor's garden: your Father had an accident there; he was put in a pie by Mrs. McGregor.

"Now run along, and don't get into mischief, I am going out."

Then old Mrs. Rabbit took a basket and her umbrella, and went through the wood to the baker's. She bought a loaf of brown bread and five currant buns.

Flopsy, Mopsy, and Cotton-tail, who were good little bunnies, went down the lane to gather blackberries;

but Peter, who was very naughty, ran straight away to Mr. McGregor's garden, and squeezed under the gate!

First he ate some lettuces and some French beans; and then he ate some radishes; and then, feeling rather sick, he went to look for some parsley. But round the end of a cucumber frame, whom should he meet but Mr. McGregor!

Mr. McGregor was on his hands and knees planting out young cabbages, but he jumped up and ran after Peter, waving a rake and calling out, "Stop thief!"

Peter was most dreadfully frightened; he rushed all over the garden, for he had forgotten the way back to the gate.

He lost one of his shoes among the cabbages, and the other shoe amongst the potatoes.

After losing them, he ran on four legs and went faster, so that I think he might have got away altogether if he had not unfortunately run into a gooseberry net, and got caught by the large buttons on his jacket. It was a blue jacket with brass buttons, quite new.

Peter gave himself up for lost, and shed big tears; but his sobs were overheard by some friendly sparrows, who flew to him in great excitement, and implored him to exert himself.

Mr. McGregor came up with a sieve, which he intended to pop upon the top of Peter; but Peter wriggled out just in time, leaving his jacket behind him.

And rushed into the toolshed, and jumped into a can. It would have been a beautiful thing to hide in, if it had not had so much water in it.

Mr. McGregor was quite sure that Peter was somewhere in the toolshed, perhaps hidden underneath a flower-pot. He began to turn them over carefully, looking under each.

Presently Peter sneezed—"Kerty-schoo!" Mr. McGregor was after him in no time, and tried to put his foot upon Peter, who jumped out of a

window, upsetting three plants. The window was too small for Mr. Mc-Gregor, and he was tired of running after Peter. He went back to his work.

Peter sat down to rest; he was out of breath and trembling with fright, and he had not the least idea which way to go. Also he was very damp with sitting in that can.

After a time he began to wander about, going lippity-lippity not very fast, and looking all around.

He found a door in a wall; but it was locked, and there was no room for a fat little rabbit to squeeze underneath.

An old mouse was running in and out over the stone doorstep, carrying peas and beans to her family in the wood. Peter asked her the way to the gate, but she had such a large pea in her mouth that she could not

answer. She only shook her head at him. Peter began to cry.

Then he tried to find his way straight across the garden, but he became more and more puzzled. Presently, he came to a pond where Mr. McGregor filled his water-cans. A white cat was staring at some goldfish; she sat very, very still, but now and then the tip of her tail twitched as if it were alive. Peter thought it best to go away without speaking to

her; he had heard about cats from his cousin, little Benjamin Bunny.

He went back towards the toolshed, but suddenly, quite close to him, he heard the noise of a hoe—scr-r-ritch, scratch, scratch, scritch. Peter scuttered underneath the bushes. But presently, as nothing happened, he came out, and climbed upon a wheelbarrow, and peeped over. The first thing he saw was Mr. McGregor hoeing onions. His back

was turned towards Peter, and beyond him was the gate!

Peter got down very quietly off the wheelbarrow, and started running as fast as he could go, along a straight walk behind some black-currant bushes.

Mr. McGregor caught sight of him at the corner, but Peter did not care. He slipped underneath the gate, and was safe at last in the wood outside the garden.

Mr. McGregor hung up the little jacket and the shoes for a scarecrow to frighten the blackbirds.

Peter never stopped running or looked behind him till he got home to the big fir-tree.

He was so tired that he flopped down upon the nice soft sand on the floor of the rabbit-hole, and shut his eyes. His mother was busy cooking; she wondered what he had done with his clothes. It was the second little

jacket and pair of shoes that Peter had lost in a fortnight!

I am sorry to say that Peter was not very well during the evening.

His mother put him to bed, and made some camomile tea; and she gave a dose of it to Peter!

"One table-spoonful to be taken at bed-time."

But Flopsy, Mopsy, and Cottontail had bread and milk and blackberries for supper.

THE HOUSE THAT JACK BUILT

THIS is the house that Jack built.

This is the malt,
That lay in the house that
Jack built.

THIS is the rat,
That ate the malt,
That lay in the house that
Jack built.

THIS is the cat,
   That killed the rat,
That ate the malt,
That lay in the house that
   Jack built.

THIS is the dog,
    That worried the cat,
That killed the rat,
That ate the malt,
That lay in the house that
    Jack built.

THIS is the cow with the crumpled horn,
   That tossed the dog,
That worried the cat,
That killed the rat,
That ate the malt,
That lay in the house that
     Jack built.

THIS is the maiden all forlorn,
  That milked the cow with the crumpled
    horn,
      That tossed the dog,
      That worried the cat,
      That killed the rat,
      That ate the malt,
    That lay in the house that
        Jack built.

THIS is the man all tattered and torn,
  That kissed the maiden all forlorn,
That milked the cow with the crumpled horn,
That tossed the dog,
That worried the cat,
That killed the rat,
That ate the malt,
That lay in the house that
      Jack built.

THIS is the priest all shaven and shorn,
  That married the man all tattered and torn,
That kissed the maiden all forlorn,
That milked the cow with the crumpled horn,
                    That tossed the dog,
                    That worried the cat,
                    That killed the rat,
                    That ate the malt,
                  That lay in the house that
                    Jack built.

THIS is the cock that crowed in the morn,
  That waked the priest all shaven and shorn,
That married the man all tattered and torn,
That kissed the maiden all forlorn,
That milked the cow with the crumpled horn,
That tossed the dog,
That worried the cat,
That killed the rat,
That ate the malt,
That lay in the house that

    Jack built.

THIS is the farmer who sowed the corn,
    That fed the cock that crowed in the morn,
That waked the priest all shaven and shorn,
That married the man all tattered and torn,
That kissed the maiden all forlorn,
That milked the cow with the crumpled horn,
        That tossed the dog,
        That worried the cat,
        That killed the rat,
        That ate the malt,
That lay in the house that

        Jack built.

FABLES

The Rat and the Elephant

A rat, of quite the smallest size,
Fix'd on an elephant his eyes,
And jeer'd the beast of high descent
Because his feet so slowly went.
Upon his back, three stories high,
There sat, beneath a canopy,
A certain sultan of renown,
   His dog, and cat, and wife sublime,
   His parrot, servant, and his wine,
All pilgrims to a distant town.
The rat profess'd to be amazed
That all the people stood and gazed
With wonder, as he pass'd the road,
Both at the creature and his load.
   "As if," said he, "to occupy
   A little more of land or sky
   Made one, in view of common sense,
   Of greater worth and consequence!
   What see ye, men in this parade,
   That food for wonder need be
     made?
   The bulk which makes a child
     afraid?
   In truth, I take myself to be,
   In all aspects as good as he."
And further might have gone his
     vaunt;
   But, darting down, the cat
   Convinced him that a rat
Is smaller than an elephant.

The Wind and the Sun

THE Wind and the Sun were disputing which was the stronger. Suddenly they saw a traveller coming down the road, and the Sun said: "I see a way to decide our dispute.

Whichever of us can cause that traveller to take off his cloak shall be regarded as the stronger. You begin." So the Sun retired behind a cloud, and the Wind began to blow as hard as it could upon the traveller. But the harder he blew the more closely did the traveller wrap his cloak round him, till at last the Wind had to give up in despair. Then the Sun came out and shone in all his glory upon the traveller, who soon found it too hot to walk with his cloak on.

*Kindness effects more
than Severity.*

The Fox and the Stork

At one time the Fox and the Stork were on visiting terms and seemed very good friends. So the Fox invited the Stork to dinner, and for a joke put nothing before her but some soup in a very shallow dish. This the Fox could easily lap up, but the Stork could only wet the end of her long bill in it, and left the meal as hungry as when she began. "I am sorry," said the Fox, "the soup is not to your liking."

"Pray do not apologise," said the Stork. "I hope you will return this visit, and come and dine with me soon." So a day was appointed when the Fox should visit the Stork; but when they were seated at table all that was for their dinner was contained in a very long-necked jar with a narrow mouth, in which the Fox could not insert his snout, so all he could manage to do was to lick the outside of the jar.

"I will not apologise for the dinner," said the Stork:

"One bad turn
deserves another."

The Fox and the Grapes

ONE hot summer's day a Fox was strolling through an orchard till he came to a bunch of Grapes just ripening on a vine which had been trained over a lofty branch. "Just the thing to quench my thirst," quoth he. Drawing back a few paces, he took a run and a jump, and just missed the bunch. Turning round again with a One, Two, Three, he jumped up, but with no greater success. Again and again he tried after the tempting morsel, but at last had to give it up, and walked away with his nose in the air, saying: "I am sure they are sour."

It is easy to despise
what you
cannot get.

The Shepherd Boy and the Wolf

THERE was once a young Shepherd Boy who tended his sheep at the foot of a mountain near a dark forest. It was rather lonely for him all day, so he thought upon a plan by which he could get a little company and some excitement. He rushed down towards the village calling out "Wolf, Wolf," and the villagers came out to meet him, and some of them stopped with him for a considerable time. This pleased the

boy so much that a few days afterwards he tried the same trick, and
again the villagers came to his help.
But shortly after this a Wolf actually did come out from the
forest, and began to worry the sheep, and the boy of course
cried out "Wolf, Wolf," still louder than before. But this time
the villagers, who had been fooled twice before, thought the
boy was again deceiving them, and nobody stirred to come to
his help. So the Wolf made a good meal off the boy's flock, and
when the boy complained, the wise man of the village said:
"A liar will not be believed,
even when
he speaks the truth."

The Lion and the Mouse

ONCE when a Lion was asleep a little Mouse began running up and down upon him; this soon wakened the Lion, who placed his huge paw upon him, and opened his big jaws to swallow him. "Pardon, O King," cried the little Mouse; "forgive me this time, I shall never forget it; who knows but what I may be able to do you a turn some of these days?" The Lion was so tickled at the idea of the Mouse being able to help him, that he lifted up his paw and let him go. Some time after the Lion was caught in a trap, and the hunters, who desired to carry him alive to the King, tied him to a tree while they went in search of a waggon to carry him on. Just then the little Mouse happened to pass by, and seeing the sad plight in which the Lion was, went up to him and soon gnawed away the ropes that bound the King of the Beasts. "Was I not right?" said the little Mouse.

*Little friends
may prove
great
friends.*

The Goose with

the Golden Eggs

ONE day a countryman going to the nest of his Goose found there an egg all yellow and glittering. When he took it up it was as heavy as lead and he was going to throw it away, because he thought a trick had been played upon him. But he took it home on second thoughts, and soon found to his delight that it was an egg of pure gold. Every morning the same thing occurred, and he soon became rich by selling his eggs. As he grew rich he grew greedy; and thinking to get at once all the gold the Goose could give, he killed it and opened it only to find,—nothing.

Greed
oft
o'erreaches
itself.

The Milkmaid and Her Pail

PATTY, the Milkmaid, was going to market carrying her milk in a Pail on her head. As she went along she began calculating what she would do with the money she would get for the milk. "I'll buy some fowls from Farmer Brown," said she, "and they will lay eggs each morning, which I will sell to the parson's wife. With the money that I get from the sale of these eggs I'll buy myself a new dimity frock and a chip hat; and when I go to market, won't all the young men come up and speak to me! Polly Shaw will be that jealous; but I don't care. I shall just look at her and toss my head like this." As she spoke, she tossed her head back, the Pail fell off it and all the milk was spilt. So she had to go home and tell her mother what had occurred.

"Ah, my child," said her mother, *"Do not count your chickens before they are hatched."*

The Fox and the Crow

A FOX once saw a crow fly off with a piece of cheese in its beak and settle on a branch of a tree. "That's for me, as I am a Fox," said Master Reynard, and he walked up to the foot of the tree. "Good-day, Mistress Crow," he cried. "How well you are looking today: how glossy your feathers; how bright your eye. I feel sure your voice must surpass that of other birds, just as your figure does; let me hear but one song from you that I may greet you as the Queen of Birds." The Crow lifted up her head and began to caw her best, but the moment she opened her mouth the piece of cheese fell to the ground, only to be snapped up by Master Fox. "That will do," said he. "That was all I wanted. In exchange for your cheese I will give you a piece of advice for the future—

DO NOT TRUST FLATTERERS."
The Flatterer doth rob
by stealth
his victim, both
of Wit and Wealth.

The Dog in the Manger

A DOG looking out for its afternoon nap jumped into the Manger of an Ox and lay there cosily upon the straw. But soon the Ox, returning from its afternoon work, came up to the Manger and wanted to eat some of the straw. The Dog

in a rage, being awakened from its slumber, stood up and barked at the Ox, and whenever it came near attempted to bite it. At last the Ox had to give up the hope of getting at the straw, and went away muttering:

"Ah, people often grudge
others what they
cannot enjoy themselves."

The Town Mouse and
The Country Mouse

Now you must know that a Town Mouse once upon a time went on a visit to his cousin in the country. He was rough and ready, this cousin, but he loved his town friend and made him heartily welcome. Beans and bacon, cheese and bread, were all he had to offer, but he offered them freely. The Town Mouse rather turned up his long nose at this country fare, and said: "I cannot understand, Cousin, how

you can put up with such poor food as this, but of course you cannot expect anything better in the country; come you with me and I will show you how to live. When you have been in town a week you will wonder how you could ever have stood a country life." No sooner said than done: the two mice set off for the town and arrived at the Town Mouse's residence late at night. "You will want some refreshment after our long journey," said the polite Town Mouse, and took his friend into the grand dining-room. There they found the remains of a fine feast, and soon the two mice were eating up jellies and cakes and all that was nice. Suddenly they heard growling and barking. "What is that?" said the Country Mouse. "It is only the dogs of the house," answered the other. "Only!" said the Country Mouse. "I do not like that music at my dinner." Just at that moment the door flew open, in came two huge mastiffs, and the two mice had to scamper down and run off.

"Good-bye, Cousin," said the Country Mouse. "What! going so soon?" said the other. "Yes," he replied;

"Better beans and bacon
in peace than
cakes and ale in fear."

The Dog and the Shadow

IT HAPPENED that a Dog had got a piece of meat and was carrying it home in his mouth to eat it in peace. Now on his way home he had to cross a plank lying across a running brook. As he crossed, he looked down and saw his own shadow reflected in the water beneath. Thinking it was another dog with another piece of meat, he made up his mind to have that also. So he made a snap at the shadow in the water, but as he opened his mouth the piece of meat fell out, dropped into the water and was never seen more.

Beware lest you lose
the substance
by grasping at the shadow.

The Crow and the Pitcher

A CROW, half-dead with thirst, came upon a Pitcher which had once been full of water; but when the Crow put its beak into the mouth of the Pitcher he found that only very little water was left in it, and that he could not reach far enough down to get at it. He tried, and he tried, but at last had to give up in despair. Then a thought came to him, and he took a pebble and dropped it into the Pitcher. Then he took another pebble and dropped it into the Pitcher. Then he took another pebble and dropped that into the Pitcher. Then he took another pebble and dropped that into the Pitcher. Then he took another pebble and dropped that into the Pitcher. Then he took another pebble and dropped that into the Pitcher. At last, at last, he saw the water mount up near him; and after casting in a few more pebbles he was able to quench his thirst and save his life.

Little by little
does the trick.

The Ant and the Grasshopper

IN A field one summer's day a Grasshopper was hopping about, chirping and singing to its heart's content. An Ant passed by, bearing along with great toil an ear of corn he was taking to the nest.

"Why not come and chat with me," said the Grasshopper, "instead of toiling and moiling in that way?"

"I am helping to lay up food for the winter," said the Ant, "and recommend you to do the same."

"Why bother about winter?" said the Grasshopper; "we have got plenty of food at present." But the Ant went on its way and continued its toil. When the winter came the Grasshopper had no food, and found itself dying of hunger, while it saw the ants distributing every day corn and grain from the stores they had collected in the summer. Then the Grasshopper knew:

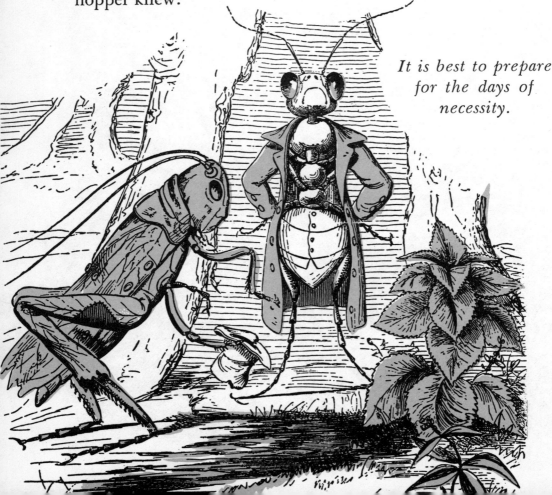

It is best to prepare for the days of necessity.

The Wolf in Sheep's Clothing

A WOLF found great difficulty in getting at the sheep owing to the vigilance of the shepherd and his dogs. But one day it found the skin of a sheep that had been flayed and thrown aside, so it put it on over its own pelt and strolled down among the sheep. The Lamb that belonged to the sheep, whose skin the Wolf was wearing, began to follow the Wolf in the Sheep's clothing; so, leading the Lamb a little apart, he soon made a meal off her, and for some time he succeeded in deceiving the sheep, and enjoying hearty meals.

Appearances
are deceptive.

Androcles

A SLAVE named Androcles once escaped from his master and fled to the forest. As he was wandering about there he came upon a Lion lying down moaning and groaning. At first he turned to flee, but finding that the Lion did not pursue him, he turned back and went up to him. As he came near, the Lion put out his paw, which was all swollen and bleeding, and Androcles found that a huge thorn had got into it, and was causing all the pain. He pulled out the thorn and bound up the paw of the Lion, who was soon able to rise and lick the hand of Androcles like a dog. Then the Lion took Androcles to his cave, and every day used to bring him meat from which

to live. But shortly afterwards both Androcles and the Lion were captured, and the slave was sentenced to be thrown to the Lion, after the latter had been kept without food for several days. The Emperor and his court came to see the spectacle, and Androcles was led out into the middle of the arena. Soon the Lion was let loose from his den, and rushed bounding and roaring towards his victim. But as soon as he came near to Androcles he recognized his friend, and fawned upon him, and licked his hands like a friendly dog. The Emperor, surprised at this, summoned Androcles to him, who told him the whole story. Whereupon the slave was pardoned and freed, and the Lion let loose to his native forest.

Gratitude is the sign
of noble souls.

Belling the Cat

Long ago, the mice held a general council to consider what measures they could take to outwit their common enemy, the Cat. Some said this, and some said that; but at last a young mouse got up and said he had a proposal to make, which he thought would meet the case. "You will all agree," said he, "that our chief danger consists in the sly and treacherous manner in which the enemy approaches us. Now, if we could receive some signal of her approach, we could easily escape from her. I venture, therefore, to propose that a small bell be procured, and attached by a ribbon round the neck of the Cat. By this means we should always know when she was about, and could easily retire while she was in the neighborhood."

This proposal met with general applause, until an old mouse got up and said: "That is all very well, but who is to bell the Cat?" The mice looked at one another and nobody spoke. Then the old mouse said:

*"It is easy to propose
impossible remedies."*

The Fox and the Goat

BY AN unlucky chance a Fox fell into a deep well from which he could not get out. A Goat passed by shortly afterwards, and asked the Fox what he was doing down there. "Oh, have you not heard?" said the Fox; "there is going to be a great drought, so I jumped down here in order to be sure to have water by me. Why don't you come down too?" The Goat thought well of this advice, and jumped down into the well. But the Fox immediately jumped on her back, and by putting his foot on her long horns managed to jump up to the edge of the well. "Good-bye, friend," said the Fox; "remember next time,

Never trust the advice
of a man in difficulties."

The Wolves
and the Sheep

"WHY should there always be this terrible fighting between us?" said the Wolves to the Sheep. "It is all the fault of those horrible Dogs. They always bark whenever we come near you, and attack us before we have done any harm. If you would only send them away, we might soon make a peace treaty and be friends forever."

The Sheep, poor silly creatures that they were, being easily fooled, dismissed the Dogs. The Wolves then proceeded at their own leisure to destroy the unguarded Sheep.

If you listen to your enemy
you will get yourself
into danger.

The Wolf and the Crane

A WOLF had been gorging on an animal he had killed, when suddenly a small bone in the meat stuck in his throat and he could not swallow it. He soon felt terrible pain in his throat, and ran up and down groaning and groaning and seeking for something to relieve the pain. He tried to induce everyone he met to remove the bone. "I would give anything," said he, "if you would take it out." At last the Crane agreed to try, and told the Wolf to lie on his side and open his jaws as wide as he could. Then the Crane put its long neck down the Wolf's throat, and with its beak loosened the bone, till at last it got it out.

"Will you kindly give me the reward you promised?" said the Crane.

The Wolf grinned and showed his teeth and said: "Be content. You have put your head inside a Wolf's mouth and taken it out again in safety; that ought to be reward enough for you."

Gratitude and greed
go not together.

The Hare and the Tortoise

THE Hare was once boasting of his speed before the other animals. "I have never yet been beaten," said he, "when I put forth my full speed. I challenge any one here to race with me."

The Tortoise said quietly: "I accept your challenge."

"That is a good joke," said the Hare; "I could dance round you all the way."

"Keep your boasting till you've beaten," answered the Tortoise. "Shall we race?"

So a course was fixed and a start was made. The Hare darted almost out of sight at once, but soon stopped and, to show his contempt for the Tortoise, lay down to have a nap. The Tortoise plodded on and plodded on, and when the Hare awoke from his nap, he saw the Tortoise just near the winning-post and could not run up in time to save the race. Then said the Tortoise:

"Plodding wins
the race."

Aladdin

AND THE WONDERFUL LAMP

ALADDIN was the son of a poor tailor in an Eastern city. He was a spoiled boy, and loved play better than work; so that when Mustapha, his father, died, he was not able to earn his living; and his poor mother had to spin cotton all day long to procure food for their support. But she dearly loved her son, knowing that he had a good heart, and she believed that as he grew older he would do better, and become at last a worthy and prosperous man. One day, when Aladdin was walking outside the town, an old man came up to him, and looking very hard in his face, said he was his father's brother, and had long been away in a distant country, but that now he wished to help his nephew to get on. He then put a ring on the boy's finger, telling him that no harm could happen to him so long as he wore it. Now, this strange man was no uncle of Aladdin, nor was he related at all to him; but he was a wicked magician, who wanted to make use of the lad's services, as we shall see presently.

The old man led Aladdin a good way into the country, until they came to a very lonely spot between two lofty black mountains. Here he lighted a fire, and threw into it some gum, all the time repeating many strange words. The ground then opened just before them, and a stone trapdoor appeared. After lifting this up, the Magician told Aladdin to go below, down some broken steps, and at the foot of these he would find three halls, in the last of which was a door leading to a garden full of beautiful trees; this he was to cross, and after mounting

some more steps, he would come to a
terrace, when he would see a niche, in
which there was a lighted Lamp. He
was then to take the Lamp, put out the
light, empty the oil, and bring it away
with him.

Aladdin. found all the Magician
had told him to be true; he passed

quickly but cautiously through the three halls, so as not even
to touch the walls with his clothes, as the Magician had
directed. He took the Lamp from the niche, threw out the
oil, and put it in his bosom. As he came back through the
garden, his eyes were dazzled with the bright colored fruits on
the trees, shining like glass. Many of these he plucked and
put in his pockets, and then returned with the Lamp, and
called upon his uncle to help him up the broken steps. "Give
me the Lamp," said the old man, angrily. "Not till I get out
safe," cried the boy. The Magician, in a passion, then slammed

down the trapdoor, and Aladdin was shut up fast enough. While crying bitterly, he by chance rubbed the ring, and a figure appeared before him, saying, "I am your slave, the Genie of the Ring; what do you desire?"

Aladdin told the Genie of the Ring that he only wanted to be set free, and to be taken back to his mother. In an instant he found himself at home, very hungry, and his poor mother was much pleased to see him again. He told her all that had happened; she then felt curious to look at the Lamp he had brought, and began rubbing it, to make it shine brighter. Both were quite amazed at seeing rise before them a strange figure; this proved to be the Genie of the Lamp, who asked for their commands. On hearing that food was what they most wanted, a black slave instantly entered with the choicest fare upon a dainty dish of silver, and with silver plates for them to eat from.

Aladdin and his mother feasted upon the rich fare brought to them, and sold the silver dish and plates, on the produce of which they lived happily for some weeks. Aladdin was now able to dress well, and in taking his usual walk, he one day chanced to see the Sultan's daughter coming with her attendants from the baths. He was so much struck with her beauty, that he fell in love with her at once, and told his mother that she must go to the Sultan, and ask him to give the Princess to be his wife. The poor woman said he must be crazy; but her son not only knew what a treasure he had got in the Magic Lamp, but he had also found how valu-

able were the shining fruits he had gathered, which he thought at the time to be only colored glass. At first he sent a bowlful of these jewels—for so they were—to the Sultan, who was amazed at their richness, and said to Aladdin's mother: "Your son shall have his wish, if he can send me, in a week, forty bowls like this, carried by twenty white and twenty black slaves, handsomely dressed." He thought by this to keep what he had got, and to hear no more of Aladdin. But the Genie of the Lamp soon brought the bowls of jewels and the slaves, and Aladdin's mother went with them to the Sultan.

The Sultan was overjoyed at receiving these rich gifts, and at once agreed that the Princess Bulbul should be the wife of Aladdin. The happy youth then summoned the Genie of the Lamp to assist him; and shortly set out for the Palace. He was dressed in a handsome suit of clothes, and rode a beautiful horse; by his side marched a number of attendants, scattering handfuls of gold among the people. As soon as they were married, Aladdin ordered the Genie of the Lamp to build, in the course of a night, a most superb Palace, and there the young couple lived quite happily for some time. One day, when Aladdin was out hunting with the Sultan, the wicked Magician, who had heard of his good luck, and wished to get hold of the Magic Lamp, cried out in the streets, "New lamps for old ones!" A silly maid in the Palace, hearing this, got leave of the Princess to change Aladdin's old Lamp, which she had seen on a cornice where he always left it, for a new one, and so the Magician got possession of it.

As soon as the Magician had safely got the Lamp, he caused the Genie to remove the Palace, and Bulbul within it, to Africa. Aladdin's grief was very great, and so was the rage of the Sultan at the loss of the Princess, and poor Aladdin's life was in some danger, for the Sultan threatened to kill him if he did not restore his daughter in three days. Aladdin first called upon the Genie of the Ring to help him, but all he could do was to take him to Africa.

The Princess was rejoiced to see him again, but was very sorry to find that she had been the cause of all their trouble by parting with the wonderful Lamp. Aladdin, however, consoled her, and told her that he had thought of a plan for getting it back. He then left her, but soon returned with a powerful sleeping-draught, and advised her to receive the Magician with pretended kindness, and pour it into his wine at dinner that day, so as to make him fall sound asleep, when they could take the Lamp from him. Everything happened as they expected; the Magician drank the wine, and when Aladdin came in, he found that he had fallen back lifeless on the couch. Aladdin took the Lamp from his bosom, and called upon the Genie to transport the Palace, the Princess, and himself, back to their native city. The Sultan was as much astonished and pleased at their return, as he had been provoked at the loss of his daughter; and Aladdin, with his Bulbul, lived long afterwards to enjoy his good fortune.

CINDERELLA

OR THE GLASS SLIPPER

ONCE upon a time there was a gentleman who
married, for his second wife, the proudest
and most haughty woman that ever was seen. She
had two daughters of her own, who were, indeed,
exactly like her in all things. The gentleman had
also a young daughter, of rare goodness and
sweetness of temper, which she took from her
mother, who was the best creature in the world.

The wedding was scarcely over, when the
stepmother's bad temper began to show itself. She
could not bear the goodness of this young girl,
because it made her own daughters appear the
more odious. The stepmother gave her the mean-
est work in the house to do; she had to scour the
dishes, tables, etc., and to scrub the floors and
clean out the bedrooms. The poor girl had to
sleep in the garret, upon a wretched straw bed,
while her sisters lay in fine rooms with inlaid
floors, upon beds of the very newest fashion, and
where they had looking-glasses so large that they
might see themselves at their full length. The
poor girl bore all patiently, and dared not com-
plain to her father, who would have scolded her
if she had done so, for his wife governed him entirely.

When she had done her work, she used to go
into the chimney corner, and sit down among the
cinders, hence she was called Cinderwench. The
younger sister of the two, who was not so
rude and uncivil as the elder, called her
Cinderella. However, Cinderella, in spite

of her mean apparel, was a hundred times more handsome than her sisters, though they were always richly dressed.

It happened that the King's son gave a ball, and invited to it all persons of fashion. Our young misses were also invited, for they cut a very grand figure among the people of the countryside. They were highly delighted with the invitation, and wonderfully busy in choosing the gowns, petticoats, and headdresses which might best become them. This made Cinderella's lot still harder, for it was she who ironed her sisters' linen and plaited their ruffles. They talked all day long of nothing but how they should be dressed.

"For my part," said the elder, "I will wear my red velvet suit with French trimmings."

"And I," said the younger, "shall wear my usual skirt; but then, to make amends for that I will put on my gold flowered mantle, and my diamond stomacher, which is far from being the most ordinary one in the world." They sent for the best hairdressers they could get to make up their hair in fashionable style, and bought patches for their cheeks. Cinderella was consulted in all these matters, for she had good taste. She advised them always for the best, and even offered her services to dress their hair, which they were very willing she should do.

As she was doing this, they said to her:—

"Cinderella, would you not be glad to go to the ball?"

"Young ladies," she said, "you only jeer at me; it is not for such as I am to go there."

"You are right," they replied; "people would laugh to see a Cinderwench at a ball."

Anyone but Cinderella would have dressed their hair awry, but she was good-natured, and arranged it perfectly well. They were almost two days without eating, so much were they transported with joy. They broke above a dozen laces in trying to lace themselves tight, that they might have a fine, slender shape, and they were continually at their looking-glass.

At last the happy day came; they went to Court, and Cinderella followed them with her eyes as long as she could, and when she had lost sight of them, she fell a-crying.

Her godmother, who saw her all in tears, asked her what was the matter.

"I wish I could—I wish I could—" but she could not finish for sobbing.

Her godmother, who was a fairy, said to her, "You wish you could go to the ball; is it not so?"

"Alas, yes," said Cinderella, sighing.

"Well," said her godmother, "be but a good girl, and I

will see that you go." Then she took her into her chamber, and said to her, "Run into the garden, and bring me a pumpkin."

Cinderella went at once to gather the finest she could get, and brought it to her godmother, not being able to imagine how this pumpkin could help her to go to the ball. Her godmother scooped out all the inside of it, leaving nothing but the rind. Then she struck it with her wand, and the pumpkin was instantly turned into a fine gilded coach.

She then went to look into the mouse-trap, where she found six mice, all alive. She ordered Cinderella to lift the trap-door, when, giving each mouse, as it went out, a little tap with her wand, it was that moment turned into a fine horse, and the six mice made a fine set of six horses of a beautiful mouse-colored, dapple gray.

Being at a loss for a coachman, Cinderella said, "I will go and see if there is not a rat in the rat-trap—we may make a coachman of him."

"You are right," replied her godmother; "go and look." Cinderella brought the rat-trap to her, and in it there were three huge rats. The fairy chose the one which had the largest beard, and, having touched him with her wand, he was turned into a fat coachman with

the finest mustache and whiskers ever seen.

    After that, she said to her:—

    "Go into the garden, and you will find six lizards behind the watering-pot; bring them to me."

She had no sooner done so than her godmother turned them into six footmen, who skipped up immediately behind the coach, with their liveries all trimmed with gold and silver, and they held on as if they had done nothing else their whole lives.

The fairy then said to Cinderella, "Well, you see here a carriage fit to go to the ball in; are you pleased with it?"

"Oh yes!" she cried; "but must I go as I am in these rags?"

Her godmother simply touched her with her wand, and, at the same moment, her clothes were turned into cloth of gold and silver, all decked with jewels. This done, she gave her a pair of the prettiest glass slippers in the whole world. Being thus attired, she got into the carriage, her godmother commanding her, above all things, not to stay till after midnight, and telling her, at the same time, that if she stayed one moment longer, the coach would be a pumpkin again, her horses mice, her coachman a rat, her footmen lizards, and her clothes would become just as they were before.

She promised her godmother she would not fail to leave the ball before midnight. She drove away, scarce able to contain herself for joy. The King's son, who was told that a great princess, whom nobody knew, was come, ran out to receive her. He gave her his hand as she alighted from the coach, and led her into the hall where the company was assembled. There was at once a profound silence; every one left off dancing, and the violins ceased to play, so attracted was everyone by the singular beauties of the unknown newcomer. Nothing was then heard but a confused sound of voices saying:—

"Ha! how beautiful she is! Ha! how beautiful she is!"

The King himself, old as he was, could not keep his eyes off her, and he told the Queen under his breath that it was a long time since he had seen so beautiful and lovely a creature.

All the ladies were busy studying her clothes and head-dress, so that they might have theirs made next day after the same pattern, provided they could meet with such fine materials and able hands to make them.

The King's son conducted her to the seat of honor, and afterwards took her out to dance with him. She danced so very gracefully that they all admired her more and more. A fine collation was served, but the young Prince ate not a morsel, so intently was he occupied with her.

She went and sat down beside her sisters, showing them a thousand civilities, and giving them among other things part of the oranges and citrons with which the Prince had regaled her. This very much surprised them, for they had not been presented to her.

Cinderella heard the clock strike a quarter to twelve. She at once made her adieus to the company and hastened away as fast as she could.

As soon as she got home, she ran to find her godmother, and, after having thanked her, she said she much wished she might go to the ball the next day, because the King's son had asked her to do so. As she was eagerly telling her god-mother all that happened at the ball, her two sisters knocked at the door; Cinderella opened it. "How long you have stayed!" said she, yawning, rubbing her eyes, and stretching herself as if she had been just awakened. She had not, however, had any desire to sleep since they went from home.

"If you had been at the ball," said one of her sisters, "you would not have been tired with it. There came thither the finest princess, the most beautiful ever was seen with mortal eyes. She showed us a thousand civilities, and gave us oranges and citrons."

Cinderella did not show any pleasure at this. Indeed, she asked them the name of the princess; but they told her they did not know it, and that the King's son was very much concerned, and would give all the world to know who she was. At this Cinderella, smiling, replied:—

"Was she then so very beautiful? How fortunate you have been! Could I not see her? Ah! dear Miss Charlotte, do lend me your yellow suit of clothes which you wear every day."

"Ay, to be sure!" cried Miss Charlotte;

"lend my clothes to such a dirty Cinderwench as thou art! I should be out of my mind to do so."

Cinderella, indeed, expected such an answer and was very glad of the refusal; for she would have been sadly troubled if her sister had lent her what she jestingly asked for. The next day the two sisters went to the ball, and so did Cinderella, but dressed more magnificently than before. The King's son was always by her side, and his pretty speeches to her never ceased. These by no means annoyed the young lady. Indeed, she quite forgot her godmother's orders to her, so that she heard the clock begin to strike twelve when she thought it could not be more than eleven. She then rose up and fled, as nimble as a deer. The Prince followed, but could not overtake her. She left behind one of her glass slippers, which the Prince took up most carefully. She got home, but quite out of breath, without her carriage, and in her old clothes, having nothing left her of all her finery but one of the little slippers, fellow to the one she had dropped. The guards at the palace gate were asked if they had not seen a princess go out, and they replied they had seen nobody go out but a young girl, very meanly dressed, and who had more the air of a poor country girl than of a young lady.

When the two sisters returned from the ball, Cinderella asked them if they had had a pleasant time, and if the fine lady had been there. They told her, yes; but that she hurried away the moment it struck twelve, and with so much haste that she dropped one of her little glass slippers, the prettiest in the world, which the King's son had taken up. They said, further, that he had done nothing but look at her all the time, and that most certainly he was very much in love with the beautiful owner of the glass slipper.

What they said was true; for a few days after the King's son caused it to be proclaimed, by sound of trumpet, that he would marry her whose foot this slipper would fit exactly. They began to try it on the princesses, then on the duchesses, and then on all the ladies of the Court; but in vain. It was brought to the two sisters, who did all they possibly could to thrust a foot into the slipper, but they could not succeed. Cinderella, who saw this, and knew her slipper, said to them, laughing:—

"Let me see if it will not fit me."

Her sisters burst out a-laughing, and began to banter her. The gentleman who was sent to try the slipper looked earnestly at Cinderella, and, finding her very handsome, said it was but just that she should try, and that he had orders to let every lady try it on.

He obliged Cinderella to sit down, and, putting the slipper to her little foot, he found it went on very easily, and fitted her as if it had been made of wax. The astonishment of her two sisters was great, but it was still greater when Cinderella pulled out of her pocket the other slipper and put it on her foot. Thereupon, in came her godmother, who, having touched Cinderella's clothes with her wand, made them more magnificent than those she had worn before.

And now her two sisters found her to be that beautiful lady they had seen at the ball. They threw themselves at her feet to beg pardon for all their ill treatment of her. Cinderella took them up, and, as she embraced them, said that she forgave them with all her heart, and begged them to love her always.

She was conducted to the young Prince, dressed as she was. He thought her more charming than ever, and, a few days after, married her. Cinderella, who was as good as she was beautiful, gave her two sisters a home in the palace, and that very same day married them to two great lords of the Court.

BEAUTY and

the BEAST

ONCE upon a time a rich Merchant, meeting with heavy losses, had to retire to a small cottage, with his three daughters. The two elder grumbled at this; but the youngest, named Beauty, tried to comfort her father and make his home happy. Once, when he was going on a journey, to try to mend his fortunes, the girls came to wish him goodbye; the two elder told him to bring them some nice presents on his return, but Beauty merely begged of him to bring her a rose. When the Merchant was on his way back he saw some fine roses, and thinking of Beauty, plucked the prettiest he could find. He had no sooner taken it than he saw a hideous Beast, armed with a deadly weapon. This fierce looking creature asked him how he dared to touch his flowers, and talked of putting him to death. The Merchant pleaded that he only took the rose to please his daughter Beauty, who had begged of him to get her one.

On this, the Beast said gruffly, "Well, I will not take your life, if you will bring one of your daughters here to die in your stead. She must come willingly, or I will not have her. You may stay and rest in my palace until to-morrow." Although the Mer-

chant found an excellent supper laid for him, he could not
eat; nor could he sleep, although everything was made ready
for his comfort. The next morning he set out on a handsome
horse, provided by the Beast.

When he came near his house his children came out to

greet him. But seeing the sadness of his face, and his eyes filled with tears, they asked the cause of his trouble. Giving Beauty the rose, he told her all. The two elder sisters laid all the blame on Beauty; but his sons, who had come from the forest to meet him, declared that they would go to the Beast instead. But Beauty said that as she was the cause of this misfortune, she alone must suffer for it, and was quite willing to go; and, in spite of the entreaties of her brothers, who loved her dearly, she set out with her father, to the secret joy of her two envious sisters.

When they arrived at the palace the doors opened of themselves; sweet music was heard, and they walked into a room where supper was prepared. Just as they had eaten their supper, the Beast entered, and said in a mild tone, "Beauty, did you come here willingly to die in place of your father?" "Willingly," she answered, with a trembling voice. "So much the better for you," said the Beast; "your father can stay here tonight, but must go home on the following morning." Beauty tried to cheer her father, at parting, by saying that she would try to soften the heart of the Beast, and get him to let her return home soon. After he was gone, she went into a fine room, on the door of which was written, in letters of gold, "Beauty's Room;" and lying on the table was a portrait of herself, under which were these words: "Beauty is Queen here; all things will obey her." All her meals were served to the sound of music, and at suppertime the Beast, drawing the curtains aside, would walk in, and talk so pleasantly that she soon lost much of her fear of him. At last, he turned towards her, and said, "Am I so very ugly?" "Yes, indeed you are," replied Beauty, "but then you are so kind that I don't mind your looks." "Will you marry me, then?" asked he. Beauty, looking away, said, "Pray don't ask me." He then bade her "Goodnight" with a sad voice, and she retired to her bedchamber.

The palace was full of galleries and apartments, containing the most beautiful works of art. In one room was a cage filled with rare birds. Not far from this room she saw a

numerous troop of monkeys of all sizes. They advanced to meet her, making her low bows. Beauty was much pleased with them, and said she would like some of them to follow her and keep her company. Instantly two tall young apes, in court dresses, advanced, and placed themselves with great gravity beside her, and two sprightly little monkeys took up her train as pages. From this time the monkeys always waited upon her with all the attention and respect that officers of a royal household are accustomed to pay to queens.

Beauty was now, in fact, quite the Queen of the palace, and all her wishes were gratified; but, excepting at supper-time, she was always alone; the Beast then appeared, and behaved so agreeably that she liked him more and more. But to his question, "Beauty, will you marry me?" he never could get any other answer than a shake of the head from her, on which he always took his leave very sadly.

Although Beauty had everything she could wish for she was not happy, as she could not forget her father, and brothers, and sisters. At last, one evening, she begged so hard of the Beast to let her go home that he agreed to her wish, on her

promising not to stay away longer than two months, and gave her a ring, telling her to place it on her dressing-table whenever she desired to go or to return; and then showed her where to find suitable clothes, as well as presents to take home. The poor Beast was more sad than ever. She tried to cheer him, saying, "Beauty will soon return," but nothing seemed to comfort him. Beauty then went to her room, and before retiring to rest she took care to place the ring on the dressing-table. When

she awoke next morning, what was her joy at finding herself in
her father's house, with the gifts and clothes from the palace
at her bedside.

At first she wondered where she was; but she soon heard
the voice of her father, and, rushing out, she flung her arms
round his neck. The father and daughter had much to say to
each other. Beauty related all that had happened to her at the

palace. Her father, enriched by the liberality of the Beast, had left his old house, and now lived in a very large city, and her sisters were engaged to be married to young men of good family.

When she had passed some weeks with her family, Beauty found that her sisters, who were secretly vexed at her good fortune, still looked upon her as a rival, and treated her with coldness. Besides this, she remembered her promise to the Beast, and resolved to return to him. But her father and brothers begged her to stay a day or two longer, and she could not resist their entreaties. But one night she dreamed that the poor Beast was lying dead in the palace garden; she awoke in a fright, looked for her ring, and placed it on the table. In the morning she was at the Palace again, but the Beast was nowhere to be found; at last she ran to the place in the garden that she had dreamed about, and there, sure enough, the poor Beast was, lying senseless on his back.

At this sight Beauty wept and reproached herself for having caused his death. She ran to a fountain and sprinkled his face with water. The Beast opened his eyes, and as soon as he could speak, he said, sorrowfully, "Now that I see you once more, I die contented." "No, no!" she cried, "you shall not die! Oh, live to be my husband, and Beauty will be your faithful wife!" The moment she had uttered these words, a dazzling light shone everywhere; the Palace windows glittered with lamps, and music was heard around. To her great wonder, a handsome young Prince stood before her, who said that her words had broken the spell of a magician, by which he had been doomed to wear the form of a Beast, until a beautiful girl should love him in spite of his ugliness. The grateful Prince now claimed Beauty as his wife. The Merchant was soon informed of his daughter's good fortune, and the Prince was married to Beauty on the following day.

Sleeping

Beauty

O<small>NCE</small> upon a time there was a king and a queen, who were very sorry that they had no children,—so sorry that it cannot be told.

At last, however, the Queen had a daughter. There was a very fine christening; and the Princess had for her godmothers all the fairies they could find in the whole kingdom (there were seven of them), so that every one of them might confer a gift upon her, as was the custom of fairies in those days. By this means the Princess had all the perfections imaginable.

After the christening was over, the company returned to the King's palace, where was prepared a great feast for the fairies. There was placed before every one of them a magnificent cover with a case of massive gold, wherein were a spoon, and a knife and fork, all of pure gold set with diamonds and rubies. But as they were all sitting down at table they saw a very old fairy come into the hall. She had not been invited, because for more than fifty years she had not been out of a certain tower, and she was believed to be either dead or enchanted.

The King ordered her a cover, but he could not give her a case of gold as the others had, because seven only had been made for the seven fairies. The old fairy fancied she was slighted, and muttered threats between her teeth. One of the young fairies who sat near heard her, and, judging that she might give the little Princess some unlucky gift, hid herself behind the curtains as soon as they left the table. She hoped that she might speak last and undo as much as she could the evil which the old fairy might do.

In the meanwhile all the fairies began to give their gifts to the Princess. The youngest gave her for her gift that she should be the most beautiful person in the world; the next, that she should have the wit of an angel; the third, that she should be able to do everything she did gracefully; the fourth, that she should dance perfectly; the fifth, that she should sing like a nightingale; and the sixth, that she should play all kinds of musical instruments to the fullest perfection.

The old fairy's turn coming next, her head shaking more with spite than with age, she said that the Princess should pierce her hand with a spindle and die of the wound. This terrible gift made the whole company tremble, and everybody fell a-crying.

At this very instant the young fairy came from behind the curtain and said these words in a loud voice:—

"Assure yourselves, O King and Queen, that your daughter shall not die of this disaster. It is true, I have no power to undo entirely what my elder has done. The Princess shall indeed pierce her hand with a spindle; but, instead of dying, she shall only fall into a deep sleep, which shall last a hundred years, at the end of which a king's son shall come and awake her."

The King, to avoid the misfortune foretold by the old fairy, issued orders forbidding any one, on pain of death, to spin with a distaff and spindle, or to have a spindle in his house. About fifteen or sixteen years after, the King and Queen being absent at one of their country villas, the young Princess was one day running up and down the palace; she went from room to room, and at last she came into a little garret on the top of the tower, where a good old woman, alone, was spinning with her spindle. This good woman had never heard of the King's orders against spindles.

"What are you doing there, my good woman?" said the Princess.

"I am spinning, my pretty child," said the old woman, who did not know who the Princess was.

"Ha!" said the Princess, "this is very pretty; how do you do it? Give it to me. Let me see if I can do it."

She had no sooner taken it into her hand then, either because she was too quick and heedless, or because the decree of the fairy had so ordained, it ran into her hand, and she fell down in a swoon.

The good old woman, not knowing what to do, cried out for help. People came in from every quarter; they threw water upon the face of the Princess, unlaced her, struck her on the palms of her hands, and rubbed her temples with cologne water; but nothing would bring her to herself.

Then the King, who came up at hearing the noise, remembered what the fairies had foretold. He knew very well that this must come to pass, since the fairies had foretold it, and he caused the Princess to be carried into the finest room in his palace, and to be laid upon a bed all embroidered with gold and silver. One would have taken her for a little angel, she was so beautiful; for her swooning had not dimmed the brightness of her complexion; her cheeks were carnation, and her lips coral. It is true her eyes were shut, but she was heard to breathe softly, which satisfied those about her that she was not dead.

The King gave orders that they should let her sleep quietly till the time came for her to awake. The good fairy who had saved her life by condemning her to sleep a hundred years was in the kingdom of Matakin, twelve thousand leagues off, when this accident befell the Princess; but she was instantly informed of it by a little dwarf, who had seven-leagued boots, that is, boots with which he could stride over seven leagues of ground at once. The fairy started off at once, and arrived, about an hour later, in a fiery chariot drawn by dragons.

The King handed her out of the chariot, and she approved everything he had done; but as she had very great foresight, she thought that when the Princess should awake she might not know what to do with herself, if she was all alone in this old palace. This was what she did: she touched with her wand everything in the palace (except the King and Queen) —governesses, maids of honor, ladies of the bedchamber, gentlemen, officers, stewards, cooks, undercooks, kitchen maids, guards with their porters, pages, and footmen; she likewise touched all the horses which were in the stables, the cart horses, the hunters and the saddle horses, the grooms, the great dogs in the outward court, and little Mopsey, too, the Princess's spaniel, which was lying on the bed.

As soon as she touched them they all fell asleep, not to awake again until their mistress did, that they might be ready to wait upon her when she wanted them. The very spits at the fire, as full as they could hold of partridges and pheasants, fell asleep, and the fire itself as well. All this was done in a moment. Fairies are not long in doing their work.

And now the King and Queen, having kissed their dear child without waking her, went out of the palace and sent forth orders that nobody should come near it.

These orders were not necessary; for in a quarter of an hour's time there grew up all round about the park such a vast number of trees, great and small, bushes and brambles, twining one within another, that neither man nor beast could pass through; so that nothing could be seen but the very top of the towers of the palace; and that, too, only from afar off. Everyone knew that this also was the work of the fairy in order that while the Princess slept she should have nothing to fear from curious people. After a hundred years the son of the King then reigning, who was of another family from that of the sleeping Princess, was a-hunting on that side of the country, and he asked what those towers were which he saw in the middle of a great thick wood. Every one answered according as they had heard. Some said that it was an old haunted castle, others that all the witches of the country held their midnight revels there, but the common opinion was that it was an ogre's dwelling, and that he carried to it all the little children he could catch, so as to eat them up at his leisure, without any one being able to follow him, for he alone had the power to make his way through the wood.

The Prince did not

know what to believe, and presently a very aged countryman spake to him thus:—

"May it please your royal Highness, more than fifty years since I heard from my father that there was then in this castle the most beautiful princess that was ever seen; that she must sleep there a hundred years, and that she should be waked by a king's son, for whom she was reserved."

The young Prince on hearing this was all on fire. He thought, without weighing the matter, that he could put an end to this rare adventure; and, pushed on by love and the desire of glory, resolved at once to look into it.

As soon as he began to get near to the wood, all the great trees, the bushes, and brambles gave way of themselves to let him pass through. He walked up to the castle which he saw at the end of a large avenue; and you can imagine he was a good deal surprised when he saw none of his people following him, because the trees closed again as soon as he had passed through them. However, he did not cease from continuing his way; a young prince in search of glory is ever valiant.

He came into a spacious outer court, and what he saw was enough to freeze him with horror. A frightful silence reigned over all; the image of death was everywhere, and there was nothing to be seen but what seemed to be the outstretched bodies of dead men and animals. He, however, very well knew, by the ruby faces and pimpled noses of the porters, that they were only asleep; and their goblets, wherein still remained some drops of wine, showed plainly that they had fallen asleep while drinking their wine.

He then crossed a court paved with marble, went up the stairs, and came into the guard chamber, where guards were standing in their ranks, with their muskets upon their shoulders, and snoring with all their might. He went through several rooms full of gentlemen and ladies, some standing and others sitting, but all were asleep. He came into a gilded chamber, where he saw upon a bed, the curtains of which were all open, the most beautiful sight ever beheld—a princess who appeared to be about fifteen or sixteen years of age, and whose bright and resplendent beauty had something divine in it. He approached with trembling and admiration, and fell down upon his knees before her.

Then, as the end of the enchantment was come, the Princess awoke, and looking on him with eyes more tender than could have been expected at first sight, said:—

"Is it you, my Prince? You have waited a long while."

The Prince, charmed with

these words, and much more with the manner in which they were spoken, knew not how to show his joy and gratitude; he assured her that he loved her better than he did himself. Their discourse was not very connected, but they were the better pleased, for where there is much love there is little eloquence. He was more at a loss than she, and we need not wonder at it; she had had time to think of what to say to him; for it is evident (though history says nothing of it) that the good fairy, during so long a sleep, had given her very pleasant dreams. In short, they talked together for four hours, and then they said not half they had to say.

In the meanwhile all the palace had woke up with the Princess; everyone thought upon his own business, and as they were not in love, they were ready to die of hunger. The lady of honor, being as sharp set as the other folks, grew very impatient, and told the Princess aloud that the meal was served. The Prince helped the Princess to rise. She was entirely and very magnificently dressed; but his royal Highness took care not to tell her that she was dressed like his great-grandmother, and had a high collar. She looked not a bit the less charming and beautiful for all that.

They went into the great mirrored hall, where they supped, and were served by the officers of the Princess's household. The violins and haut-boys played old tunes, but they were excellent, though they had not been played for a hundred years; and after supper, without losing any time, the lord almoner married them in the chapel of the castle. They had two lovely children, a boy and a girl, and lived happily ever after.

Rumpelstiltskin

THERE was once a miller who was poor, but he had one beautiful daughter. It happened one day that he came to speak with the king, and, to give himself consequence, he told him that he had a daughter who could spin gold out of straw. The king said to the miller,

"That is an art that pleases me well; if thy daughter is as clever as you say, bring her to my castle tomorrow, that I may put her to the proof."

When the girl was brought to him, he led her into a room that was quite full of straw, and gave her a wheel and spindle, and said,

"Now set to work, and if by the early morning thou hast not spun this straw to gold thou shalt die." And he shut the door himself, and left her there alone.

And so the poor miller's daughter was left there sitting, and could not think what to do for her life. She had no notion how to set to work to spin gold from straw, and her distress grew so great that she began to weep. Then all at once the door opened, and in came a little man, who said,

"Good evening, miller's daughter; why are you crying?"

"Oh!" answered the girl, "I have got to spin gold out of straw, and I don't understand the business."

Then the little man said,

"What will you give me if I spin it for you?"

"My necklace," said the girl.

The little man took the necklace, seated himself before the wheel, and whirr, whirr, whirr! Three times round and the bobbin was full; then he took up another, and whirr, whirr, whirr! Three times round, and that was full; and so he

went on till the morning, when all the straw had been spun, and all the bobbins were full of gold. At sunrise came the king, and when he saw the gold he was astonished and very much rejoiced, for he was very avaricious. He had the miller's daughter taken into another room filled with straw, much bigger than the last, and told her that as she valued her life she must spin it all in one night. The girl did not know what to do, so she began to cry, and then the door opened, and the little man appeared and said,

"What will you give me if I spin all this straw into gold?"

"The ring from my finger," answered the girl.

So the little man took the ring, and began again to send the wheel whirring round, and by next morning all the straw was spun into glistening gold. The king was rejoiced beyond measure at the sight, but as he could never have enough of gold, he had the miller's daughter taken into a still larger room full of straw, and said,

"This, too, must be spun in one night, and if you accomplish it you shall be my wife." For he thought, "Although she is but a miller's daughter, I am not likely to find anyone richer in the whole world."

As soon as the girl was left alone, the little man appeared for the third time and said,

"What will you give me if I spin the straw for you this time?"

"I have nothing left to give," answered the girl.

"Then you must promise me the first child you have after you are queen," said the little man.

"But who knows whether that will happen?" thought the girl; but as she did not know what else to do in her necessity, she promised the little man what he desired, upon which he began to spin, until all the straw was gold. And when in the morning the king came and found all done according to his wish, he caused the wedding to be held at once, and the miller's pretty daughter became a queen.

In a year's time she brought a fine child into the world,

and thought no more of the little man; but one day he came suddenly into her room, and said,

"Now give me what you promised me."

The queen was terrified greatly, and offered the little man all the riches of the kingdom if he would only leave the child; but the little man said,

"No, I would rather have something living than all the treasures of the world."

Then the queen began to lament and to weep, so that the little man had pity upon her.

"I will give you three days," said he, "and if at the end of that time you cannot tell my name, you must give up the child to me."

Then the queen spent the whole night in thinking over all the names that she had ever heard, and sent a messenger through the land to ask far and wide for all the names that could be found. And when the little man came next day, (beginning with Caspar, Melchior, Balthazar) she repeated all she knew, and went through the whole list, but after each the little man said,

"That is not my name."

The second day the queen sent to inquire of all the neighbors what the servants were called, and told the little man all the most unusual and singular names, saying,

"Perhaps you are called Roast-ribs, or Sheepshanks, or Spindleshanks?" But he answered nothing but,

"That is not my name."

The third day the messenger came back again, and said, "I have not been able to find one single new name; but as I passed through the woods I came to a high hill, and near it was a little house, and before the house burned a fire, and round the fire danced a comical little man, and he hopped on one leg and cried,

"To-day do I bake, tomorrow I brew,
The day after that the queen's child
      comes in;
And oh! I am glad that nobody knew
That the name I am called is
      Rumpelstiltskin!"

You cannot think how pleased the queen was to hear that name, and soon afterwards, when the little man walked in and said, "Now, Mrs. Queen, what is my name?" she said at first,

"Are you called Jack?"

"No," answered he.

"Are you called Harry?" she asked again.

"No," answered he. And then she said,

"Then perhaps your name is Rumpelstiltskin!"

"The devil told you that! the devil told you that!" cried the little man, and in his anger he stamped with his right foot so hard that it went into the ground above his knee; then he seized his left foot with both his hands in such a fury that he split in two, and there was an end of him.

PUSS IN BOOTS

ONCE upon a time there was a miller who left no more riches to the three sons he had than his mill, his ass, and his cat. The division was soon made. Neither the lawyer nor the attorney was sent for. They would soon have eaten up all the poor property. The eldest had the mill, the second the ass, and the youngest nothing but the cat.

The youngest, as we can understand, was quite unhappy at having so poor a share.

"My brothers," said he, "may get their living handsomely enough by joining their stocks together; but, for my part, when I have eaten up my cat, and made me a muff of his skin, I must die of hunger."

The Cat, who heard all this, without appearing to take any notice, said to him with a grave and serious air:—

"Do not thus afflict yourself, my master; you have nothing else to do but to give me a bag, and get a pair of boots made for me, that I may scamper through the brambles, and you shall see that you have not so poor a portion in me as you think."

Though the Cat's master did not think much of what he said, he had seen him play such cunning tricks to catch rats and mice—hanging himself by the heels, or hiding himself in

the meal, to make believe he was dead—that he did not altogether despair of his helping him in his misery. When the Cat had what he asked for, he booted himself very gallantly, and putting his bag about his neck, he held the strings of it in his two forepaws, and went into a warren where there was a great number of rabbits. He put bran and sow-thistle into his bag, and, stretching out at length, as if he were dead, he waited for some young rabbits, not yet acquainted with the deceits of the world, to come and rummage his bag for what he had put into it.

Scarcely was he settled but he had what he wanted. A rash and foolish young rabbit jumped into his bag, and Monsieur Puss, immediately drawing close the strings, took him and killed him at once. Proud of his prey, he went with it to the palace, and asked to speak with the King. He was shown upstairs into his Majesty's apartment, and, making a low bow to the King, he said:—

"I have brought you, sire, a rabbit which my noble Lord, the Master of Carabas" (for that was the title which Puss was pleased to give his master) "has commanded me to present to your Majesty from him."

"Tell thy master," said the King, "that I thank him, and that I am pleased with his gift."

Another time he went and hid himself among some standing corn, still holding his bag open; and when a brace of partridges ran into it, he drew the strings, and so caught them both. He then went and made a present of these to the King, as he had done before of the rabbit which he took in the warren. The King, in like manner, received the partridges with great pleasure, and ordered his servants to reward him.

The Cat continued for two or three months thus to carry to his Majesty, from time to time, some of his master's game. One day when he knew that the King was to take the air along the riverside, with his daughter, the most beautiful princess in the world, he said to his master:—

"If you will follow my advice, your fortune is made. You have nothing else to do but go and bathe in the river, just at the spot I shall show you, and leave the rest to me."

The Marquis of Carabas did what the Cat advised him to, without knowing what could be the use of doing it. While he was bathing, the King passed by, and the Cat cried out with all his might:—

"Help! help! My Lord the Marquis of Carabas is drowning!"

At this noise the King put his head out of the coach window, and seeing the Cat who had so often brought him game, he commanded his guards to run immediately to the assistance of his Lordship the Marquis of Carabas.

While they were drawing the poor Marquis out of the river, the Cat came up to the coach and told the King that, while his master was bathing, there came by some rogues, who ran off with his clothes, though he had cried out, "Thieves! thieves!" several times, as loud as he could. The cunning Cat had hidden the clothes under a great stone. The King immediately commanded the officers of his wardrobe to run and fetch one of his best suits for the Lord Marquis of Carabas.

The King was extremely polite to him, and as the fine clothes he had given him set off his good looks (for he was well made and handsome), the King's daughter found him very much to her liking, and the Marquis of Carabas had no sooner cast two or three respectful and somewhat tender glances than she fell in love with him to distraction. The King would have him come into the coach and take part in the airing. The Cat, overjoyed to see his plan begin to succeed, marched on before, and, meeting with some countrymen, who were mowing a meadow, he said to them:—

"Good people, you who are mowing, if you do not tell the King that the meadow you mow belongs to my Lord Marquis of Carabas, you shall be chopped as small as herbs for the pot."

The King did not fail to ask the mowers to whom the meadow they were mowing belonged.

"To my Lord Marquis of Carabas," answered they all

together, for the Cat's threat had made them afraid.

"You have a good property there," said the King to the Marquis of Carabas.

"You see, sire," said the Marquis, "this is a meadow which never fails to yield a plentiful harvest every year."

The Master Cat, who went still on before, met with some reapers, and said to them:—

"Good people, you who are reaping, if you do not say that all this corn belongs to the Marquis of Carabas, you shall be chopped as small as herbs for the pot."

The King, who passed by a moment after, wished to know to whom belonged all that corn, which he then saw.

"To my Lord Marquis of Carabas," replied the reapers, and the King was very well pleased with it, as well as the Marquis, whom he congratulated thereupon. The Master Cat, who went always before, said the same thing to all he met, and the King was astonished at the vast estates of my Lord Marquis of Carabas.

Monsieur Puss came at last to a stately castle, the master of which was an Ogre, the richest ever known; for all the lands which the King had then passed through belonged to this castle. The Cat, who had taken care to inform himself who this Ogre was and what he could do, asked to speak with him, saying he could not pass so near his castle without having the honor of paying his respects to him.

The Ogre received him as civilly as an Ogre could do, and made him sit down.

"I have been assured," said the Cat, "that you have the gift of being able to change yourself into all sorts of creatures you have a mind to; that you can, for example, transform yourself into a lion, or elephant, and the like."

"That is true," answered the Ogre, roughly; "and to convince you, you shall see me now become a lion."

Puss was so terrified at the sight of a lion so near him that he immediately climbed into the gutter, not without much trouble and danger, because of his boots, which were of no use at all to him for walking upon the tiles. A little while after, when Puss saw that the Ogre had resumed his natural form, he came down, and owned he had been very much frightened.

"I have, moreover, been informed," said the Cat, "but I know not how to believe it, that you have also the power to take on you the shape of the smallest animals; for example, to change yourself into a rat or a mouse, but I must own to you I take this to be impossible."

"Impossible!" cried the Ogre; "you shall see." And at the same time he changed himself into a mouse, and began to run about the floor. Puss no sooner perceived this then he fell upon him and ate him up.

Meanwhile, the King, who saw, as he passed, this fine castle of the Ogre's, had a mind to go into it. Puss, who heard the noise of his Majesty's coach coming over the drawbridge, ran out, and said to the King, "Your Majesty is welcome to this castle of my Lord Marquis of Carabas."

"What! my Lord Marquis," cried the King, "and does this castle also belong to you? There can be nothing finer than this courtyard and all the stately buildings which surround it; let us see the interior, if you please."

The Marquis gave his hand to the young Princess, and followed the King, who went first. They passed into the great hall, where they found a magnificent collation, which the Ogre had prepared for his friends, who were that very day to visit him, but dared not to enter, knowing the King was there. His Majesty, charmed with the good qualities of my Lord of Carabas, as was also his daughter, who had fallen violently in love with him, and seeing the vast estate he possessed, said to him:—

"It will be owing to yourself only, my Lord Marquis, if you are not my son-in-law."

The Marquis, with low bows, accepted the honor which his Majesty conferred upon him, and forthwith that very same day married the Princess.

Puss became a great lord, and never ran after mice anymore except for his diversion.

Dick Whittington and His Cat

IN THE reign of the famous King Edward III, there was a little boy called Dick Whittington, whose father and mother died when he was very young. As poor Dick was not old enough to work, he was very badly off; he got but little for his dinner, and sometimes nothing at all for his breakfast; for the people who lived in the village were very poor indeed, and could not spare him much more than the parings of potatoes, and now and then a hard crust of bread.

Now Dick had heard many, many very strange things about the great city called London; for the country people at that time thought that folks in London were all fine gentlemen and ladies; and that there was singing and music there all day long; and that the streets were all paved with gold.

One day a large waggon and eight horses, all with bells at their heads, drove through the village while Dick was standing by the sign-post. He thought that this waggon must be going to the fine town of London; so he took courage, and asked the waggoner to let him walk with him by the side of the waggon. As soon as the waggoner heard that poor Dick had no father or mother, and saw by his ragged clothes that he could not be worse off than he was, he told him he might go if he would, so off they set together.

So Dick got safe to London, and was in such a hurry to see the fine streets paved all over with gold, that he did not

even stay to thank the kind
waggoner, but ran off as fast as
his legs would carry him,
through many of the streets,
thinking every moment to
come to those that were paved
with gold; for Dick had seen a
guinea three times in his own
little village, and remembered
what a deal of money it brought in change; so he thought he
had nothing to do but to take up some little bits of the pavement, and should then have as much money as he could wish
for.

Poor Dick ran till he was tired, and had quite forgot his
friend the waggoner; but at last, finding it grow dark, and
that every way he turned he saw nothing but dirt instead of
gold, he sat down in a dark corner and cried himself to
sleep.

Little Dick was all night in the streets; and next morning, being very hungry, he got up and walked about, and
asked everybody he met to give him a halfpenny to keep him
from starving; but nobody stayed to answer him, and only
two or three gave him a halfpenny; so that the poor boy was
soon quite weak and faint for the want of victuals.

In this distress he asked charity of several people and one
of them said crossly: "Go to work for an idle rogue." "That I
will," said Dick, "I will go to work for you, if you will let me."
But the man only cursed at him and went on.

At last a good-natured looking gentleman saw how hungry
he looked. "Why don't you go to work, my lad?" said he to
Dick. "That I would, but I do not know how to get any,"
answered Dick. "If you are willing, come along with me,"
said the gentleman, and took him to a hayfield, where Dick
worked briskly, and lived merrily till the hay was made.

After this he found himself as badly off as before; and
being almost starved again, he laid himself down at the door

of Mr. Fitzwarren, a rich merchant. Here he was soon seen by the cook-maid, who was an ill-tempered creature, and happened just then to be very busy dressing dinner for her master and mistress; so she called out to poor Dick: "What business have you there, you lazy rogue? There is nothing else but beggars; if you do not take yourself away, we will see how you will like a sousing of some dish-water; I have some here hot enough to make you jump."

Just at that time Mr. Fitzwarren himself came home to dinner; and when he saw a dirty ragged boy lying at the door, he said to him: "Why do you lie there, my boy? You seem old enough to work; I am afraid you are inclined to be lazy."

"No, indeed, sir," said Dick to him, "that is not the case, for I would work with all my heart, but I do not know anybody, and I believe I am very sick for the want of food."

"Poor fellow, get up; let me see what ails you." Dick now tried to rise, but was obliged to lie down again, being too weak to stand, for he had not eaten any food for three days, and was no longer able to run about and beg a halfpenny of people in the street. So the kind merchant ordered him to be taken into the house, and have a good dinner given him, and be kept to do what work he was able to do for the cook.

Little Dick would have lived very happy in this good family if it had not been for the ill-natured cook. She used to say: "You are under me, so look sharp; clean the spit and the dripping-pan, make the fires, wind up the jack, and do all the scullery work nimbly, or ——" and she would shake the ladle at him. Besides, she was so fond of basting, that when she had no meat to baste, she would baste poor Dick's head and shoulders with a broom, or anything else that happened to fall in her way. At last her ill-usage of him was told to Alice, Mr. Fitzwarren's daughter, who told the cook she should be turned away if she did not treat him kinder.

The behavior of the cook was now a little better; but besides this, Dick had another hardship to get over. His bed stood in a garret, where there were so many holes in the floor and the walls that every night he was tormented with rats and mice. A gentleman having given Dick a penny for cleaning his shoes, he thought he would buy a cat with it. The next day he saw a girl with a cat, and asked her, "Will you let me have that cat for a penny?" The girl said: "Yes, that I will, master, though she is an excellent mouser."

Dick hid his cat in the garret, and always took care to carry a part of his dinner to her; and in a short time he had no more trouble with the rats and mice, but slept quite sound every night.

Soon after this, his master had a ship ready to sail; and as it was the custom that all his servants should have some chance for good fortune as well as himself, he called them all into the parlor and asked them what they would send out.

They all had something that they were willing to venture except poor Dick, who had neither money nor goods, and therefore could send nothing. For this reason he did not

235

come into the parlor with the rest; but Miss Alice guessed what was the matter, and ordered him to be called in. She then said: "I will lay down some money for him, from my own purse; but her father told her: "This will not do, for it must be something of his own."

When poor Dick heard this, he said: "I have nothing but

a cat which I bought for a penny some time since of a little girl."

"Fetch your cat then, my lad," said Mr. Fitzwarren, "and let her go."

Dick went upstairs and brought down poor puss, with tears in his eyes, and gave her to the captain; "For," he said, "I shall now be kept awake all night by the rats and mice." All the company laughed at Dick's odd venture; and Miss Alice, who felt pity for him, gave him some money to buy another cat.

This, and many other marks of kindness shown him by Miss Alice, made the ill-tempered cook jealous of poor Dick, and she began to use him more cruelly than ever, and always made game of him for sending his cat to sea. She asked him: "Do you think your cat will sell for as much money as would buy a stick to beat you?"

At last poor Dick could not bear this usage any longer, and he thought he would run away from his place; so he packed up his few things, and started very early in the morning, on All-hallows Day, the first of November. He walked as far as Halloway; and there sat down on a stone, which to this day is called "Whittington's Stone," and began to think to himself which road he should take.

While he was thinking what he should do, the Bells of Bow Church, which at that time were only six, began to ring, and at their sound seemed to say to him:

"Turn again, Whittington,
Thrice Lord Mayor of London."

"Lord Mayor of London!" said he to himself. "Why, to be sure, I would put up with almost anything now, to be Lord Mayor of London, and ride in a fine coach, when I grow to be a man! Well, I will go back, and think nothing of the cuffing and scolding of the old cook, if I am to be Lord Mayor of London at last."

Dick went back, and was lucky enough to get into the house, and set about his work, before the old cook came downstairs.

We must now follow Miss Puss to the coast of Africa. The ship with the cat on board was a long time at sea; and was at last driven by the winds on a part of the coast of Barbary, where the only people were the Moors, unknown to the English. The people came in great numbers to see the sailors, because they were of different color to themselves, and treated them civilly; and, when they became better acquainted, were very eager to buy the fine things that the ship was loaded with.

When the captain saw this, he sent patterns of the best things he had to the king of the country; who was so much pleased with them, that he sent for the captain to the palace. Here they were placed, as it is the custom of the country, on rich carpets flowered with gold and silver. The king and queen were seated at the upper end of the room; and a number of dishes were brought in for dinner. They had not sat long, when a vast number of rats and mice rushed in, and devoured all the meat in an instant. The captain wondered at this, and asked if these vermin were not unpleasant.

"Oh yes," said they, "very offensive; and the king would give half his treasure to be freed of them, for they not only destroy his dinner, as you see, but they assault him in his chamber, and even in bed, so that he is obliged to be watched while he is sleeping, for fear of them."

The captain jumped for joy; he remembered poor Whittington and his cat, and told the king he had a creature on board the ship that would despatch all these vermin immediately. The king jumped so high at the joy which the news gave him, that his turban dropped off his head. "Bring this creature to me," says he; "vermin are dreadful in a court, and if she will perform what you say, I will load your ship with gold and jewels in exchange for her."

The captain, who knew his business, took this opportunity to set forth the merits of Mrs. Puss. He told his majesty: "It is not very convenient to part with her, as, when she is gone, the rats and mice may destroy the goods in the ship—but to oblige your majesty, I will fetch her."

"Run, run!" said the queen; "I am impatient to see the dear creature."

Away went the captain to the ship, while another dinner was got ready. He put Puss under his arm, and arrived at the palace just in time to see the table full of rats. When the cat saw them, she did not wait for bidding, but jumped out of the captain's arms, and in a few minutes laid almost all the rats and mice dead at her feet. The rest of them in their fright scampered away to their holes.

The king was quite charmed to get rid so easily of such plagues, and the queen desired that the creature who had done them so great a kindness might be brought to her, that she might look at her. Upon which the captain called: "Pussy, pussy, pussy!" and she came to him. He then presented her to the queen, who started back, and was afraid to touch a creature who had made such a havoc among the rats and mice. How-

ever, when the captain stroked the cat and called: "Pussy, pussy," the queen also touched her and cried: "Putty, putty," for she had not learned English. He then put her down on the queen's lap, where she purred and played with her majesty's hand, and then purred herself to sleep.

The king, having seen the exploits of Mrs. Puss, and being informed that her kittens would stock the whole country, and keep it free from rats, bargained with the captain for the whole ship's cargo, and then gave him ten times as much for the cat as all the rest amounted to.

The captain then took leave of the royal party, and set sail with a fair wind for England, and after a happy voyage arrived safe in London.

One morning, early, Mr. Fitzwarren had just come to his counting-house and seated himself at the desk, to count over the cash, and settle the business for the day, when somebody came tap, tap, at the door. "Who's there?" said Mr. Fitzwarren. "A friend," answered the other; "I come to bring you good news of your ship *Unicorn*. The merchant, bustling up in such a hurry that he forgot his gout, opened the door, and who should he see waiting but the captain and factor, with a cabinet of jewels and a bill of lading; when he looked at this the merchant lifted up his eyes and thanked Heaven for sending him such a prosperous voyage.

They then told the story of the cat, and showed the rich present that the king and queen had sent for her to poor Dick. As soon as the merchant heard this, he called out to his servants:

"Go send him in, and tell him of his fame;

Pray call him Mr. Whittington by name."

Mr. Fitzwarren now showed himself to be a good man; for when some of his servants said so great a treasure was too much for him, he answered; "God forbid I should deprive him of the value of a single penny; it is his own, and he shall have it to a farthing."

He then sent for Dick, who at that time was scouring pots for the cook, and was quite dirty. He would have excused himself from coming into the counting-house, saying, "The room is swept, and my shoes are dirty and full of hob-nails." But the merchant ordered him to come in.

Mr. Fitzwarren ordered a chair to be set for him, and so he began to think they were making game of him, and at the same time said to them: "Do not play tricks with a poor simple boy, but let me go down again, if you please, to my work."

"Indeed, Mr. Whittington," said the merchant, "we are all quite in earnest with you, and I most heartily rejoice in the news that these gentlemen have brought you; for the captain has sold your cat to the King of Barbary, and brought you in return for her more riches than I possess in the whole world; and I wish you may long enjoy them!"

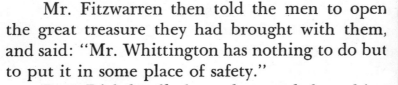

Mr. Fitzwarren then told the men to open the great treasure they had brought with them, and said: "Mr. Whittington has nothing to do but to put it in some place of safety."

Poor Dick hardly knew how to behave himself for joy. He begged his master to take what part of it he pleased, since he owed it all to his kindness. "No, no," answered Mr. Fitzwarren, "this is all your own; and I have no doubt but you will use it well."

Dick next asked his mistress, and then Miss Alice, to accept a part of his good fortune; but they would not, and at the same time told him they felt great joy at his good success. But this poor fellow was too kind-hearted to keep it all to himself; so he made a present to the captain, the mate, and the rest of Mr. Fitzwarren's servants; and even to the ill-natured old cook.

After this Mr. Fitzwarren advised him to send for a proper tailor, and get himself dressed like a gentleman; and told him he was welcome to live in his house till he could provide himself with a better.

When Whittington's face was washed, his hair curled, his hat cocked, and he was dressed in a nice suit of clothes he was as handsome and genteel as any young man who visited at Mr. Fitzwarren's; so that Miss Alice, who had once been so kind to him, and thought of him with pity, now looked upon him as fit to be her sweetheart; and the more so, no doubt, because Whittington was now always thinking what he could do to oblige her, and making her the prettiest presents that could be.

Mr. Fitzwarren soon saw their love for each other, and proposed to join them in marriage; and to this they both readily agreed. A day for the wedding was soon fixed; and they were attended to church by the Lord Mayor, the court of aldermen, the sheriffs, and a great number of the richest merchants in London, whom they afterwards treated with a very rich feast.

History tells us that Mr. Whittington and his lady lived in great splendor, and were very happy. They had several children. He was Sheriff of London, thrice Lord Mayor, and received the honor of knighthood by Henry V.

He entertained this king and his queen at dinner, after his conquest of France, so grandly, that the king said: "Never had prince such a subject;" when Sir Richard heard this, he said: "Never had subject such a prince."

The figure of Sir Richard Whittington with his cat in his arms, carved in stone, was to be seen till the year 1780 over the archway of the old prison at Newgate, which he built for criminals.

THE REAL PRINCESS

T HERE was once a prince, and he wanted a princess, but then she must be a *real* princess. He travelled right round the world to find one, but there was always something wrong. There were plenty of princesses, but whether they were real princesses he had great difficulty in discovering; there was always something which was not quite right about them. So at last he had to come home again, and he was very sad because he wanted a real princess so badly.

One evening there was a terrible storm; it thundered and lightened and the rain poured down in torrents; indeed it was a fearful night.

In the middle of the storm somebody knocked at the town gate, and the old King himself went to open it.

It was a princess who stood outside, but she was in a terrible state from the rain and the storm. The water streamed out of her hair and her clothes; it ran in at the top of her shoes and out at the heel, but she said that she was a real princess.

"Well we shall soon see if that is true," thought the old Queen, but she said nothing. She went into the bedroom, took all the bedclothes off and laid a pea on the bedstead; then she took twenty mattresses and piled them on the top of the pea, and then twenty feather beds on the top of the mattresses. This was where the princess was

to sleep that night. In the morning they asked her how she had slept.

"Oh terribly badly!" said the princess. "I have hardly closed my eyes the whole night! Heaven knows what was in the bed. I seemed to be lying upon some hard thing, and my whole body is black and blue this morning. It is terrible!"

They saw at once that she must be a real princess when she had felt the pea through twenty mattresses and twenty feather beds. Nobody but a real princess could have such a delicate skin.

So the prince took her to be his wife, for now he was sure that he had found a real princess, and the pea was put into the Museum, where it may still be seen if no one has stolen it.

Now this is a true story.

The Tinder Box

A soldier came marching along the high road. One, two! One, two! He had his knapsack on his back and his sword at his side, for he had been to the wars and he was on his way home now. He met an old witch on the road; she was so ugly, her lower lip hung right down on to her chin.

She said, "Good evening, soldier! What a nice sword you've got, and such a big knapsack; you are a real soldier! You shall have as much money as ever you like!"

"Thank you kindly, you old witch!" said the soldier.

"Do you see that big tree?" said the witch, pointing to a tree close by. "It is hollow inside!" Climb up to the top and you will see a hole into which you can let yourself down, right down under the tree! I will tie a rope round your waist so that I can haul you up again when you call!"

"What am I to do down under the tree?" asked the soldier.

"Fetch money!" said the witch. "You must know that when you get down to the bottom of the tree you will find yourself in a wide passage; it's quite light there, for there are over a hundred blazing lamps. You will see three doors which you can open, for the keys are there. If you go into the first room you will see a big box in the middle of the floor. A dog is sitting on the top of it, and he has eyes as big as saucers, but you needn't mind that. I will give you my blue checked apron, which you can spread out on the floor; then go quickly forward, take up the dog and put him on my apron, open the box and take out as much money as ever you like. It is all copper, but if you like silver better, go into the next room. There you will find a dog with eyes as big as millstones; but never mind that, put him on my apron and take the money. If you prefer gold you can have it too, and as much as you can carry, if you go into the third room. But the dog sitting on that box has eyes each as big as the Round Tower. He *is* a dog, indeed, as you may imagine! But don't let it trouble you; you only have to put him on to my apron and then he won't hurt you, and you can take as much gold out of the box as you like!"

"That's not so bad!" said the soldier. "But what am I to give you, old witch? For you'll want something, I'll be bound."

"No," said the witch, "not a single penny do I want; I only want you to bring me an old tinder box that my grandmother forgot the last time she was down there!"

"Well, tie the rope round my waist!" said the soldier.

"Here it is," said the witch, "and here is my blue checked apron."

Then the soldier climbed up the tree, let himself slide down the hollow trunk, and found himself, as the witch had said, in the wide passage where the many hundred lamps were burning.

Now he opened the first door. Ugh! There sat the dog with eyes as big as saucers staring at him.

"You are a nice fellow!" said the soldier, as he put him on to the witch's apron, and took out as many pennies as he could cram into his pockets. Then he shut the box, and put the dog on the top of it again, and went into the next room. There sat the dog with eyes as big as millstones.

"You shouldn't stare at me so hard; you might get a pain in your eyes!" Then he put the dog on the apron, but when he saw all the silver in the box he threw away all the coppers and stuffed his pockets and his knapsack with silver. Then he went on into the third room. Oh! how horrible! that dog really had two eyes as big as the Round Tower, and they rolled round and round like wheels.

"Good evening!" said the soldier, saluting, for he had never seen such a dog in his life; but after looking at him for a bit he thought "that will do," and then he lifted him down on to the apron and opened the chest. Preserve us! What a lot of gold! He could buy the whole of Copenhagen with it, and all the sugar pigs from the cake women, all the tin soldiers, whips and rocking horses in the world! That was money indeed! Now the soldier threw away all the silver he had filled his pockets and his knapsack with, and put gold in its place. Yes, he crammed all his pockets, his knapsack, his cap and his boots so full that he could hardly walk! Now, he really had got a lot of money. He put the dog back on to the box, shut the door, and shouted up through the tree, "Haul me up, you old witch!"

"Have you got the tinder box?"

"Oh! to be sure!" said the soldier. "I had quite forgotten it." And he went back to fetch it. The witch hauled him up, and there he was standing on the high road again with his pockets, boots, knapsack and cap full of gold.

"What do you want the tinder box for?" asked the soldier.

"That's no business of yours," said the witch. "You've got the money; give me the tinder box!"

"Rubbish!" said the soldier. "Tell me directly what you want with it, or I will draw my sword and cut off your head."

"I won't!" said the witch.

Then the soldier cut off her head; there she lay! But he tied all the money up in her apron, slung it on his back like a pack, put the tinder box in his pocket, and marched off to the town.

It was a beautiful town, and he went straight to the finest hotel, ordered the grandest rooms and all the food he liked best, because he was a rich man now that he had so much money.

Certainly the servant who had to clean his boots thought they were very funny old things for such a rich gentleman, but he had not had time yet to buy any new ones; the next day he bought new boots and fine clothes. The soldier now became a fine gentleman, and the people told him all about the grand things in the town, and about their king, and what a lovely princess his daughter was.

"Where is she to be seen?" asked the soldier.

"You can't see her at all!" they all said; "she lives in a great copper castle surrounded with walls and towers. Nobody but the king dare go in and out, for it has been prophesied that she will marry a common soldier, and the king doesn't like that!"

"I should like to see her well enough!" thought the soldier. But there was no way of getting leave for that.

He now led a very merry life; went to theatres, drove about in the King's Park, and gave away a lot of money to poor people, which was very nice of him; for he remembered how disagreeable it used to be not to have a penny in his pocket. Now he was rich, wore fine clothes, and had a great many friends, who all said what a nice fellow he was—a thorough gentleman —and he liked to be told that.

But as he went on spending money every day and his store was never renewed, he at last found himself with only two pence left. Then he was obliged to move out of his fine rooms. He had to take a tiny little attic up under the roof, clean his own boots, and mend them himself with a darning needle. None of his friends went to see him, because there were far too many stairs.

One dark evening when he had not even enough money to buy a candle with, he suddenly remembered that there was a little bit in the old tinder box he had brought out of the hollow tree, when the witch held him down. He got out the tinder box with the candle end in it and struck fire, but as the sparks flew out from the flint the door burst open and the dog with eyes as big as saucers, which he had seen down under the tree, stood before him and said, "What does my lord command?"

"By heaven!" said the soldier, "this is a nice kind of tinder box, if I can get whatever I want like this! Get me some money," he said to the dog, and away it went.

It was back in a twinkling with a big bag full of pennies in its mouth.

Now the soldier saw what a treasure he had in the tinder box. If he struck once, the dog which sat on the box of copper came; if he struck twice, the dog on the silver box came, and if he struck three times, the one from the box of gold.

He now moved down to the grand rooms and got his fine clothes again, and then all his friends knew him once more and liked him as much as ever.

Then he suddenly began to think: After all it's a curious thing that no man can get a sight of the princess! Everyone says she is so beautiful! But what is the good of that, when she always has to be shut up in that big copper palace with all the towers. Can I not somehow manage to see her? Where is my tinder box? Then he struck the flint, and, whisk, came the dog with eyes as big as saucers.

"It certainly is the middle of the night," said the soldier, "but I am very anxious to see the princess, if only for a single moment."

The dog was out of the door in an instant, and before the soldier had time to think about it, he was back again with the princess. There she was fast asleep on the dog's back, and she was so lovely that anybody could see that she must be a real princess! The soldier could not help it, but he was obliged to kiss her, for he was a true soldier.

Then the dog ran back again with the princess, but in the morning, when the king and queen were having breakfast, the princess said that she had had such a wonderful dream about a dog and a soldier. She had ridden on the dog's back, and the soldier had kissed her.

"That's a pretty tale," said the queen.

After this an old lady-in-waiting had to sit by her bed at night to see if this was really a dream, or what it could be.

The soldier longed so intensely to see the princess again that at night the dog came to fetch her. He took her up and ran off with her as fast as he could, but the old lady-in-waiting put on her galoshes and ran just as fast behind them; when she saw that they disappeared into a large house, she thought now I know where it is, and made a big cross with chalk on the gate. Then she went home and lay down, and presently the dog came back, too, with the princess. When he saw that there was a cross on the gate, he took a bit of chalk, too, and made crosses on all the gates in the town; now this was very clever of him, for the lady-in-waiting could not possibly find the gate when there were crosses on all the gates.

Early next morning the king, the queen, the lady-in-waiting, and all the court officials went to see where the princess had been.

"There it is," said the king, when he saw the first door with the cross on it.

"No, my dear husband, it is there," said the queen, who saw another door with a cross on it.

"But there is one, and there is another!" they all cried out. They soon saw that it was hopeless to try and find it.

Now the queen was a very clever woman; she knew more than how to drive in a chariot. She took her big gold scissors and cut up a large piece of silk into small pieces, and made a pretty little bag, which she filled with fine grains of buckwheat. She then tied it on to the back of the princess, and when that was done she cut a little hole in the bag, so that the grains could drop out all the way wherever the princess went.

At night the dog came again, took the princess on his back, and ran off with her to the soldier, who was so fond of her that he longed to be a prince, so that he might have her for his wife.

The dog never noticed how the grain dropped out all along the road from the palace to the soldier's window, where he ran up the wall with the princess.

In the morning the king and queen easily saw where their daughter had been, and they seized the soldier and threw him into the dungeons.

There he lay! Oh, how dark and tiresome it was, and then one day they said to him, "Tomorrow you are to be hanged." It was not amusing to be told that, especially as he had left his tinder box behind him at the hotel.

In the morning he could see through the bars in the little window that the people were hurrying out of the town to see him hanged. He heard the drums and saw the soldiers marching along. All the world was going; among them was a shoemaker's boy in his leather apron and slippers. He was in such a hurry that he lost one of his slippers, and it fell close under the soldier's window where he was peeping out through the bars.

"I say, you boy! Don't be in such a hurry," said the soldier to him. "Nothing will happen till I get there! But if you will run to the house where I used to live, and fetch me my tinder box, you shall have a penny! You must put your best foot foremost!"

The boy was only too glad to have the penny, and tore off to get the tinder box, gave it to the soldier, and—yes, now we shall hear.

Outside the town a high scaffold had been raised, and the soldiers were drawn up round about it, as well as crowds of the townspeople. The king and the queen sat upon a beautiful throne exactly opposite the judge and all the councillors.

The soldier mounted the ladder, but when they were about to put the rope round his neck, he said that before undergoing his punishment a criminal was always allowed the gratification of a harmless wish, and he wanted very much to smoke a pipe, as it would be his last pipe in this world.

The king would not deny him this, so the soldier took out his tinder box and struck fire, once, twice, three times, and there were all the dogs. The one with eyes like saucers, the one with eyes like millstones, and the one whose eyes were as big as the Round Tower.

"Help me! Save me from being hanged!" cried the soldier.

And then the dogs rushed at the soldiers and the councillors; they took one by the legs, and another by the nose, and threw them up many fathoms into the air; and when they fell down, they were broken all to pieces.

"I won't!" cried the king, but the biggest dog took both him and the queen and threw them after all the others. Then the soldiers became alarmed, and the people shouted, "Oh! good soldier, you shall be our king and marry the beautiful princess!"

Then they conducted the soldier to the king's chariot, and all three dogs danced along in front of him and shouted "Hurrah!" The boys all put their fingers in their mouths and whistled,, and the soldiers presented arms. The princess came out of the copper palace and became queen, which pleased her very much. The wedding took place in a week, and the dogs all had seats at the table, where they sat staring with all their eyes.

JACK AND
THE BEANSTALK

THERE was once upon a time a poor widow who had an
only son named Jack, and a cow named Milky-white. And
all they had to live on was the milk the cow gave every morning, which they carried to the market and sold. But one morning Milky-white gave no milk, and they didn't know what to do.

"What shall we do, what shall we do?" said the widow,
wringing her hands.

"Cheer up, mother, I'll go and get work somewhere,"
said Jack.

"We've tried that before, and nobody would take you,"
said his mother; "we must sell Milky-white and with the
money start shop, or something."

"All right mother," says Jack; "it's market-day today, and
I'll soon sell Milky-white, and then we'll see what we can do."

So he took the cow's halter in his hand, and off he started.
He hadn't gone far when he met a funny-looking old man, who
said to him: "Good morning, Jack."

"Good morning to you," said Jack, and wondered how
he knew his name.

"Well, Jack, and where are you off to?" said the man.

"I'm going to market to sell our cow here."

"Oh, you look the proper sort of chap to sell cows," said
the man; "I wonder if you know how many beans make five."

"Two in each hand and one in your mouth," says Jack, as
sharp as a needle.

"Right you are," says the man, "and here they are, the very beans themselves," he went on, pulling out of his pocket a number of strange-looking beans.

"As you are so sharp," says he, "I don't mind doing a swop with you—your cow for these beans."

"Go along," says Jack; "wouldn't you like it?"

"Ah! you don't know what these beans are," said the man; "if you plant them overnight, by morning they grow right up to the sky."

"Really?" said Jack; "you don't say so."

"Yes, that is so, and if it doesn't turn out to be true you can have your cow back."

"Right," says Jack, and hands him over Milky-white's halter and pockets the beans.

Back goes Jack home, and as he hadn't gone very far it wasn't dusk by the time he got to his door.

"Back already, Jack?" said his mother; "I see you haven't got Milky-white, so you've sold her. How much did you get for her?"

"You'll never guess, mother," says Jack.

"No, you don't say so. Good boy! Five pounds, ten, fif-teen, no, it can't be twenty."

"I told you you couldn't guess. What do you say to these beans; they're magical, plant them overnight and—"

"What!" says Jack's mother, "have you been such a fool, such a dolt, such an idiot, as to give away my Milky-white, the best milker in the parish, and prime beef to boot, for a set of paltry beans? Take that! Take that! Take that! And as for your precious beans here they go out of the window. And now off with you to bed. Not a sup shall you drink, and not a bit shall you swallow this very night."

So Jack went upstairs to his little room in the attic, and sad and sorry he was, to be sure, as much for his mother's sake, as for the loss of his supper.

At last he dropped off to sleep.

When he woke up, the room looked so funny. The sun was shining into part of it, and yet all the rest was quite dark and shady. So Jack jumped up and dressed himself and went to the window. And what do you think he saw? Why, the beans his mother had thrown out of the window into the garden, had sprung up into a big beanstalk which went up and up and up till it reached the sky. So the man spoke truth after all.

The beanstalk grew up quite close past Jack's window, so all he had to do was to open it and give a jump on to the beanstalk which ran up just like a big ladder. So Jack climbed, and he climbed and he climbed and he climbed and he climbed and he climbed and he climbed till at last he reached the sky. And when he got there he found a long broad road going as straight as a dart. So he walked along and he walked along and he walked along till he came to a great big tall house, and on the doorstep there was a great big tall woman.

"Good morning, mum," says Jack, quite polite-like. "Could you be so kind as to give me some breakfast?" For he hadn't had anything to eat, you know, the night before and was as hungry as a hunter.

"It's breakfast you want, is it?" says the great big tall woman, "it's breakfast you'll be if you don't move off from here. My man is an ogre and there's nothing he likes better than boys broiled on toast. You'd better be moving on or he'll soon be coming."

"Oh! please mum, do give me something to eat, mum. I've had nothing to eat since yesterday morning, really and truly, mum," says Jack. "I may as well be broiled as die of hunger."

Well, the ogre's wife was not half so bad after all. So she took Jack into the kitchen, and gave him a chunk of bread and cheese and a jug of milk. But Jack hadn't half finished these when thump! thump! thump! the whole house began to tremble with the noise of someone coming.

"Goodness gracious me! It's my old man," said the ogre's wife, "what on earth shall I do? Come along quick and jump in here." And she bundled Jack into the oven just as the ogre came in.

He was a big one, to be sure. At his belt he had three calves strung up by the heels, and he unhooked them and threw them down on the table and said: "Here wife, broil me a couple of these for breakfast. Ah! what's this I smell?

Fee-fi-fo-fum,
I smell the blood of an Englishman,
Be he alive, or be he dead
I'll have his bones to grind my bread."

"Nonsense, dear," said his wife, "you're dreaming. Or perhaps you smell the scraps of that little boy you liked so much for yesterday's dinner. Here, you go and have a wash and tidy up, and by the time you come back your breakfast'll be ready for you."

So off the ogre went, and Jack was just going to jump out of the oven and run away when the woman told him not. "Wait till he's asleep," says she; "he always has a doze after breakfast."

Well, the ogre had his breakfast, and after that he goes to a big chest and takes out of it a couple of bags of gold, and down he sits and counts till at last his head began to nod and he began to snore till the whole house shook again.

Then Jack crept out on tiptoe from his oven, and as he was passing the ogre he took one of the bags of gold under his arm, and off he pelters till he came to the beanstalk, and then he threw down the bag of gold, which of course fell into his mother's garden, and then he climbed down and climbed down till at last he got home and told his mother and showed her the gold and said: "Well, mother, wasn't I right about the beans? They are really magical, you see."

So they lived on the bag of gold for sometime, but at last they came to the end of it, and Jack made up his mind to try his luck once more up at the top of the beanstalk. So one fine morning he rose up early, and got on to the beanstalk, and he climbed and he climbed and he climbed and he climbed and he climbed and he climbed till at last he came out on to the road again and up to the great big tall house he had been to before. There, sure enough, was the great big tall woman a-standing on the doorstep.

"Good morning, mum," says Jack, as bold as brass, "could you be so good as to give me something to eat?"

"Go away, my boy," said the big tall woman, or else my man will eat you up for breakfast. But aren't you the youngster who came here once before? Do you know, that very day, my man missed one of his bags of gold."

"That's strange, mum," said Jack, "I dare say I could tell you something about that, but I'm so hungry I can't speak till I've had something to eat."

Well the big tall woman was so curious that she took him

in and gave him something to eat. But he had scarcely begun munching it as slowly as he could when thump! thump! thump! they heard the giant's footstep, and his wife hid Jack away in the oven.

All happened as it did before. In came the ogre as he did before, said: "Fee-fi-fo-fum," and had his breakfast off three broiled oxen. Then he said: "Wife, bring me the hen that lays the golden eggs." So she brought it, and the ogre said: "Lay," and it laid an egg all of gold. And then the ogre began to nod his head, and to snore till the house shook.

Then Jack crept out of the oven on tiptoe and caught hold of the golden hen, and was off before you could say "Jack Robinson." But this time the hen gave a cackle which woke the ogre, and just as Jack got out of the house he heard him calling: "Wife, wife, what have you done with my golden hen?"

And the wife said: "Why, my dear?"

But that was all Jack heard, for he rushed off to the beanstalk and climbed down like a house on fire. And when he got home he showed his mother the wonderful hen, and said "Lay" to it; and it laid a golden egg every time he said "Lay."

Well, Jack was not content, and it wasn't very long before he determined to have another try at his luck up there at the top of the beanstalk. So one fine morning, he rose up early, and got on to the beanstalk, and he climbed and he climbed and he climbed and he climbed

till he got to the top. But this time he knew better than to go straight to the ogre's house. And when he got near it, he waited behind a bush till he saw the ogre's wife come out with a pail to get some water, and then he crept into the house and got into the copper. He hadn't been there long when he heard thump! thump! thump! as before, and in came the ogre and his wife.

"Fee-fi-fo-fum, I smell the blood of an Englishman," cried out the ogre. "I smell him, wife, I smell him."

"Do you, my dearie?" says the ogre's wife. "Then, if it's that little rogue that stole your gold and the hen that laid the golden eggs he's sure to have got into the oven." And they both rushed to the oven. But Jack wasn't there, luckily, and the ogre's wife said: "There you are again with your fee-fi-fo-fum. Why of course it's the boy you caught last night that I've just broiled for your breakfast. How forgetful I am, and how careless you are not to know the difference between live and dead after all these years."

So the ogre sat down to the breakfast and ate it, but every now and then he would mutter: "Well, I could have sworn—" and he'd get up and search the larder and the cupboards and everything, only, luckily, he didn't think of the copper.

After breakfast was over, the ogre called out: "Wife, wife, bring me my golden harp." So she brought it and put it on the table before him. Then he said: "Sing!" and the golden harp sang most beautifully. And it went on singing till the ogre fell asleep, and commenced to snore like thunder.

Then Jack lifted up the copper-lid very quietly and got down like a mouse and crept on hands and knees till he came to the table, when up he crawled, caught hold of the golden harp and dashed with it towards the door. But the harp called out quite loud: "Master! Master!" and the ogre woke up just in time to see Jack running off with his harp.

Jack ran as fast as he could, and the ogre came rushing after, and would soon have caught him only Jack had a start and dodged him a bit and knew where he was going. When he got to the beanstalk the ogre was not more than twenty yards away when suddenly he saw Jack disappear like, and when he came to the end of the road he saw Jack underneath climbing down for dear life. Well, the ogre didn't like trusting himself to such a ladder, and he stood and waited, so Jack got another start. But just then the harp cried out: "Master! Master!" and the ogre swung himself down on to the beanstalk, which shook with his weight. Down climbs Jack, and after him climbed the ogre. By this time Jack had climbed down and climbed down and climbed down till he was very nearly home. So he called out: "Mother! Mother! bring me an axe, bring me an axe." And his mother came rushing out with the axe in her hand, but when she came to the beanstalk she stood stock still with fright for there she saw the ogre with his legs just through the clouds.

But Jack jumped down and got hold of the axe and gave a chop at the beanstalk which cut it half in two. The ogre felt the beanstalk shake and quiver so he stopped to see what was the matter. Then Jack gave another chop with the axe, and the beanstalk was cut in two and began to topple over. Then the ogre fell down and broke his crown, and the beanstalk came toppling after.

Then Jack showed his mother his golden harp, and what with showing that and selling the golden eggs, Jack and his mother became very rich, and he married a great princess, and they lived happy ever after.

The Shoemaker and the Elves

THERE was once a shoemaker, who, through no fault of his own, became so poor that at last he had nothing left but just enough leather to make one pair of shoes. He cut out the shoes at night, so as to set to work upon them next morning; and as he had a good conscience, he laid himself quietly down in his bed, committed himself to heaven, and fell asleep. In the morning, after he had said his prayers, and was going to get to work, he found the pair of shoes made and finished, and standing on his table. He was very much astonished, and could not tell what to think, and he took the shoes in his hand to examine them more closely; and they were so well made that every stitch was in its right place, just as if they had come from the hand of a master workman.

Soon after a purchaser entered, and as the shoes fitted him very well, he gave more than the usual price for them, so that the shoemaker had enough money to buy leather for two more pairs of shoes. He cut them out at night, and intended to set to work the next morning with fresh spirit; but that was not to be, for when he got up they were already finished, and a customer even was not lacking, who gave him so much money that he was able to buy leather enough for four new pairs. Early next morning he found the four pairs also finished, and so it always happened; whatever he cut out in the evening was worked up by the morning, so that he was soon in the way of making a good living, and in the end became very well to do.

One night, not long before Christmas, when the shoemaker had finished cutting out, and before he went to bed, he said to his wife:

"How would it be if we were to sit up tonight and see who it is that does us this service?"

His wife agreed, and set a light to burn. Then they both hid in a corner of the room, behind some coats that were hanging up, and then they began to watch. As soon as it was midnight they saw come in two neatly-formed naked little men, who seated themselves before the shoemaker's table, and took

up the work that was already prepared, and began to stitch, to pierce, and to hammer so cleverly and quickly with their little fingers that the shoemaker's eyes could scarcely follow them, so full of wonder was he. And they never left off until everything was finished and was standing ready on the table, and then they jumped up and ran off.

The next morning the shoemaker's wife said to her husband, "Those little men have made us rich, and we ought to show ourselves grateful. With all their running about, and having nothing to cover them, they must be very cold. I'll tell you what; I will make little shirts, coats, waistcoats, and breeches for them, and knit each of them a pair of stockings, and you shall make each of them a pair of shoes."

The husband consented willingly, and at night, when everything was finished, they laid the gifts together on the table, instead of the cut-out work, and placed themselves so that they could observe how the little men would behave. When midnight came, they rushed in, ready to set to work, but when they found, instead of the pieces of prepared leather, the neat little garments put ready for them, they stood a moment in surprise, and then they testified the greatest delight. With the greatest swiftness they took up the pretty garments and slipped them on, singing:

"What spruce and dandy boys are we!
No longer cobblers we will be."

They then hopped and danced about, jumping over the chairs and tables, and at last they danced out at the door.

From that time they were never seen again; but it always went well with the shoemaker as long as he lived, and whatever he took in hand prospered.

THE ELVES

AND THE CHANGELING

THE elves once took a child away from its mother, and left in its place a changeling with a big head and staring eyes, who did nothing but eat and drink. The mother in her trouble went to her neighbors and asked their advice. The neighbors told her to take the changeling into the kitchen and put it near the hearth, and then to make up the fire, and boil water in two eggshells; that would make the changeling laugh, and if he laughed, it would be all over with him. So the woman did as her neighbors advised. And when she set the eggshells of water on the fire, the changeling said:

"Though old I be
As forest tree,
Cooking in an eggshell never did I see!"

and began to laugh. And directly there came in a crowd of elves bringing in the right child; and they laid it near the hearth, and carried the changeling away with them.

THE SERVANT MAID
AND THE ELVES

THERE was once a poor servant maid, who was very cleanly and industrious; she swept down the house every day, and put the sweepings on a great heap by the door. One morning, before she began her work, she found a letter, and as she could not read, she laid her broom in the corner, and took the letter to her master and mistress, to see what it was about; and it was an invitation from the elves, who wished the maid to come and stand godmother to one of their children. The maid did not know what to do; and as she was told that no one ought to refuse the elves anything, she made up her mind to go. So there came three little elves, who conducted her into the middle of a high mountain, where the little people lived. Here everything was of a very small size, but more fine and elegant than can be told. The mother of the child lay in a bed made of ebony, studded with pearls, the counterpane was embroidered with gold, the cradle was of ivory, and the bathing tub of gold. So the maid stood godmother, and was then for going home, but the elves begged her to stay at least three more days with them; and so she consented, and spent the time in mirth and jollity, and the elves seemed very fond of her. At last, when she was ready to go away, they filled her pockets full of gold, and led her back again out of the mountain. When she got back to the house, she was going to begin working again, and took her broom in her hand; it was still standing in the corner where she had left it, and began to sweep. Then came up some strangers and asked her who she was, and what she was doing. And she found that instead of three days, she had been seven years with the elves in the mountain, and that during that time her master and mistress had died.

The Wonderful Tar Baby Story

By Joel Chandler Harris

"Didn't the fox never catch the rabbit, Uncle Remus?" asked the little boy the next evening.

"He come might nigh it, honey, sho's you born—Brer Fox did. One day atter Brer Rabbit fool 'im wid dat calamus root, Brer Fox went ter wuk en got 'im some tar, en mix it wid some turkentime, en fix up a contrapshun wat he call a Tar-

Baby, en he tuck dish yer Tar-Baby en he sot 'er in de big road, en den he lay off in de bushes fer to see what de news wuz gwineter be. En he didn't hatter wait long, nudder, kaze bimeby here come Brer Rabbit pacin' down de road—lippity-clippity, clippity-lippity—dez ez sassy ez a jay bird. Brer Fox, he lay low. Brer Rabbit come prancin' 'long twel he spy de Tar-Baby, en den he fotch up on his behime legs like he wus 'stonished. De Tar-Baby, she sot dar, she did, en Brer Fox, he lay low.

"Mawnin'! sez Brer Rabbit, sezee—nice wedder dis mawnin', sezee.

"Tar-Baby ain't sayin' nothin', en Brer Fox, he lay low.

"How duz yo' sym'tums seem ter segashuate? sez Brer Rabbit, sezee.

"Brer Fox, he wink his eye slow, en lay low, en de Tar-Baby, she ain't sayin' nothin'.

"How you come on, den? Is you deaf? sez Brer Rabbit, sezee. Kaze if you is, I kin holler louder, sezee.

"Tar-Baby stay still, en Brer Fox, he lay low.

"Youer stuck up, dat's w'at you is, sez Brer Rabbit, sezee, 'en I'm gwineter kyore you, dats w'at I'm a gwineter do, sezee.

"Brer Fox, he sorter chuckle in his stummick, he did, but Tar-Baby ain't sayin' nothin'.

"I'm gwineter larn you howter talk ter 'specttubble fokes ef hit's de las' ack, sez Brer Rabbit, sezee. Ef you don't take off dat hat en tell me howdy, I'm gwineter bus' you wide open, sezee.

"Tar-Baby stay still, en Brer Fox, he lay low.

"Brer Rabbit keep on axin' 'im, en de Tar-Baby, she keep on sayin' nothin', twel present'y Brer Rabbit draw back wid his fis', he did, en blip he tuck 'er side er de head. Right dar's whar he broke his merlasses jug. His fis' stuck, en he can't pull loose. De tar hilt 'im. But Tar-Baby, she stay still, en Brer Fox, he lay low.

"Ef you don't lemme loose, I'll knock you agin, sez Brer Rabbit, sezee, en wid dat he fotch 'er a wipe wid de udder han', en dat stuck. Tar-Baby, she ain't sayin' nothin', en Brer Fox, he lay low.

"Tu'n me loose, fo' I kick de natal stuffin' outen you, sez Brer Rabbit, sezee, but de Tar-Baby, she ain't sayin' nothin'. She des hilt on, en den Brer Rabbit lose de use er his feet in de same way. Brer Fox, he lay low. Den Brer Rabbit squall out dat ef de Tar-Baby don't tu'n 'im loose he butt 'er cranksided. En den he butted, en his head got stuck. Den Brer Fox, he sa'ntered fort', lookin' des ez innercent ez one er yo' mammy's mockin'-birds.

"Howdy, Brer Rabbit, sez Brer Fox, sezee. You look sorter stuck up dis mawnin', sezee, en den he rolled on de groun', en laughed en laughed twel he couldn't laugh no mo'. I speck you'll take dinner wid me dis time, Brer Rabbit. I done laid in some calamus root, en I ain't gwineter take no skuse, sez Brer Fox, sezee."

Here Uncle Remus paused, and drew a two pound yam out of the ashes.

"Did the fox eat the rabbit?" asked the little boy to whom the story had been told.

"Dat's all de fur de tale goes," replied the old man. "He mout, en den again he moutent. Some say Jedge B'ar come long en loosed 'im—some say he didn't. I hear Miss Sally callin'. You better run 'long."

272

THE HISTORY OF
TOM THUMB

IN THE days of the great Prince Arthur, there lived a mighty magician, called Merlin, the most learned and skillful enchanter the world has ever seen.

This famous magician, who could take any form he pleased, was travelling about as a poor beggar, and being very tired, he stopped at the cottage of a ploughman to rest himself, and asked for some food.

The countryman bade him welcome, and his wife, who was a very good-hearted woman, soon brought him some milk in a wooden bowl, and some coarse brown bread on a platter.

Merlin was much pleased with the kindness of the ploughman and his wife; but he could not help noticing that though everything was neat and comfortable in the cottage, they both seemed to be very unhappy. He therefore asked them why they were so melancholy, and learned that they were miserable because they had no children.

The poor woman said, with tears in her eyes: "I should be the happiest creature in the world if I had a son; although he was no bigger than my husband's thumb, I would be satisfied."

Merlin was so much amused with the idea of a boy no bigger than a man's thumb, that he determined to grant

the poor woman's wish. Accordingly, in a short time after, the ploughman's wife had a son, who, wonderful to relate! was not a bit bigger than his father's thumb.

The queen of the fairies, wishing to see the little fellow, came in at the window while the mother was sitting up in the bed admiring him. The queen kissed the child, and, giving it the name of Tom Thumb, sent for some of the fairies, who dressed her little godson according to her orders:

"An oak-leaf hat he had for his crown;
His shirt of web by spiders spun;
With jacket wove of thistle's down;
His trousers were of feathers done.
His stockings, of apple-rind, they tie
With eyelash from his mother's eye:
His shoes were made of mouse's skin,
Tann'd with the downy hair within."

Tom never grew any larger than his father's thumb, which was only of ordinary size; but as he got older he became very cunning and full of tricks. When he was old enough to play with the boys, and had lost all his own cherry-stones, he used to creep into the bags of his playfellows, fill his pockets, and, getting out without their noticing him, would again join in the game.

One day, however, as he was coming out of a bag of cherry-stones, where he had been stealing as usual, the boy to whom it belonged chanced to see him. "Ah, ah! my little Tommy," said the boy, "so I have caught you stealing my cherry-stones at last, and you shall be rewarded for your thievish tricks." On saying this, he drew the string tight round his neck, and gave the bag such a hearty shake, that poor little Tom's legs, thighs, and body were sadly bruised. He roared out with pain, and begged to be let out, promising never to steal again.

A short time afterwards his mother was making a batter-pudding, and Tom, being very anxious to see how it was made, climbed up to the edge of the bowl; but his foot slipped, and he plumped over head and ears into the batter, without his mother noticing him, who stirred him into the pudding-bag, and put him in the pot to boil.

The batter filled Tom's mouth, and prevented him from crying; but, on feeling the hot water, he kicked and struggled so much in the pot, that his mother thought that the pudding was bewitched, and, pulling it out of the pot, she threw it outside the door. A poor tinker, who was passing by, lifted up the pudding, and, putting it into his budget, he then walked off. As Tom had now got his mouth cleared of the batter, he then began to cry aloud, which so frightened the tinker that he flung down the pudding and ran away. The pudding being broke to pieces by the fall, Tom crept out covered all over with the batter, and walked home. His mother, who was very sorry to see her darling in such a woeful state, put him into a teacup, and soon washed off the batter; after which she kissed him, and laid him in bed.

Soon after the adventure of the pudding, Tom's mother went to milk her cow in the meadow, and she took him along with her. As the wind was very high, for fear of being blown away, she tied him to a thistle with a piece of fine thread. The cow soon observed Tom's oak-leaf hat, and liking the appearance of it, took poor Tom and the thistle at one mouthful. While the cow was chewing the thistle, Tom was afraid of her great teeth, which threatened to crush him in pieces, and he roared out as loud as he could: "Mother, mother!"

"Where are you, Tommy, my dear Tommy?" said his mother.

"Here, mother," replied he, "in the red cow's mouth."

His mother began to cry and wring her hands; but the cow, surprised at the odd noise in her throat, opened her mouth and let Tom drop out. Fortunately his mother caught him in her apron as he was falling to the ground, or he would have been dreadfully hurt. She then put Tom in her bosom and ran home with him.

Tom's father made him a whip of a barley straw to drive the cattle with, and having one day gone into the fields, Tom slipped a foot and rolled into the furrow. A raven, which was flying over, picked him up, and flew with him over the sea, and there dropped him.

A large fish swallowed Tom the moment he fell into the sea, which was soon after caught, and bought for the table of King Arthur. When they opened the fish in order to cook it, every one was astonished at finding such a little boy, and Tom was quite de-

lighted at being free again. They carried him to the king, who made Tom his dwarf, and he soon grew a great favorite at court; for by his tricks and gambols he not only amused the king and queen, but also all the Knights of the Round Table.

It is said that when the king rode out on horseback, he often took Tom along with him, and if a shower came on, he used to creep into his majesty's waist coat pocket, where he slept till the rain was over.

King Arthur one day asked Tom about his parents, wishing to know if they were as small as he was, and whether they were well off. Tom told the king that his father and mother were as tall as anybody about the court, but in rather poor circumstances. On hearing this, the king carried Tom to his treasury, the place where he kept all his money, and told him to take as much money as he could carry home to his parents, which made the poor little fellow caper with joy. Tom went immediately to procure a purse, which was made of a water-bubble, and then returned to the treasury, where he received a silver three-penny-piece to put into it.

Our little hero had some difficulty in lifting the burden upon his back; but he at last succeeded in getting it placed to his mind, and set forward on his journey. However, without meeting with any accident, and after resting himself more

than a hundred times by the way, in two days and two nights he reached his father's house in safety.

Tom had travelled forty-eight hours with a huge silver-piece on his back, and was almost tired to death, when his mother ran out to meet him, and carried him into the house. But he soon returned to court.

As Tom's clothes had suffered much in the batter-pudding, and the inside of the fish, his majesty ordered him a new suit of clothes, and to be mounted as a knight on a mouse.

> Of Butterfly's wings his shirt was made,
>   His boots of chicken's hide;
> And by a nimble fairy blade,
> Well learned in the tailoring trade,
>   His clothing was supplied.
>   A needle dangled by his side;
>   A dapper mouse he used to ride,
>   Thus strutted Tom in stately pride!

279

It was certainly very diverting to see Tom in this dress and mounted on the mouse, as he rode out a-hunting with the king and nobility, who were all ready to expire with laughter at Tom and his fine prancing charger.

The king was so charmed with his dress that he ordered a little chair to be made, in order that Tom might sit upon his table, and also a palace of gold, a span high, with a door an inch wide, to live in. He also gave him a coach, drawn by six small mice.

The queen was so enraged at the honors conferred on Sir Thomas that she resolved to ruin him, and told the king that the little knight had been saucy to her.

The king sent for Tom in great haste, but being fully aware of the danger of royal anger, he crept into an empty snail-shell, where he lay for a long time until he was almost starved with hunger; but at last he ventured to peep out, and seeing a fine large butterfly on the ground, near the place of his concealment, he got close to it and jumping astride on it, was carried up into the air. The butterfly flew with him from tree to tree and from field to field, and at last returned to the court, where the king and nobility all strove to catch him; but at last poor Tom fell from his seat into a watering pot, in which he was almost drowned.

When the queen saw him, she was in a rage, and said he should be beheaded; and he

was then put into a mouse trap until the time of his execution.

However, a cat, observing something alive in the trap, patted it about till the wires broke, and set Thomas at liberty.

The king received Tom again into favor, which he did not live to enjoy, for a large spider one day attacked him; and although he drew his sword and fought well, yet the spider's poisonous breath at last overcame him.

> He fell dead on the ground where he stood,
> And the spider suck'd every drop of his blood.

King Arthur and his whole court were so sorry at the loss of their little favorite that they went into mourning and raised a fine white marble monument over his grave with the following epitaph:

> Here lies Tom Thumb, King Arthur's knight,
> Who died by a spider's cruel bite.
> He was well known in Arthur's court,
> Where he afforded gallant sport;
> He rode a tilt and tournament,
> And on a mouse a-hunting went.
> Alive he filled the court with mirth;
> His death to sorrow soon gave birth.
> Wipe, wipe your eyes, and shake your head
> And cry,—Alas! Tom Thumb is dead!

JACK THE GIANT KILLER

WHEN good King Arthur reigned, there lived near the Land's End of England, in the County of Cornwall, a farmer who had one only son called Jack. He was brisk and of ready, lively wit, so that nobody or nothing could worst him.

In those days the Mount of Cornwall was kept by a huge giant named Cormoran. He was eighteen feet in height, and about three yards round the waist, of a fierce and grim countenance, the terror of all the neighboring towns and villages. He lived in a cave in the midst of the Mount, and whenever he wanted food he would wade over to the mainland, where he would furnish himself with whatever came in his way. Everybody at his approach ran out of their houses, while he seized on their cattle, making nothing of carrying half-a-dozen oxen on his back at a time; and as for their sheep and hogs, he would tie them round his waist like a bunch of tallow-dips. He had done this for many years, so that all Cornwall was in despair.

One day Jack happened to be at the town hall when the magistrates were sitting in council about the Giant. He asked: "What reward will be given to the man who kills Cormoran?" "The giant's treasure," they said, "will be the reward." Quoth Jack: "Then let me undertake it."

So he got a horn, shovel, and pickaxe, and went over to the Mount in the beginning of a dark winter's evening, when he fell to work, and before morning had dug a pit twenty-two feet deep, and nearly as broad, covering it over with long sticks and straw. Then he strewed a little mould over it, so that it appeared like plain ground. Jack then placed himself on the opposite side of the pit, farthest from the giant's lodging, and, just at the break of day, he put the horn to his mouth, and blew. Tantivy, Tantivy. This noise roused the giant, who rushed from his cave, crying: "You incorrigible villain, are you come here to disturb my rest?

You shall pay dearly for this. Satisfaction I will have, and this it shall be; I will take you whole and broil you for breakfast." He had no sooner uttered this, than he tumbled into the pit, and made the very foundations of the Mount to shake. "Oh Giant," quoth Jack, "where are you now? Oh, faith, you are gotten now into Lob's Pound, where I will surely plague you for your threatening words; what do you think now of broiling me for your breakfast? Will no other diet serve you but poor Jack?" Then having tantalized the giant for a while, he gave him a most weighty knock with his pickaxe on the very crown of his head, and killed him on the spot.

Jack then filled up the pit with earth, and went to search the cave, which he found contained much treasure. When the magistrates heard of this they made a declaration he should henceforth be termed

JACK THE GIANT-KILLER

and presented him with a sword and a belt, on which were written these words embroidered in letters of gold:

"Here's the right valiant Cornish man,
Who slew the giant Cormoran."

The news of Jack's victory soon spread over all the West of England, so that another giant, named Blunderbore, hearing of it, vowed to be revenged on Jack, if ever he should light on him. This giant was the lord of an enchanted castle situated in the midst of a lonesome wood. Now Jack, about four months afterwards, walking near this wood in his journey to

Wales, being weary, seated himself near a pleasant fountain and fell fast asleep. While he was sleeping, the giant, coming there for water, discovered him, and knew him to be the far-famed Jack the Giant-Killer by the lines written on the belt. Without ado, he took Jack on his shoulders and carried him towards his castle. Now, as they passed through a thicket, the rustling of the boughs awakened Jack, who was strangely surprised to find himself in the clutches of the giant. His terror was only begun, for, on entering the castle, he saw the ground strewed with human bones, and the giant told him his own would ere long be among them. After this the giant locked poor Jack in an immense chamber, leaving him there while he went to fetch another giant, his brother, living in the same wood, who might share in the meal on Jack.

After waiting some time Jack, on going to the window, beheld afar off the two giants coming towards the castle. "Now," quoth Jack to himself, "my death or my deliverance is at hand." Now, there were strong cords in a corner of the room in which Jack was, and two of these he took, and made a strong noose at the end; and while the giants were unlocking the iron gate of the castle he threw the ropes over each of their heads. Then he drew the other ends across a beam, and pulled with all his might, so that he throttled them. Then, when he saw they were black in the face, he slid down the rope, and drawing his sword, slew them both. Then, taking the giant's keys, and unlocking the rooms, he found three fair ladies tied by the hair of their heads, almost starved to death. "Sweet ladies," quoth Jack, "I have destroyed this monster and his brutish brother, and obtained your liberties." This said, he presented them with the keys, and so proceeded on his journey to Wales.

Jack made the best of his way by travelling as fast as he could, but lost his road, and was benighted, and could find no habitation until, coming into a narrow valley, he found a large house, and in order to get shelter took courage to knock at the gate. But what was his surprise when there came forth a monstrous giant with two heads; yet he did not appear so fiery as

the others were, for he was a Welsh giant, and what he did was
by private and secret malice under the false show of friendship.
Jack, having told his condition to the giant, was shown into a
bedroom, where, in the dead of night, he heard his host in
another apartment muttering these words;

"Though here you lodge with me this night,
     You shall not see the morning light:
     My club shall dash your brains outright!"

"Say'st thou so," quoth Jack; "that is like one of your

Welsh tricks, yet I hope to be cunning enough for you." Then, getting out of bed, he laid a billet in the bed in his stead, and hid himself in a corner of the room. At the dead time of the night in came the Welsh giant, who struck several heavy blows on the bed with his club, thinking he had broken every bone in Jack's skin. The next morning Jack, laughing in his sleeve, gave him hearty thanks for his night's lodging. "How have you rested?" quoth the giant; "did you not feel anything in the night?" "No," quoth Jack, "nothing but a rat, which gave me two or three slaps with her tail." With that, greatly wondering, the giant led Jack to breakfast, bringing him a bowl containing four gallons of hasty pudding. Being loth to let the giant think it too much for him, Jack put a large leather bag under his loose coat, in such a way that he could convey the pudding into it without its being perceived. Then, telling the giant he would show him a trick, taking a knife, Jack ripped open the bag, and out came all the hasty pudding. Whereupon, saying, "Odds splutters her nails, hur can do that trick hursELF," the monster took the knife, and ripping open his belly, fell down dead.

Now, it happened in these days that King Arthur's only son asked his father to give him a large sum of money, in order that he might go and seek his fortune in the principality of Wales, where lived a beautiful lady possessed with seven evil spirits. The king did his best to persuade his son from it, but in vain; so at last gave way and the prince set out with two horses, one loaded with money, the other for himself to ride upon. Now, after several days' travel, he came to a market-town in Wales, where he beheld a vast crowd of people gathered together. The prince asked the reason of it, and was told that they had arrested a corpse for several large sums of money which the deceased owed when he died. The prince replied that it was a pity creditors should be so cruel, and said: "Go bury the dead, and let his creditors come to my lodging, and there their debts shall be paid." They came, in such great numbers that before night he had only twopence left for himself.

Now Jack the Giant-Killer, coming that way, was so taken with the generosity of the prince, that he desired to be his servant. This being agreed upon, the next morning they set forward on their journey together, when, as they were riding out of the town, an old woman called after the prince, saying, "He has owed me twopence these seven years; pray pay me as well as the rest." Putting his hand into his pocket, the prince gave the woman all he had left, so that after their day's food, which cost what small store Jack had by him, they were without a penny between them.

When the sun got low, the king's son said: "Jack, since we have no money, where can we lodge this night?"

But Jack replied: "Master, we'll do well enough, for I have an uncle lives within two miles of this place; he is a huge and monstrous giant with three heads; he'll fight five hundred men in armor, and make them to fly before him."

"Alas!" quoth the prince, "what shall we do there? He'll certainly chop us up at a mouthful. Nay, we are scarce enough to fill one of his hollow teeth!"

"It is no matter for that," quoth Jack; "I myself will go before and prepare the way for you; therefore stop here and wait till I return." Jack then rode away at full speed, and coming to the gate of the castle, he knocked so loud that he made the neighboring hills resound. The giant roared out at this like thunder: "Who's there?"

Jack answered: "None but your poor cousin Jack."

Quoth he: "What news with my poor cousin Jack?"

He replied: "Dear uncle, heavy news, God

wot!''

"Prithee,'' quoth the giant, "what heavy news can come to me? I am a giant with three heads, and besides thou knowest I can fight five hundred men in armor, and make them fly like chaff before the wind.''

"Oh, but,'' quoth Jack, " here's the king's son a-coming with a thousand men in armor to kill you and destroy all that you have!''

"Oh, cousin Jack,'' said the giant, "this is heavy news indeed! I will immediately run and hide myself, and thou shalt lock, bolt, and bar me in, and keep the keys until the prince is gone.'' Having secured the giant, Jack fetched his master, when they made themselves heartily merry whilst the poor giant lay trembling in a vault under the ground.

Early in the morning Jack furnished his master with a fresh supply of gold and silver, and then sent him three miles forward on his journey, at which time the prince was pretty well out of the smell of the giant. Jack then returned, and let the giant out of the vault, who asked what he should give him for keeping the castle from destruction. "Why,'' quoth Jack, "I want nothing but the old coat and cap, together with the old rusty sword and slippers which are at your bed's head.'' Quoth the giant: "You know not what you ask; they are the most precious things I have. The coat will keep you invisible, the cap will tell you all you want to know, the sword cuts asunder whatever you strike, and the shoes are of extraordinary swiftness. But you have been very serviceable to me, therefore take them with all my heart.'' Jack thanked his uncle, and then went off with them. He soon overtook his master and they quickly arrived at the house of the lady the prince sought, who, finding the prince to be a suitor, prepared a splendid banquet for him. After the repast was concluded, she told him she had a task for him. She wiped his mouth with a handkerchief, saying: "You must show me that handkerchief tomorrow morning, or else you will lose your head." With that she put it in her bosom. The prince went to bed in great sorrow, but Jack's cap of knowledge informed him how it was to be obtained. In the middle of the night she called upon her familiar spirit to carry her to Lucifer. But Jack put on his coat of darkness and his shoes of swiftness, and was there as soon as she was. When she entered the place of the demon, she gave the handkerchief to him, and he laid it upon a shelf, whence Jack took it and brought it to his master, who showed it to the lady next day, and so saved his life. On that day, she gave the prince a kiss and told him he must show her the lips tomorrow morning that she kissed last night, or lose his head.

"Ah!" he replied, "if you kiss none but mine, I will."

"That is neither here nor there," said she; "if you do not, death's your portion!"

At midnight she went as before, and was angry with the demon for letting the handkerchief go. "But now," quoth she, "I will be too hard for the king's son, for I will kiss thee, and he is to show me thy lips." Which she did, and Jack, when she was not standing by, cut off Lucifer's head and brought it under his invisible coat to his master, who the next morning pulled it out by the horns before the lady. This broke the enchantment and the evil spirit left her, and she appeared in all her beauty. They were married the next morning, and soon after went to the Court of King Arthur, where Jack for his many great exploits, was made one of the Knights of the Round Table.

Jack soon went searching for giants again, but he had not ridden far, when he saw a cave, near the entrance of which he beheld a giant sitting upon a block of timber, with a knotted iron club by his side. His goggle eyes were like flames of fire, his countenance grim and ugly, and his cheeks like a couple of large flitches of bacon, while the bristles of his beard resembled rods of iron wire, and the locks that hung down upon his brawny shoulders were like curled snakes or hissing adders. Jack alighted from his horse, and, putting on the coat of darkness, went up close to the giant, and said softly: "Oh! are you there? It will not be long before I take you fast by the beard." The giant all this while could not see him, on account of his invisible coat, so that Jack, coming up close to the monster, struck a blow with his sword at his head, but, missing his aim, he cut off the nose instead. At this, the giant roared like claps of thunder, and began to lay about him with his iron club like one stark mad. But Jack, running behind, drove his sword up to the hilt in the giant's back, so that he fell down dead. This done, Jack cut off the giant's head, and sent it, with his brother's also, to King Arthur, by a waggoner he hired for that purpose.

Jack now resolved to enter the giant's cave in search of his treasure, and, passing along through a great many windings and turnings, he came at length to a large room paved with freestone, at the upper end of which was a boiling caldron, and on the right hand a large table, at which the giant used to dine. Then he came to a window, barred with iron, through which he looked and beheld a vast number of miserable captives, who, seeing him, cried out: "Alas! young man, art thou come to be one amongst us in this miserable den?"

"Ay," quoth Jack, "but pray tell me what is the meaning of your captivity?"

"We are kept here," said one, "till such time as the giants have a wish to feast, and then the fattest among us is slaughtered! And many are the times they have dined upon murdered men!"

"Say you so," quoth Jack, and straightway unlocked the gate and let them free, who all rejoiced like condemned men at sight of a pardon. Then searching the giant's coffers, he shared the gold and silver equally amongst them and took them to a neighboring castle, where they all feasted and made

merry over their deliverance.

But in the midst of all this mirth a messenger brought news that one Thunderdell, a giant with two heads, having heard of the death of his kinsmen, had come from the northern dales to be revenged on Jack, and was within a mile of the castle, the country people flying before him like chaff. But Jack was not a bit daunted, and said: "Let him come! I have a tool to pick his teeth; and you, ladies and gentlemen, walk out into the garden, and you shall witness this giant Thunderdell's death and destruction."

The castle was situated in the midst of a small island surrounded by a moat thirty feet deep and twenty feet wide, over which lay a drawbridge. So Jack employed men to cut through this bridge on both sides, nearly to the middle; and then, dressing himself in his invisible coat, he marched against the giant with his sword of sharpness. Although the giant could not see Jack, he smelt his approach, and cried out in these words:

"Fee, fi, fo, fum!
I smell the blood of an Englishman!
Be he alive or be he dead,
I'll grind his bones to make me bread!"

"Say'st thou so," said Jack; "then thou art a monstrous miller indeed."

The giant cried out again: "Art thou that villain who killed my kinsmen? Then I will tear thee with my teeth, suck thy blood, and grind thy bones to powder."

"You'll have to catch me first," quoth Jack, and throwing off his invisible coat, so that the giant might see him, and putting on his shoes of swiftness, he ran from the giant, who followed like a walking castle, so that the very foundations of the earth seemed to shake at every step. Jack led him a long dance, in order that the gentlemen and ladies might see; and at last to end the matter, ran lightly over the drawbridge, the giant in full speed, pursuing him with his club. Then, coming to the middle of the bridge, the giant's great weight broke it down, and he tumbled headlong into the water, where he rolled and wallowed like a whale. Jack, standing by the moat, laughed at him all the while; but though the giant foamed to hear him scoff, and plunged from place to place in the moat, yet he could not get out to be revenged. Jack at length got a cart rope and cast it over the two heads of the giant and drew him ashore by a team of horses, and then cut off both his heads with his sword of sharpness, and sent them to King Arthur.

After some time spent in mirth and pastime, Jack, taking leave of the knights and ladies, set out for new adventures. Through many woods he passed, and came at length to the foot of a high mountain. Here, late at night, he found a lonesome house, and knocked at the door, which was opened by an aged man with a head as white as snow. "Father," said Jack, "can you lodge a benighted traveller that has lost his way?" "Yes," said the old man, "you are right welcome to my poor cottage." Whereupon Jack entered, and down they sat together, and the old man began to speak as follows: "Son, I see by your belt you are the great conqueror of giants, and behold, my son, on the top of this mountain is an enchanted castle; this is kept by a giant named Galligantua, and he, by the help of an old conjurer, betrays many knights and ladies into his castle, where by magic art they are transformed into sundry shapes and forms. But above all, I grieve for a duke's daughter, whom they fetched from her father's garden, carrying her through the air in a burning chariot drawn by fiery dragons, when they secured her within the castle, and transformed her into a white hind. And though many knights have tried to break the enchantment, and work her deliverance, yet no one could accomplish it, on account of two dreadful griffins which are placed at the castle gate and which destroy everyone who comes near. But you, my son, may pass by them undiscovered, where on the gates of the castle you will find engraven in large letters how the spell may be broken." Jack gave the old man his hand, and promised that in the morning he would venture his life to free the lady.

In the morning Jack arose and put on his invisible coat and magic cap and shoes, and prepared himself for the fray. Now, when he had reached the top of the mountain he soon discovered the two fiery griffins, but passed them without fear, because of his invisible coat. When he had got beyond them, he found upon the gates of the castle a golden trumpet hung by a silver chain, under which these lines were engraved:

"Whoever shall this trumpet blow,
Shall soon the giant overthrow
And break the black enchantment straight:
So all shall be in happy state."

Jack had no sooner read this but he blew the trumpet, at which the castle trembled to its vast foundations, and the giant and conjurer were in horrid confusion, biting their thumbs and tearing their hair, knowing their wicked reign was at an end. Then, the giant stooping to take up his club, Jack at one blow cut off his head; whereupon the conjurer, mounting up into the air, was carried away in a whirlwind. Then the enchantment was broken, and all the lords and ladies who had so long been transformed into birds and beasts returned to their proper shapes, and the castle vanished away in a cloud of smoke. This being done, the head of Galligantua was likewise, in the usual manner, conveyed to the Court of King Arthur, where, the very next day, Jack followed, with the knights and ladies who had been delivered. Whereupon, as a reward for his good services, the king prevailed upon the duke to bestow his daughter in marriage on honest Jack. So married they were, and the whole kingdom was filled with joy at

the wedding. Furthermore, the king bestowed on Jack a noble castle, with a very beautiful estate thereto belonging, where he and his lady lived in great joy and happiness all the rest of their days.

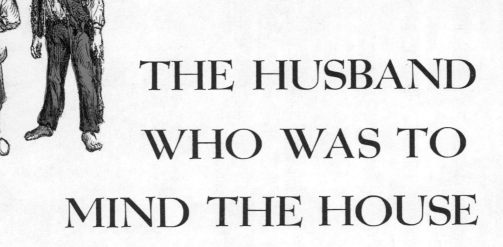

THE HUSBAND
WHO WAS TO
MIND THE HOUSE

ONCE on a time there was a man, so surly and cross, he never thought his wife did anything right in the house. So one evening, in hay-making time, he came home, scolding and swearing, and showing his teeth and making a dust.

"Dear love, don't be so angry; there's a good man," said his goody; "tomorrow let's change our work. I'll go out with the mowers and mow, and you shall mind the house at home."

Yes, the husband thought that would do very well. He was quite willing, he said.

So, early next morning, his goody took a scythe over her neck, and went out into the hay-field with the mowers and began to mow; but the man was to mind the house, and do the work at home.

First of all he wanted to churn the butter; but when he had churned awhile, he got thirsty, and went down to the cellar to tap a barrel of ale. So, just when he had knocked in the bung, and was putting the tap into the cask, he heard overhead the pig come into the kitchen. Then off he ran up the cellar steps, with the tap in his hand, as fast as he could, to look after the pig, lest it should upset the churn; but when he got up, and saw the pig had already knocked the churn over, and stood there, routing and grunting amongst the cream which was running all over the floor, he got so wild with rage that he quite forgot the ale-barrel, and ran at the pig as hard as he could. He caught it, too, just as it ran out of doors, and gave it such a kick that piggy lay for dead on the spot. Then all at once he remembered he had the tap in his hand; but when he got down to the cellar, every drop of ale had run out of the cask.

Then he went into the dairy and found enough cream left to fill the churn again, and so he began to churn, for butter

they must have at dinner. When he had churned a bit, he remembered that their milking cow was still shut up in the byre, and hadn't had a bit to eat or a drop to drink all the morning, though the sun was high. Then all at once he thought 'twas too far to take her down to the meadow, so he'd just get her up on the housetop—for the house, you must know, was thatched with sods, and a fine crop of grass was growing there. Now their house lay close up against a steep down, and he thought if he laid a plank across to the thatch at the back he'd easily get the cow up.

But still he couldn't leave the churn, for there was his little babe crawling about on the floor, and "if I leave it," he thought, "the child is safe to upset it." So he took the churn on his back, and went out with it; but then he thought he'd better first water the cow before he turned her out on the thatch; so he took up a bucket to draw water out of the well; but, as he stooped down at the well's brink, all the cream ran out of the churn over his shoulders, and so down into the well.

Now it was near dinnertime, and he hadn't even got the butter yet; so he thought he'd best boil the porridge, and filled the pot with water, and hung it over the fire. When he had done that, he thought the cow might perhaps fall off the thatch and break her

legs or her neck. So he got up on the house to tie her up. One end of the rope he made fast to the cow's neck, and the other he slipped down the chimney and tied round his own thigh; and he had to make haste, for the water now began to boil in the pot, and he had still to grind the oatmeal.

So he began to grind away; but while he was hard at it, down fell the cow off the house top after all, and as she fell, she dragged the man up the chimney by the rope. There he stuck fast; and as for the cow, she hung halfway down the wall, swinging between heaven and earth, for she could neither get down nor up.

And now the goody had waited seven lengths and seven breadths for her husband to come and call them home to dinner; but never a call they had. At last she thought she'd waited long enough, and went home. But when she got there and saw the cow hanging in such an ugly place, she ran up and cut the rope in two with her scythe. But as she did this, down came her husband out of the chimney; and so when his old dame came inside the kitchen, there she found him standing on his head in the porridge-pot.

THE EMPEROR'S NEW CLOTHES

MANY years ago there was an Emperor who was so excessively fond of new clothes that he spent all his money on them. He cared nothing about his soldiers, nor for the theatre, nor for driving in the woods except for the sake of showing off his new clothes. He had a costume for every hour in the day, and instead of saying as one does about any other King or Emperor, "He is in his council chamber," here one always said, "The Emperor is in his dressing-room."

Life was very gay in the great town where he lived; hosts of strangers came to visit it every day, and among them one day two swindlers. They gave themselves out as weavers, and said that they knew how to weave the most beautiful stuffs imaginable. Not only were the colors and patterns unusually fine, but the clothes that were made of these stuffs had the peculiar quality of becoming invisible to every person who was not fit for the office he held, or if he was impossibly dull.

"Those must be splendid clothes," thought the Emperor. "By wearing them I should be able to discover which men in my kingdom are unfitted for their posts. I shall distinguish the wise men from the fools. Yes, I certainly must order some of that stuff to be woven for me."

He paid the two swindlers a lot of money in advance so that they might begin their work at once.

They did put up two looms and pretended to weave, but they had nothing whatever upon their shuttles. At the outset they asked for a quantity of the finest silk and the purest gold thread, all of which they put into their own bags while they worked away at the empty looms far into the night.

"I should like to know how those weavers are getting on with the stuff," thought the Emperor; but he felt a little queer when he reflected that anyone who was stupid or unfit for his post would not be able to see it. He certainly thought that he need have no fears for himself, but still he thought he would send somebody else first to see how it was getting on. Everybody in the town knew what wonderful power the stuff possessed, and everyone was anxious to see how stupid his neighbor was.

"I will send my faithful old minister to the weavers," thought the Emperor. "He will be best able to see how the stuff looks, for he is a clever man and no one fulfills his duties better than he does!"

So the good old minister went into the room where the two swindlers sat working at the empty loom.

"Heaven preserve us!" thought the old minister, opening his eyes very wide. "Why, I can't see a thing!" But he took care not to say so.

Both the swindlers begged him to be good enough to step a little nearer, and asked if he did not think it a good pattern and beautiful coloring. They pointed to the empty loom, and the poor old minister stared as hard as he could but he could not see anything, for of course there was nothing to see.

"Good heavens!" thought he, "is it possible that I am a fool. I have never thought so and nobody must know it. Am I not fit for my post? It will never do to say that I cannot see the stuffs."

"Well, sir, you don't say anything about the

stuff," said the one who was pretending to weave.

"Oh, it is beautiful! quite charming!" said the old minister looking through his spectacles; "this pattern and these colors! I will certainly tell the Emperor that the stuff pleases me very much."

"We are delighted to hear you say so," said the swindlers, and then they named all the colors and described the peculiar pattern. The old minister paid great attention to what they said, so as to be able to repeat it when he got home to the Emperor.

Then the swindlers went on to demand more money, more silk, and more gold, to be able to proceed with the weaving; but they put it all into their own pockets—not a single strand was ever put into the loom, but they went on as before weaving at the empty loom.

The Emperor soon sent another faithful official to see how the stuff was getting on, and if it would soon be ready. The same thing happened to him as to the minister; he looked and looked, but as there was only the empty loom, he could see nothing at all.

"Is not this a beautiful piece of stuff?" said both the swindlers, showing and explaining the beautiful pattern and colors which were not there to be seen.

"I know I am not a fool!" thought the man, "so it must be that I am unfit for my good post! It is very strange though! however one must not let it appear!" So he praised the stuff he did not see, and assured them of his delight in the beautiful colors and the originality of the design. "It is absolutely charming!" he said to the Emperor. Everybody in the town was talking about this splendid stuff.

Now the Emperor thought he would like to see it while it was still on the loom. So, accompanied by a number of selected courtiers, among whom were the two faithful officials who had already seen the imaginary stuff, he went to visit the crafty imposters, who were working away as hard as ever they could at the empty loom.

"It is magnificent!" said both the honest officials. "Only see, your Majesty, what a design! What colors!" And they pointed to the empty loom, for they thought that no doubt the others could see the stuff.

"What!" thought the Emperor; "I see nothing at all!

This is terrible! Am I a fool? Am I not fit to be Emperor? Why, nothing worse could happen to me!"

"Oh, it is beautiful!" said the Emperor. "It has my highest approval!" and he nodded his satisfaction as he gazed at the empty loom. Nothing would induce him to say that he could not see anything.

The whole suite gazed and gazed, but saw nothing more than all the others. However, they all exclaimed with his Majesty, "It is very beautiful!" and they advised him to wear a suit made of this wonderful cloth on the occasion of a great procession which was just about to take place. "It is magnificent! gorgeous! excellent!" went from mouth to mouth; they were all equally delighted with it. The Emperor gave each of the rogues an order of knighthood to be worn in their buttonholes and the title of "Gentlemen Weavers."

The swindlers sat up the whole night, before the day on which the procession was to take place, burning sixteen candles; so that people might see how anxious they were to get the Emperor's new clothes ready. They pretended to take the stuff off the loom. They cut it out in the air with a huge pair of scissors, and they stitched away with needles without any thread in them. At last they said: "Now the Emperor's new clothes are ready!"

The Emperor, with his grandest courtiers, went to them himself, and both the swindlers raised one arm in the air, as if they were holding something, and said: "See, these are the trousers, this is the coat, here is the mantle!" and so on. "It is as light as a spider's web. One might think one had nothing on, but that is the very beauty of it!"

"Yes!" said all the courtiers, but they could not see anything, for there was nothing to see.

"Will your imperial majesty be graciously pleased to take off your clothes," said the imposters, "so that we may put on the new ones, along here before the great mirror."

The Emperor took off all his clothes, and the imposters pretended to give him one article of dress after the other, of

the new ones which they had pretended to make. They pretended to fasten something round his waist and to tie on something; this was the train, and the Emperor turned round and round in front of the mirror.

"How well his majesty looks in the new clothes! How becoming they are!" cried all the people round. "What a design, and what colors! They are most gorgeous robes!"

"The canopy is waiting outside which is to be carried over your majesty in the procession," said the master of the ceremonies.

"Well, I am quite ready," said the Emperor. "Don't the clothes fit well?" and then he turned round again in front of the mirror, so that he should seem to be looking at his grand things.

The chamberlains who were to carry the train stooped and pretended to lift it from the ground with both hands, and they walked along with their hands in the air. They dared not let it appear that they could not see anything.

Then the Emperor walked along in the procession under the gorgeous canopy, and everybody in the streets and at the windows exclaimed, "How beautiful the Emperor's new clothes are! What a splendid train! And they fit to perfection!" Nobody would let it appear that he could see nothing, for then he would not be fit for his post, or else he was a fool.

None of the Emperor's clothes had been so successful before.

"But he has got nothing on," said a little child.

"Oh, listen to the innocent," said its father; and one person whispered to the other what the child had said. "He has nothing on, a child says he has nothing on!"

"But he has nothing on!" at last cried all the people.

The Emperor writhed, for he knew it was true, but he thought "the procession must go on now," so he held himself stiffer than ever, and the chamberlains held up the invisible train.

THE BREMEN
TOWN MUSICIANS

THERE was once an ass whose master had made him carry sacks to the mill for many a long year, but whose strength began at last to fail, so that each day as it came found him less capable of work. Then his master began to think of turning him out, but the ass, guessing that something was in the wind that boded him no good, ran away, taking the road to Bremen; for there he thought he might get an engagement as town musician. When he had gone a little way he found a hound lying by the side of the road panting, as if he had run a long way.

"Now, hold fast, what are you so out of breath about?" said the ass.

"Oh dear!" said the dog, "now I am old, I get weaker every day, and can do no good in the hunt, so, as my master was going to have me killed, I have made my escape; but now, how am I to gain a living?"

"I will tell you what," said the ass, "I am going to Bremen to become town musician. You may as well go with me, and take up music too. I can play the lute, and you can beat the drum."

And the dog consented, and they walked on together. It was not long before they came to a cat sitting in the road, looking as dismal as three wet days.

"Now then, what is the matter with you, old shaver?" said the ass.

"I should like to know who would be cheerful when his neck is in danger," answered the cat. "Now that I am old and my teeth are getting blunt, and I would rather sit by the oven and purr than run about after mice, and my mistress wanted to drown me; so I took myself off; but good advice is scarce, and I do not know what is to become of me."

"Go with us to Bremen," said the ass, "and become town musician. You understand serenading."

The cat thought well of the idea, and went with them accordingly. After that the three travellers passed by a yard, and a cock was perched on the gate crowing with all his might.

"Your cries are enough to pierce bone and marrow," said the ass; "what is the matter?"

"I have foretold good weather for Lady-day, so that all the shirts may be washed and dried; and now on Sunday morning company is coming, and the mistress has told the cook that I must be made into soup, and this evening my neck is to be wrung, so that I am crowing with all my might while I can."

"You had much better go with us, Chanticleer," said the ass. "We are going to Bremen. At any rate that will be better than dying. You have a powerful voice, and when we are all performing together it will have a very good effect."

So the cock consented, and they went on all four together.

But Bremen was too far off to be reached in one day, and towards evening they came to a wood, where they determined to pass the night. The ass and the dog lay down under a large tree; the cat got up among the branches, and the cock flew up to the top, as that was the safest place for him. Before he went to sleep he looked all round him to the four points of the compass, and perceived in the distance a little light shining, and he called out to his companions that there must be a house not far off, as he could see a light, so the ass said,

"We had better get up and go there, for these are uncomfortable quarters." The dog began to fancy a few bones, not quite bare, would do him good. And they all set off in the direction of the light, and it grew larger and brighter, until at last it led them to a robber's house, all lighted up. The ass, being the biggest, went up to the window, and looked in.

"Well, what do you see?" asked the dog.

"What do I see?" answered the ass; "here is a table set out with splendid eatables and drinkables, and robbers sitting at it and making themselves very comfortable."

"That would just suit us," said the cock.

"Yes, indeed, I wish we were there," said the ass. Then they consulted together how it should be managed so as to get the robbers out of the house, and at last they hit on a plan. The ass was to place his forefeet on the window-sill, the dog was to get on the ass's back, the cat on the top of the dog, and lastly the cock was to fly up and perch on the cat's head. When that was done, at a given signal they all began to perform their music. The ass brayed, the dog barked, the cat mewed, and the cock crowed; then they burst through into the room, breaking all the panes of glass. The robbers fled at the dreadful sound; they thought it was some goblin, and fled to the wood in the utmost terror. Then the four companions sat down to table, made free with the remains of the meal, and feasted as if they had been hungry for a month. And when they had finished they put out the lights, and each sought out a sleeping-place to suit his nature and habits. The ass laid himself down outside on the dunghill, the dog behind the door, the cat on the hearth by the warm ashes, and the cock settled himself in the cock-loft, and as they were all tired with their long journey they soon fell fast asleep.

When midnight drew near, and the robbers from afar saw that no light was burning, and that everything appeared quiet, their captain said to them that he thought that they had run away without reason, telling one of them to go and reconnoitre. So one of them went, and found everything quite quiet; he went into the kitchen to strike a light, and taking the glowing fiery eyes of the cat for burning coals, he held a match to them in order to kindle it. But the cat, not seeing the joke, flew into his face, spitting and scratching. Then he cried out in terror, and ran to get out at the back door, but the dog, who was lying there, ran at him and bit his leg; and as he was rushing through the yard by the dunghill the ass struck out and gave him a great kick with his hindfoot; and the cock, who had been wakened with the noise, and felt quite brisk, cried out, "Cock-a-doodle-doo!"

Then the robber got back as well as he could to his captain, and said, "Oh, dear! in that house there is a grewsome witch, and I felt her breath and her long nails in my face; and by the door there stands a man who stabbed me in the leg with a knife; and in the yard there lies a black spectre, who beat me with his wooden club; and above, upon the roof, there sits the justice, who cried, 'Bring that rogue here!' And so I ran away from the place as fast as I could."

From that time forward the robbers never ventured to that house, and the four Bremen town musicians found themselves so well off where they were, that there they stayed. And the person who last related this tale is still living, as you see.

HANSEL AND GRETEL

NEAR a great forest there lived a poor woodcutter and his wife, and his two children; the boy's name was Hansel and the girl's Gretel. They had very little to bite or to sup, and once, when there was great dearth in the land, the man could not even gain the daily bread. As he lay in bed one night thinking of this, and turning and tossing, he sighed heavily, and said to his wife,

"What will become of us? We cannot even feed our children; there is nothing left for ourselves."

"I will tell you what, husband," answered the wife; "we will take the children early in the morning into the forest, where it is thickest; we will make them a fire, and we will give each of them a piece of bread, then we will go to our work and leave them alone; they will never find the way home again, and we shall be quit of them."

"No, wife," said the man, "I cannot do that; I cannot find in my heart to take my children into the forest and to leave them there alone; the wild animals would soon come and devour them."

"O you fool," said she, "then we will all four starve; you had better get the coffins ready "—and she left him no peace until he consented.

"But I really pity the poor children," said the man.

The two children had not been able to sleep for hunger, and had heard what their step-mother had said to their father. Gretel wept bitterly, and said to Hansel, "It is all over with us."

"Do be quiet, Gretel," said Hansel, "and do not fret; I will manage something." And when the parents had gone to sleep he got up, put on his little coat, opened the back door, and slipped out. The moon was shining brightly, and the white flints that lay in front of the house glistened like pieces of silver. Hansel stooped and filled the little pocket of his coat as full as it would hold. Then he went back again, and said to Gretel,

"Be easy, dear little sister, and go to sleep quietly; God will not forsake us," and laid himself down again in his bed.

When the day was breaking, and before the sun had risen, the wife came and awakened the two children, saying,

"Get up, you lazy bones; we are going into the forest to cut wood."

Then she gave each of them a piece of bread, and said,

"That is for dinner, and you must not eat it before then, for you will get no more."

Gretel carried the bread under her apron, for Hansel had his pockets full of the flints. Then they set off all together on their way to the forest. When they had gone a little way Hansel stood still and looked back towards the house, and this he did again and again, till his father said to him,

"Hansel, what are you looking at? Take care not to forget your legs."

"O father," said Hansel, "I am looking at my little white kitten, who is sitting up on the roof to bid me good-bye."

"You young fool," said the woman, "that is not your kitten, but the sunshine on the chimney-pot."

Of course Hansel had not been looking at his kitten, but had been taking every now and then a flint from his pocket and dropping it on the road.

When they reached the middle of the forest the father told the children to collect wood to make a fire to keep them warm; and Hansel and Gretel gathered brushwood enough for a little mountain; and it was set on fire, and when the flame was burning quite high the wife said,

"Now lie down by the fire and rest yourselves, you children, and we will go and cut wood; and when we are ready we will come and fetch you."

So Hansel and Gretel sat by the fire, and at noon they each ate their piece of bread. They thought their father was in the wood all the time, as they seemed to hear the strokes of the axe; but really it was only a dry branch hanging to a withered tree that the wind moved to and fro. So when they had stayed there a long time their eyelids closed with weariness, and they fell fast asleep. When at last they woke it was night, and Gretel began to cry, and said,

"How shall we ever get out of this wood?" But Hansel comforted her, saying,

"Wait a little while longer, until the moon rises, and then we can easily find the way home."

And when the full moon got up Hansel took his little sister by the hand, and followed the way where the flint stones shone like silver, and showed them the road. They walked on the whole night through, and at the break of day they came to their father's house. They knocked at the door, and when the wife opened it and saw that it was Hansel and Gretel she said,

"You naughty children, why did you sleep so long in the wood? We thought you were never coming home again!"

But the father was glad, for it had gone to his heart to leave them both in the woods alone.

Not very long after that there was again great scarcity in those parts, and the children heard their mother say at night in bed to their father,

"Everything is finished up; we have only half a loaf, and after that the tale comes to an end. The children must be off; we will take them farther into the wood this time, so that they shall not be able to find the way back again; there is no other way to manage."

The man felt sad at heart, and he thought,

"It would be better to share one's last morsel with one's children."

But the wife would listen to nothing that he said, but scolded and reproached him. He who says A must say B too, and when a man has given in once he has to do it a second time.

But the children were not asleep, and had heard all the talk. When the parents had gone to sleep Hansel got up to go out and get more flint stones, as he did before, but the wife had locked the door, and Hansel could not get out; but he comforted his little sister, and said,

"Don't cry, Gretel, and go to sleep quietly, and God will help us."

Early the next morning the wife came and pulled the children out of bed. She gave them each a little piece of bread—less than before; and on the way to the wood Hansel crumbled the bread in his pocket, and often stopped to throw a crumb on the ground.

"Hansel, what are you stopping behind and staring for?" said the father.

"I am looking at my little pigeon sitting on the roof, to say good-bye to me," answered Hansel.

"You fool," said the wife, "that is no pigeon, but the morning sun shining on the chimney pots."

Hansel went on as before, and strewed bread crumbs all along the road.

The woman led the children far into the wood, where they had never been before in all their lives. And again there was a large fire made, and the mother said,

"Sit still there, you children, and when you are tired, you can go to sleep; we are going into the forest to cut wood, and in the evening, when we are ready to go home we will come and fetch you."

So when noon came Gretel shared her bread with Hansel, who had strewed his along the road. Then they went to sleep, and the evening passed, and no one came for the poor children. When they awoke it was dark night, and Hansel comforted his little sister, and said,

"Wait a little, Gretel, until the moon gets up, then we shall be able to see the way home by the crumbs of bread that I have scattered along it."

So when the moon rose they got up, but they could find no crumbs of bread, for the birds of the woods and of the fields had come and picked them up. Hansel thought they might find the way all the same, but they could not. They went on all that night, and the next day from the morning until the evening, but they could not find the way out of the wood, and they were very hungry, for they had nothing to eat but the few berries they could pick up. And when they were so tired that they could no longer drag themselves along, they lay down under a tree and fell asleep.

It was now the third morning since they had left their father's house. They were always trying to get back to it, but instead of that they only found themselves farther in the wood, and if help had not soon come they would have been starved. About noon they saw a pretty snow-white bird sitting on a bough, and singing so sweetly that they stopped to listen. And when he had finished, the bird spread his wings and flew before them, and they followed after him until they came to a little house, and the bird perched on the roof, and when they came nearer they saw that the house was built of bread, and roofed with cakes; and the window was of transparent sugar.

"We will have some of this," said Hansel, "and make a fine meal. I will eat a piece of the roof, Gretel, and you can have some of the window—that will taste sweet."

So Hansel reached up and broke off a bit of the roof, just to see how it tasted, and Gretel stood by the window and gnawed at it. Then they heard a thin voice call out from inside,

> "Nibble, nibble, like a mouse,
> Who is nibbling at my house?"

And the children answered,

> "Never mind,
> It is the wind."

And they went on eating, never disturbing themselves. Hansel, who found that the roof tasted very nice, took down a great piece of it, and Gretel pulled out a large round windowpane, and sat her down and began upon it. Then the door opened, and an aged woman came out, leaning upon a crutch. Hansel and Gretel felt very frightened, and let fall what they had in their hands. The old woman, however, nodded her head, and said,

"Ah, my dear children, how come you here? You must come indoors and stay with me, you will be no trouble."

So she took them each by the hand, and led them into her little house. And there they found a good meal laid out, of milk and pancakes, with sugar, apples, and nuts. After that she showed them two little white beds, and Hansel and Gretel laid themselves down on them, and thought they were in heaven.

The old woman, although her behavior was so kind, was a wicked witch, who lay in wait for children, and had built the little house on purpose to entice them. When they were once inside she used to kill them, cook them, and eat them, and then it was a feastday with her. The witch's eyes were red, and she could not see very far, but she had a keen scent, like the beasts, and knew very well when human creatures were near. When she knew that Hansel and Gretel were coming, she gave a spiteful laugh, and said triumphantly,

"I have them, and they shall not escape me!"

Early in the morning before the children were awake, she got up to look at them, and as they lay sleeping so peacefully with round rosy cheeks, she said to herself,

"What a fine feast I shall have!"

Then she grasped Hansel with her withered hand, and led him into a little stable, and shut him up behind a grating; and call and scream as he might, it was no good. Then she went back to Gretel and shook her, crying,

"Get up, lazy bones; fetch water, and cook something nice for your brother; he is outside in the stable, and must be fattened up. And when he is fat enough I will eat him."

Gretel began to weep bitterly, but it was of no use, she had to do what the wicked witch bade her.

And so the best kind of victuals was cooked for poor Hansel, while Gretel got nothing but crab-shells. Each morning the old woman visited the little stable, and cried,

"Hansel, stretch out your finger, that I may tell if you will soon be fat enough."

Hansel, however, used to hold out a little bone, and the old woman, who had weak eyes, could not see what it was, and supposing it to be Hansel's finger, wondered very much that it was not getting fatter. When four weeks had passed and Hansel seemed to remain so thin, she lost patience and could wait no longer.

"Now then, Gretel," cried she to the little girl; "be quick and draw water; be Hansel fat or be he lean, tomorrow I must kill and cook him."

Oh what a grief for the poor little sister to have to fetch water, and how the tears flowed down over her cheeks!

"Dear God, pray help us!" cried she; "if we had been devoured by wild beasts in the wood at least we should have died together "

"Spare me your lamentations," said the old woman; "they are of no avail."

Early next morning Gretel had to get up, make the fire, and fill the kettle.

"First we will do the baking," said the old woman; I have heated the oven already, and kneaded the dough."

She pushed poor Gretel towards the oven, out of which the flames were already shining.

"Creep in," said the witch, "and see if it is properly hot, so that the bread may be baked."

And Gretel once in, she meant to shut the door upon her and let her be baked, and then she would have eaten her. But Gretel perceived her intention, and said,

"I don't know how to do it; how shall I get in?"

"Stupid goose," said the old woman, "the opening is big enough, do you see? I could get in myself!" and she stooped down and put her head in the oven's mouth. Then Gretel gave her a push, so that she went in farther, and she shut the iron door upon her, and put up the bar. Oh how frightfully she howled! but Gretel ran away, and left the wicked witch to burn miserably. Gretel went straight to Hansel, opened the stable-door, and cried,

"Hansel, we are free! the old witch is dead!"

Then out flew Hansel like a bird from its cage as soon as the door is opened. How rejoiced they both were! how they fell each on the other's neck! and danced about, and kissed each other! And as they had nothing more to fear they went over all the old witch's house, and in every corner there stood chests of pearls and precious stones.

"This is something better than flint stones," said Hansel, as he filled his pockets, and Gretel, thinking she also would like to carry something home with her, filled her apron full.

"Now, away we go," said Hansel —"if we only can get out of the witch's wood."

When they had journeyed a few hours they came to a great piece of water.

"We can never get across this," said Hansel, "I see no stepping-stones and no bridge."

"And there is no boat either," said Gretel; "but here comes a white duck; if I ask her she will help us over." So she cried,

> "Duck, duck, here we stand,
> Hansel and Gretel, on the land,
> Stepping-stones and bridge we lack,
> Carry us over on your nice white back."

And the duck came accordingly, and Hansel got upon her and told his sister to come too.

"No," answered Gretel, "that would be too hard upon the duck; we can go separately, one after the other."

And that was how it was managed, and after that they went on happily, until they came to the wood, and the way grew more and more familiar, till at last they saw in the distance their father's house. Then they ran till they came up to it, rushed in at the door, and fell on their father's neck. The man had not had a quiet hour since he left his children in the wood; but the wife was dead. And when Gretel opened her apron the pearls and precious stones were scattered all over the room, and Hansel took one handful after another out of his pocket. Then was all care at an end, and they lived in great joy together.

> *Sing every one,*
> *My story is done,*
> *And look! round the house*
> *There runs a little mouse,*
> *He that can catch her before she scampers in,*
> *May make himself a very very large*
> *fur-cap out of her skin.*

SNOW WHITE

I T WAS the middle of winter, and the snowflakes were falling
like feathers from the sky, and a queen sat at her window
working, and her embroidery frame was of ebony. And as she
worked, gazing at times out on the snow, she pricked her finger,
and there fell from it three drops of blood on the snow. And
when she saw how bright and red it looked, she said to herself,
"Oh that I had a child as white as snow, as red as blood, and as
black as the wood of the embroidery frame!"

Not very long after she had a daughter, with a skin as
white as snow, lips as red as blood, and hair as black as ebony,
and she was named Snow White. And when she was born the
queen died.

After a year had gone by the king took another wife, a
beautiful woman, but proud and overbearing, and she could
not bear to be surpassed in beauty by anyone. She had a magic
looking glass, and she used to stand before it, and look in it,
and say,

"Looking-glass upon the wall,
Who is fairest of us all?"
And the looking-glass would answer,
"You are fairest of them all."
And she was contented, for she knew that the looking-glass spoke the truth.

Now, Snow-White was growing prettier and prettier, and when she was seven years old she was as beautiful as day, far more so than the queen herself. So one day when the queen went to her mirror and said,

"Looking-glass upon the wall
Who is fairest of us all?"
It answered,
"Queen, you are full fair, 'tis true,
But Snow White fairer is than you."
This gave the queen a great shock, and she became yellow and green with envy, and from that hour her heart turned against Snow White, and she hated her. And envy and pride like ill weeds grew in her heart higher every day, until she had no peace day or night. At last she sent for a huntsman, and said,

"Take the child out into the woods, so that I may set eyes on her no more. You must put her to death, and bring

me her heart for a token.''

The huntsman consented, and led her away; but when he drew his cutlass to pierce Snow White's innocent heart, she began to weep, and to say,

"Oh, dear huntsman, do not take my life; I will go away into the wild wood, and never come home again.''

And as she was so lovely the huntsman had pity on her, and said,

"Away with you then, poor child;''for he thought the wild animals would be sure to devour her, and it was as if a stone had been rolled away from his heart when he spared to put her to death. Just at that moment a young wild boar came running by, so he caught and killed it, and taking out its heart, he brought it to the queen for a token. And it was salted and cooked, and the wicked woman ate it up, thinking that there was an end of Snow White.

Now, when the poor child found herself quite alone in the wild woods, she felt full of terror, even of the very leaves on the trees, and she did not know what to do for fright. Then she began to run over the sharp stones and through the thorn bushes, and the wild beasts after her, but they did her no harm. She ran as long as her feet would carry her; and when the evening drew near she came to a little house, and she went inside to rest. Everything there was very small, but as pretty and clean

as possible. There stood the little table ready laid, and covered with a white cloth, and seven little plates, and seven knives and forks, and drinking cups. By the wall stood seven little beds, side by side, covered with clean white quilts. Snow White, being very hungry and thirsty, ate from each plate a little porridge and bread, and drank out of each little cup a drop of wine, so as not to finish up one portion alone. After that she felt so tired that she lay down on one of the beds, but it did not seem to suit her; one was too long, another too short, but at last the seventh was quite right; and so she lay down upon it, committed herself to heaven, and fell asleep.

When it was quite dark, the masters of the house came home. They were seven dwarfs, whose occupation was to dig underground among the mountains. When they had lighted their seven candles, and it was quite light in the little house, they saw that some one must have been in, as everything was not in the same order in which they left it. The first said,

"Who has been sitting in my little chair?"

The second said,

"Who has been eating from my little plate?"

The third said,

"Who has been taking my little loaf?"

The fourth said,

"Who has been tasting my porridge?"

The fifth said,

"Who has been using my little fork?"

The sixth said,

"Who has been cutting with my little knife?"

The seventh said,

"Who has been drinking from my little cup?"

Then the first one, looking round, saw a hollow in his bed, and cried,

"Who has been lying on my bed?"

And the others came running, and cried,

"Some one has been on our beds too!"

But when the seventh looked at his bed, he saw little Snow White lying there asleep. Then he told the others, who came running up, crying out in their astonishment, and holding up their seven little candles to throw a light upon Snow White.

"O goodness! O gracious!" cried they, "what beautiful child is this?" and were so full of joy to see her that they did not wake her, but let her sleep on. And the seventh dwarf slept with his comrades, an hour at a time with each, until the night had passed.

When it was morning, and Snow White awoke and saw the seven dwarfs, she was very frightened; but they seemed quite friendly, and asked her what her name was, and she told

them; and then they asked how she came to be in their house.
And she related to them how her stepmother had wished her
to be put to death, and how the huntsman had spared her life,
and how she had run the whole day long, until at last she had
found their little house. Then the dwarfs said,

"If you will keep our house for us, and cook, and wash,
and make the beds, and sew and knit, and keep everything tidy
and clean, you may stay with us, and you shall lack nothing."

"With all my heart," said Snow White; and so she stayed,
and kept the house in good order. In the morning the dwarfs
went to the mountain to dig for gold; in the evening they came
home, and their supper had to be ready for them. All the day
long the maiden was left alone, and the good little dwarfs
warned her, saying,

"Beware of your stepmother, she will soon know you are
here. Let no one into the house."

Now the queen, having eaten Snow White's heart, as she
supposed, felt quite sure that now she was the first and fairest,
and so she came to her mirror, and said,

> "Looking-glass upon the wall,
> Who is fairest of us all?"

And the glass answered,

> "Queen, thou art of beauty rare,
> But Snow White living in the glen

With the seven little men
Is a thousand times more fair."

Then she was very angry, for the glass always spoke the truth, and she knew that the huntsman must have deceived her, and that Snow White must still be living. And she thought and thought how she could manage to make an end of her, for as long as she was not the fairest in the land, envy left her no rest. At last she thought of a plan; she painted her face and dressed herself like an old pedlar woman, so that no one would have known her. In this disguise she went across

the seven mountains, until she came to the house of the seven
little dwarfs, and she knocked at the door and cried,

"Fine wares to sell! fine wares to sell!"

Snow White peeped out of the window and cried, "Good-
day, good woman, what have you to sell?"

"Good wares, fine wares," answered she, "laces of all
colors," and she held up a piece that was woven of variegated
silk.

"I need not be afraid of letting in this good woman,"
thought Snow White, and she unbarred the door and bought

the pretty lace.

"What a figure you are, child!" said the old woman, "come and let me lace you properly for once."

Snow White, suspecting nothing, stood up before her, and let her lace her with the new lace; but the old woman laced so quick and tight that it took Snow White's breath away, and she fell down as dead.

"Now you have done with being the fairest," said the old woman as she hastened away.

Not long after that, towards evening, the seven dwarfs came home, and were terrified to see their dear Snow White lying on the ground, without life or motion; they raised her up, and when they saw how tightly she was laced they cut the lace in two; then she began to draw breath, and little by little

she returned to life. When the dwarfs heard what had happened they said,

"The old pedlar woman was no other than the wicked queen; you must beware of letting anyone in when we are not here!"

And when the wicked woman got home she went to her glass and said,

"Looking-glass against the wall,
Who is fairest of us all?"

And it answered as before,

"Queen, thou art of beauty rare,
But Snow White living in the glen
With the seven little men
Is a thousand times more fair."

When she heard that she was so struck with surprise that all the blood left her heart, for she knew that Snow White must still be living.

"But now," she said, "I will think of something that will be her ruin." And by witchcraft she made a poisoned comb. Then she dressed herself up to look like another different sort

of old woman. So she went across the seven mountains and
came to the house of the seven dwarfs, and knocked at the door
and cried,

"Good wares to sell! good wares to sell!"

Snow White looked out and said,

"Go away, I must not let anybody in."

"But you are not forbidden to look," said the old woman, taking out the poisoned comb, and holding it up. It pleased the poor child so much that she was tempted to open the door; and when the bargain was made the old woman said,

"Now, for once your hair shall be properly combed."

Poor Snow White, thinking no harm, let the old woman do as she would, but no sooner was the comb put in her hair then the poison began to work, and the poor girl fell down senseless.

"Now, you paragon of beauty," said the wicked woman, "this is the end of you," and went off. By good luck it was now near evening, and the seven little dwarfs came home. When they saw Snow White lying on the ground as dead, they thought directly that it was the stepmother's doing, and looked about, found the poisoned comb, and no sooner had they drawn it out of her hair than Snow White came to herself, and related all that had passed. Then they warned her once more to be on her guard, and never again to let anyone in at the door.

And the queen went home and stood before the looking-glass and said,

"Looking-glass against the wall,
Who is fairest of us all?"

And the looking-glass answered as before,

"Queen, thou art of beauty rare,
But Snow White living in the glen
With the seven little men
Is a thousand times more fair."

When she heard the looking-glass speak thus she trembled and shook with anger.

"Snow White shall die," cried she, "though it should cost me my own life!" And then she went to a secret lonely chamber, where no one was likely to come, and there she made a poisonous apple. It was beautiful to look upon, being white with red cheeks, so that anyone who should see it must long for it, but whoever ate even a little bit of it must die. When the apple was ready she painted her face and clothed herself like a peasant woman, and went across the seven mountains to where the seven dwarfs lived. And when she knocked at the door Snow White put her head out of the window and said,

"I dare not let anybody in; the seven dwarfs told me not."

"All right," answered the woman; "I can easily get rid of

my apples elsewhere. There, I will give you one."

"No," answered Snow White, "I dare not take anything."

"Are you afraid of poison?" said the woman, "look here, I will cut the apple in two pieces; you shall have the red side, I will have the white one."

For the apple was so cunningly made, that all the poison was in the rosy half of it. Snow White longed for the beautiful apple, and as she saw the peasant woman eating a piece of it she could no longer refrain, but stretched out her hand and took the poisoned half. But no sooner had she taken a morsel of it into her mouth than she fell to the earth as dead. And the queen, casting on her a terrible glance, laughed aloud and cried,

"As white as snow, as red as blood, as black as ebony! this time the dwarfs will not be able to bring you to life again."

And when she went home and asked the looking-glass,

"Looking-glass against the wall,
Who is fairest of us all?"
at last it answered,

"You are the fairest now of all."

Then her envious heart had peace, as much as an envious heart can have.

The dwarfs, when they came home in the evening, found Snow White lying on the ground, and there came no breath out of her mouth, and she was dead. They lifted her up, sought if anything poisonous was to be found, cut her laces, combed her hair, washed her with water and wine, but all was of no avail, the poor child was dead, and remained dead. Then they laid her on a bier, and sat all seven of them round it, and wept and lamented three whole days. And then they would have buried her, but that she looked still as if she were living, with her beautiful blooming cheeks. So they said,

"We cannot hide her away in the black ground." And they had made a coffin of clear glass, so as to be looked into from all sides, and they laid her in it, and wrote in golden letters upon it her name, and that she was a king's daughter. They then set the coffin out upon the mountain, and one of them always remained by it to watch. And the birds came too, and mourned for Snow White, first an owl, then a raven, and lastly, a dove.

Now, for a long while Snow White lay in the coffin and never changed, but looked as if she were asleep, for she was still as white as snow, as red as blood, and her hair was as black as ebony. It happened, however, that one day a king's son rode through the wood and up to the dwarfs' house, which was near it. He saw on the mountain the coffin, and beautiful Snow White within it, and he read what was written in golden letters upon it. Then he said to the dwarfs,

"Let me have the coffin, and I will give you whatever you like to ask for it."

But the dwarfs told him that they could not part with it for all the gold in the world. But he said,

"I beseech you to give it me, for I cannot live without looking upon Snow White; if you consent I will bring you to great honor, and care for you as if you were my brethren."

When he so spoke the good little dwarfs had pity upon him and gave him the coffin, and the king's son called his servants and bid them carry it away on their shoulders. Now it happened that as they were going along they stumbled over a bush, and with the shaking the bit of poisoned apple flew out of her throat. It was not long before she opened her eyes, threw up the cover of the coffin, and sat up, alive and well.

"Oh dear! where am I?" cried she. The king's son answered, full of joy, "You are near me," and, relating all that had happened, he said,

"I would rather have you than anything in the world; come with me to my father's castle and you shall be my bride."

And Snow White was kind, and went with him, and their wedding was held with pomp and great splendor.

But Snow White's wicked stepmother was also bidden to the feast, and when she had dressed herself in beautiful clothes she went to her looking-glass and said,

"Looking-glass upon the wall,
Who is fairest of us all?"
The looking-glass answered,
"O Queen, although you are of beauty rare,
The young bride is a thousand times more fair."
Then she railed and cursed, and was beside herself with disappointment and anger. First she thought she would not go to the wedding; but then she felt she should have no peace until she went and saw the bride. And when she saw her she knew her for Snow White, and could not stir from the place for anger and terror. For they had ready red-hot iron shoes, in which she had to dance until she fell down dead.

THE UGLY DUCKLING

The country was lovely just then; it was summer. The wheat was golden and the oats still green; the hay was stacked in the rich low-lying meadows, where the stork was marching about on his long red legs, chattering Egyptian, the language his mother had taught him.

Round about field and meadow lay great woods, in the midst of which were deep lakes. Yes, the country certainly was delicious. In the sunniest spot stood an old mansion surrounded by a deep moat, and great dock leaves grew from the walls of the house right down to the water's edge; some of them were so tall that a small child could stand upright under them. In amongst the leaves it was as secluded as in the depths of a forest; and there a duck was sitting on her nest. Her little ducklings were just about to be hatched, but she was nearly tired of sitting, for it had lasted such a long time. Moreover, she had very few visitors, as the other ducks liked swimming about in the moat better than waddling up to sit under the dock leaves and gossip with her.

At last one egg after another began to crack. "Cheep, cheep!" they said. All the chicks had come to life, and were poking their heads out.

"Quack! quack!" said the duck; and then they all quacked their hardest, and looked about them on all sides among the green leaves; their mother allowed them to look as much as they liked, for green is good for the eyes.

"How big the world is to be sure!" said all the young ones; for they certainly had ever so much more room to move about, than when they were inside the eggshell.

"Do you imagine this is the whole world?" said the mother. "It stretches a long way on the other side of the garden, right into the parson's field; but I have never been as far as that! I suppose you are all here now?" and she got up. "No! I declare I have not got you all yet! The biggest egg is still there; how long is it going to last?" and then she settled herself on the nest again.

"Well, how are you getting on?" said an old duck who had come to pay her a visit.

"This one egg is taking such a long time," answered the sitting duck, "the shell will not crack; but now you must look at the others; they are the finest ducklings I have ever seen! they are all exactly like their father, the rascal! He never comes to see me."

"Let me look at the egg which won't crack," said the old duck. "You may be sure that it is a turkey's egg! I have been cheated like that once, and I had no end of trouble and worry with the creatures, for I may tell you that they are afraid of the water. I could not get them into it, I quacked and snapped at them, but it was no good. Let me see the egg! Yes, it is a turkey's egg! You just leave it alone and teach the other children to swim."

"I will sit on it a little longer, I have sat so long already, that I may as well go on till the Midsummer Fair comes round."

"Please yourself," said the old duck, and she went away.

At last the big egg cracked. "Cheep, cheep!" said the young one and tumbled out; how big and ugly he was! The duck looked at him.

"That is a monstrous big duckling," she said; "none of the others looked like that; can he be a turkey chick? Well, we shall soon find that out; into the water he shall go, if I have to kick him in myself."

Next day was gloriously fine, and the sun shone on all the green dock leaves. The mother duck with her whole family went down to the moat.

Splash, into the water she sprang. "Quack, quack!" she said, and one duckling plumped in after the other. The water dashed over their heads, but they came up again and floated beautifully; their legs went of themselves, and they were all there, even the big ugly grey one swam about with them.

"No, that is no turkey," she said; "see how beautifully he uses his legs and how erect he holds himself; he is my own chick! after all, he is not so bad when you come to look at him properly. Quack, quack! Now come with me and I will take you into the world, and introduce you to the duckyard; but keep close to me all the time, so that no one may tread upon you, and beware of the cat!"

Then they went into the duckyard. There was a fearful uproar going on, for two broods were fighting for the head of an eel, and in the end the cat captured it.

"That's how things go in this world," said the mother duck, and she licked her bill for she wanted the eel's head herself.

"Use your legs," said she; "mind you quack properly, and bend your necks to the old duck over there! She is the grandest of them all; she has Spanish blood in her veins and that accounts for her size, and, do you see, she has a red rag round her leg; that is a wonderfully fine thing, and the most extraordinary mark of distinction any duck can have. It shows clearly that she is not to be parted with, and that she is worthy of recognition both by beasts and men! Quack now! don't turn your toes in, a well brought up duckling keeps his legs wide apart just like father and mother; that's it, now bend your necks, and say quack!"

They did as they were bid, but the other ducks round about looked at them and said, quite loud; "Just look there! now we are to have that tribe! just as if there were not enough of us already; and oh dear! how ugly that duckling is, we won't stand him!" and a duck flew at him at once and bit him in the neck.

"Let him be," said the mother; "he is doing no harm."

"Very likely not, but he is so ungainly and queer," said the biter; "he must be whacked."

"They are handsome children mother has," said the old duck with the rag round her leg; "all good looking except this one, and he is not a good specimen; it's a pity you can't make him over again."

"That can't be done, your grace," said the mother duck; "he is not handsome, but he is a thorough good creature, and he swims as beautifully as any of the others; nay, I think I might venture even to add that I think he will improve as he goes on, or perhaps in time he may grow smaller. He was too long in the egg, and so he has not come out with a very good figure." And then she patted his neck and stroked him down. "Besides he is a drake," said she; "so it does not matter so much. I believe he will be very strong, and I don't doubt but he will make his way in the world."

"The other ducklings are very pretty," said the old duck. "Now make yourselves quite at home, and if you find the head of an eel you may bring it to me!"

After that they felt quite at home. But the poor duckling which had been the last to come out of the shell, and who was so ugly, was bitten, pushed about, and made fun of both by the ducks and the hens. "He is too big," they all said; and the turkey-cock, who was born with his spurs on, and therefore thought himself quite an emperor, puffed himself up like a vessel in full sail, made for him, and gobbled and gobbled till he became quite red in the face. The poor duckling was at his wit's end, and did not know which way to turn; he was in despair because he was so ugly, and the butt of the whole duckyard.

So the first day passed, and afterwards matters grew worse and worse. The poor duckling was chased and hustled by all of them, even his brothers and sisters ill-used him; and they were always saying, "If only the cat would get hold of you, you hideous object!" Even his mother said, "I wish to goodness you were miles away." The ducks bit him, the hens pecked him, and the girl who fed them kicked him aside.

Then he ran off and flew right over the hedge, where the little birds flew up into the air in a fright.

"That is because I am so ugly," thought the poor duckling, shutting his eyes, but he ran on all the same. Then he came to a great marsh where the wild ducks lived; he was so tired and miserable that he stayed there the whole night.

In the morning the wild ducks flew up to inspect their new comrade.

"What sort of a creature are you?" they inquired, as the duckling turned from side to side and greeted them as well as he could. "You are frightfully ugly," said the wild ducks; "but that does not matter to us, so long as you do not marry into our family!" Poor fellow! he had no thought of marriage, all he wanted was permission to lie among the rushes, and to drink a little of the marsh water.

He stayed there two whole days, then two wild geese came, or rather two wild ganders, they were not long out of the shell, and therefore rather pert.

"I say comrade," they said, "you are so ugly that we have taken quite a fancy to you; will you join us and be a bird of passage? There is another marsh close by, and there are some charming wild geese there; all sweet young ladies, who can say quack! You are ugly enough to make your fortune among them." Just at that moment, bang! bang! was heard up above, and both the wild geese fell dead among the reeds, and the water turned blood red. Bang! bang! went the guns, and whole flocks of wild geese flew up from the rushes and the shot peppered among them again.

There was a grand shooting party, and the sportsmen lay hidden round the marsh, some even sat on the branches of the trees which overhung the water; the blue smoke rose like clouds among the dark trees and swept over the pool.

The water-dogs wandered about in the swamp, splash!

splash! The rushes and reeds bent beneath their tread on all sides. It was terribly alarming to the poor duckling. He twisted his head round to get it under his wing and just at that moment a frightful, big dog appeared close beside him; his tongue hung right out of his mouth and his eyes glared wickedly. He opened his great chasm of a mouth close to the duckling, showed his sharp teeth—and—splash—went on without touching him.

"Oh, thank Heaven!" sighed the duckling, "I am so ugly that even the dog won't bite me!"

Then he lay quite still while the shot whistled among the bushes, and bang after bang rent the air. It only became quiet late in the day, but even then the poor duckling did not dare to get up; he waited several hours more before he looked about and then he hurried away from the marsh as fast as he could. He ran across fields and meadows, and there was such a wind that he had hard work to make his way.

Towards night he reached a poor little cottage; it was such a miserable hovel that it could not make up its mind which way to fall even, and so it remained standing. The wind whistled so fiercely round the duckling that he had to sit on his tail to resist it, and it blew harder and harder; then he saw that the door had fallen off one hinge and hung so crookedly that he could creep into the house through the crack and by this means he made his way into the room. An old woman lived there with her cat and her hen. The cat, which she called "Sonnie," could arch his back, purr, and give off electric sparks, that is to say if you stroked his fur the wrong way. The hen had quite tiny short legs and so she was called "Chuckie-low-legs." She laid good eggs, and the old woman was as fond of her as if she had been her own child.

In the morning the strange duckling was dis-covered immediately, and the cat began to purr and the hen to cluck.

"What on earth is that!" said the old woman looking round, but her sight was not good and she thought the duckling was a fat duck which had escaped. "This is a capital find," said she; "now I shall have duck's eggs if only it is not a drake! we must find out about that!"

So she took the duckling on trial for three weeks, but no eggs made their appearance. The cat was the master of the house and the hen the mistress, and they always spoke of "we and the world," for they thought that they represented the half of the world, and that quite the better half.

The duckling thought there might be two opinions on the subject, but the cat would not hear of it.

"Can you lay eggs?" she asked.

"No!"

"Will you have the goodness to hold your tongue then!"

And the cat said, "Can you arch your back, purr, or give off sparks?"

"No."

"Then you had better keep your opinions to yourself when people of sense are speaking!"

The duckling sat in the corner nursing his ill-humor; then he began to think of the fresh air and the sunshine, an uncontrollable longing seized him to float on the water, and at last he could not help telling the hen about it.

"What on earth possesses you?" she asked; "you have nothing to do, that is why you get these freaks into your head. Lay some eggs or take to purring, and you will get over it."

"But it is so delicious to float on the water," said the duckling; "so delicious to feel it rushing over your head when you dive to the bottom."

"That would be a fine amusement," said the hen.

"I think you have gone mad. Ask the cat about it, he is the wisest creature I know; ask him if he is fond of floating on the water or diving under it. I say nothing about myself. Ask our mistress yourself, the old woman, there is no one in the world cleverer than she is. Do you suppose she has any desire to float on the water, or to duck underneath it?"

"You do not understand me," said the duckling.

"Well, if we don't understand you, who should? I suppose you don't consider yourself cleverer than the cat or the old woman, not to mention me. Don't make a fool of yourself, child, and thank your stars for all the good we have done you! Have you not lived in this warm room, and in such society that you might have learnt something? But you are an idiot, and there is no pleasure in associating with you. You may believe me I mean you well, I tell you home truths, and there is no surer way than that, of knowing who are one's friends. You just see about laying some eggs, or learn to purr, or to emit sparks."

"I think I will go out into the wide world," said the duckling.

"Oh, do so by all means," said the hen.

So away went the duckling, he floated on the water and ducked underneath it, but he was looked askance at by every living creature for his ugliness. Now the autumn came on, the leaves in the woods turned yellow and brown; the wind took hold of them, and they danced about. The sky looked very cold, and the clouds hung heavy with snow and hail. A raven stood on the fence and croaked Caw! Caw! from sheer cold; it made one shiver only to think of it, the poor duckling certainly was in a bad case.

One evening, the sun was just setting in wintry splendor, when a flock of beautiful large birds appeared out of the bushes; the duckling had never seen anything so beautiful. They were dazzlingly white with long waving necks; they were swans, and uttering a peculiar cry they spread out their magnificent broad wings and flew away from the cold regions to warmer lands and open seas. They mounted so high, so very high, and the ugly little duckling became strangely uneasy, he circled round and round in the water like a wheel, craning his neck up into the air after them. Then he uttered a shriek so piercing and so strange, that he was quite frightened by it himself. Oh, he could not forget those beautiful birds, those happy birds, and as soon as they were out of sight he ducked right down to the bottom, and when he came up again he was quite beside himself. He did not know what the birds were, or whither they flew, but all the same he was more drawn towards them than he had ever been by any creatures before. He did not envy them in the least, how could it occur to him even to wish to be such a marvel of beauty; he would have been thankful if only the ducks would have tolerated him among them—the poor ugly creature!

The winter was so bitterly cold that the duckling was obliged to swim about in the water to keep it from freezing; but every night the hole in which he swam got smaller and smaller. Then it froze so hard that the surface ice cracked, and the duckling had to use his legs all the time, so that the ice should not close in round him; at last he was so weary that he could move no more, and he was frozen fast into the ice.

Early in the morning a peasant came along and saw him; he went out on to the ice and hammered a hole in it with his heavy wooden shoe, and carried the duckling home to his wife. There it soon revived. The children wanted to play with it, but the duckling thought they were going to ill-use him, and rushed in his fright into the milk pan, and the milk spurted out all over the room. The woman shrieked and threw up her hands, then it flew into the butter cask, and down into the meal tub and out again. Just imagine what it looked like by this time! The woman screamed and tried to hit it with the tongs, and the children tumbled over one another in trying to catch it, and they screamed with laughter— by good luck the door stood open, and the duckling flew out among the bushes and the new fallen snow— and it lay there thoroughly exhausted.

But it would be too sad to mention all the privation and misery it had to go through during that hard winter. When the sun began to shine warmly again, the duckling was in the marsh, lying among the rushes; the larks were singing and the beautiful spring had come.

Then all at once it raised its wings and they flapped with much greater strength than before, and bore him off vigorously. Before he knew where he was, he found himself in a large garden where the apple trees were in full blossom, and the air was scented with lilacs, the long branches of which overhung the indented shores of the lake. Oh! the spring freshness was so delicious!

Just in front of him he saw three beautiful white swans advancing towards him from a thicket; with rustling feathers they swam lightly over the water. The duckling recognized the majestic birds, and he was overcome by a strange melancholy.

"I will fly to them, the royal birds, and they will hack me to pieces, because I, who am so ugly, venture to approach them! But it won't matter; better be killed by them than be snapped at by the ducks, pecked by the hens, or spurned by the henwife, or suffer so much misery in the winter."

So he flew into the water and swam towards the stately swans; they saw him and darted towards him with ruffled feathers.

"Kill me, oh, kill me!" said the poor creature, and bowing his head towards the water he awaited his death. But what did he see reflected in the transparent water?

He saw below him his own image, but he was no longer a clumsy dark grey bird, ugly and ungainly, he was himself a swan! It does not matter in the least having been born in a duckyard, if only you come out of a swan's egg!

He felt quite glad of all the misery and tribulation he had gone through; he was the better able to appreciate his good fortune now, and all the beauty which greeted him. The big swans swam round and round him, and stroked him with their bills.

Some little children came into the garden with corn and pieces of bread, which they threw into the water; and the smallest one cried out: "There is a new one!" The other children shouted with joy, "Yes, a new one has come!" And they clapped their hands and danced about, running after their father and mother. They threw the bread into the water, and one and all said that "the new one was the prettiest; he was so young and handsome." And the old swans bent their heads and did homage before him.

He felt quite shy, and hid his head under his wing; he did not know what to think; he was so very happy, but not at all proud; a good heart never becomes proud. He thought of how he had been pursued and scorned, and now he heard them all say that he was the most beautiful of all beautiful birds. The

lilacs bent their boughs right down into the water before him, and the bright sun was warm and cheering, and he rustled his feathers and raised his slender neck aloft, saying with exultation in his heart: "I never dreamt of so much happiness when I was the Ugly Duckling!"

The Steadfast Tin Soldier

THERE were once five and twenty tin soldiers, all brothers, for they were the offspring of the same old tin spoon. Each man shouldered his gun, kept his eyes well to the front, and wore the smartest red and blue uniform imaginable. The first thing they heard in their new world, when the lid was taken off the box, was a little boy clapping his hands and crying, "Soldiers, soldiers!" It was his birthday and they had just been given to him; so he lost no time in setting them up on the table. All the soldiers were exactly alike with one exception, and he differed from the rest in having only one leg. For he was made last, and there was not quite enough tin left, to finish him. However, he stood just as well on his one leg, as the others on two, in fact he is the very one who is to become famous. On the table where they were being set up, were many other toys; but the chief thing which caught the eye was a delightful paper castle. You could see through the tiny windows, right into the rooms. Outside there were some little trees surrounding a small mirror, representing a lake, whose surface reflected the waxen swans which were swim-

358

ming about on it. It was altogether charming, but the prettiest thing of all was a little maiden standing at the open door of the castle. She, too, was cut out of paper, but she wore a dress of the lightest gauze, with a dainty little blue ribbon over her shoulders, by way of a scarf, set off by a brilliant spangle, as big as her whole face. The little maid was stretching out both arms, for she was a dancer, and in the dance, one of her legs was raised so high into the air that the tin soldier could see absolutely nothing of it, and supposed that she, like himself, had but one leg.

"That would be the very wife for me!" he thought; "but she is much too grand; she lives in a palace, while I only have a box, and then there are five and twenty of us to share it. No, that would be no place for her! but I must try to make her acquaintance!" Then he lay down full length behind a snuff box, which stood on the table. From that point he could have a good look at the little lady, who continued to stand on one leg without losing her balance.

Late in the evening the other soldiers were put into their box, and the people of the house went to bed. Now was the time for the toys to play; they amused themselves with paying visits, fighting battles, and giving balls. The tin soldiers rustled about in their box, for they wanted to join the games, but they could not get the lid off. The nutcrackers turned somersaults, and the pencil scribbled nonsense on the slate. There was such a noise that the canary woke up and joined in, but his remarks were in verse. The only two who did not move were the tin soldier and the little dancer. She stood as stiff as ever on tip-toe, with her arms spread out; he was equally firm on his one leg, and he did not take his eyes off her for a moment.

Then the clock struck twelve, when pop! up flew the lid of the snuff box, but there was no snuff in it, no! There was a little black goblin, a sort of Jack-in-the-box.

"Tin soldier!" said the goblin, "have the goodness to keep your eyes to yourself."

But the tin soldier pretended not to hear.

"Ah, you just wait till tomorrow," said the goblin.

In the morning when the children got up they put the tin soldier on the window frame, and, whether it was caused by the goblin or by a puff of wind, I do not know, but all at once the window burst open, and the soldier fell headforemost from the third story.

It was a terrific descent, and he landed at last, with his leg in the air, and rested on his cap, with his bayonet fixed between two paving stones. The maid-servant and the little boy ran down at once to look for him; but although they almost trod on him, they could not see him. Had the soldier only called out, "here I am," they would easily have found him, but he did not think it proper to shout when he was in uniform.

Presently it began to rain, and the drops fell faster and

faster, till there was a regular torrent. When it was over two street boys came along.

"Look out!" said one; "there is a tin soldier! He shall go for a sail."

So they made a boat out of a newspaper and put the soldier into the middle of it, and he sailed away down the gutter; both boys ran alongside clapping their hands. Good heavens! what waves there were in the gutter, and what a current, but then it certainly had rained cats and dogs. The paper boat danced up and down, and now and then whirled round and round. A shudder ran through the tin soldier, but he remained undaunted, and did not move a muscle, only looked straight before him with his gun shouldered. All at once the boat drifted under a long wooden tunnel, and it became as dark as it was in his box.

"Where on earth am I going to now!" thought he. "Well, well, it is all the fault of that goblin! Oh, if only the little maiden were with me in the boat it might be twice as dark for all I should care!"

At this moment a big water rat, who lived in the tunnel, came up.

"Have you a pass?" asked the rat. "Hand up your pass!"

The tin soldier did not speak, but clung still tighter to his gun. The boat rushed on, the rat close behind. Phew, how he gnashed his teeth and shouted to the bits of stick and straw.

"Stop him, stop him, he hasn't paid the toll! he hasn't

shown his pass!"

But the current grew stronger and stronger, the tin soldier could already see daylight before him at the end of the tunnel; but he also heard a roaring sound, fit to strike terror to the bravest heart. Just imagine! Where the tunnel ended the stream rushed straight into the big canal. That would be just as dangerous for him as it would be for us to shoot a great rapid.

He was so near the end now that it was impossible to stop. The boat dashed out; the poor tin soldier held himself as stiff as he could; no one should say of him that he even winced.

The boat swirled round three or four times, and filled with water to the edge; it must sink. The tin soldier stood up to his neck in water, and the boat sank deeper and deeper. The paper became limper and limper, and at last ·the water went over his head—then he thought of the pretty little dancer, whom he was never to see again, and this refrain rang in his ears:

"Onward! Onward! Soldier!
For death thou canst not shun."

At last the paper gave way entirely and the soldier fell through—but at the same moment he was swallowed by a big fish.

Oh! how dark it was inside the fish, it was worse than being in the tunnel even; and then it was so narrow! But the tin soldier was as dauntless as ever, and lay full length, shouldering his gun.

The fish rushed about and made the most frantic movements. At last it became quite quiet, and after a time, a flash

like lightning pierced it. The soldier was once more in the broad daylight, and some one called out loudly, "a tin soldier!" The fish had been caught, taken to market, sold, and brought into the kitchen, where the cook cut it open with a large knife. She took the soldier up by the waist, with two fingers, and carried him into the parlor, where everyone wanted to see the wonderful man, who had travelled about in the stomach of a fish; but the tin soldier was not at all proud. They set him up on the table, and wonder of wonders! he found himself in the very same room that he had been in before. He saw the very same children, and the toys were still standing on the table, as well as the beautiful castle with the pretty little dancer.

She still stood on one leg, and held the other up in the air. You see she also was unbending. The soldier was so much moved that he was ready to shed tears of tin, but that would not have been fitting. He looked at her, and she looked at him, but they said never a word. At this moment one of the little boys took up the tin soldier, and without rhyme or reason, threw him into the fire. No doubt the little goblin in the snuff box was to blame for that. The tin soldier stood there, lighted up by the flame, and in the most horrible heat; but whether it was the heat of the real fire, or the warmth of his feelings he did not know. He had lost all his gay color; it might have been from his perilous journey, or it might have been from grief, who can tell?

He looked at the little maiden, and she looked at him; and he felt that he was melting away, but he still managed to keep himself erect, shouldering his gun bravely.

A door was suddenly opened, the draught caught the little dancer and she fluttered like a sylph, straight into the fire, to the soldier, blazed up and was gone!

By this time the soldier was reduced to a mere lump, and when the maid took away the ashes next morning she found him, in the shape of a small tin heart. All that was left of the dancer, was her spangle, and that was burnt as black as a coal.

Rapunzel

THERE once lived a man and his wife, who had long wished for a child, but in vain. Now there was at the back of their house a little window which overlooked a beautiful garden full of the finest vegetables and flowers; but there was a high wall all round it, and no one ventured into it, for it belonged to a witch of great might, and of whom all the world was afraid. One day that the wife was standing at the window, and looking into the garden, she saw a bed filled with the finest rampion; and it looked so fresh and green that she began to wish for some; and at length she longed for it greatly. This went on for days, and as she knew she could not get the rampion, she pined away, and grew pale and miserable. Then the man was uneasy, and asked,

"What is the matter, dear wife?"

"Oh," answered she, "I shall die unless I can have some of that rampion to eat that grows in the garden at the back of our house." The man, who loved her very much, thought to himself,

"Rather than lose my wife I will get some rampion, cost what it will."

So in the twilight he climbed over the wall into the witch's garden, plucked hastily a handful of rampion and brought it to his wife. She made a salad of it at once, and ate of it to her heart's content. But she liked it so much, and it tasted so good, that the next day she longed for it thrice as much as she had done before; if she was to have any rest the man must climb over the wall once more. So he went in the twilight again; and as he was climbing back, he saw, all at once, the witch standing before him, and was terribly frightened, as she cried, with angry eyes,

"How dare you climb over into my garden like a thief, and steal my rampion! it shall be the worse for you!"

"Oh," answered he, "be merciful rather than just, I have only done it through necessity; for my wife saw your rampion out of the window, and became possessed with so great a longing that she would have died if she could not have had some to eat." Then the witch said,

"If it is all as you say you may have as much rampion as you like, on one condition—the child that will come into the world must be given to me. It shall go well with the child, and I will care for it like a mother."

In his distress of mind the man promised everything; and when the time came when the child was born the witch appeared, and, giving the child the name of Rapunzel (which is the same as rampion), she took it away with her.

Rapunzel was the most beautiful child in the world. When she was twelve years old the witch shut her up in a tower in the midst of a wood, and it had neither steps nor door, only a small window above. When the witch wished to be let in, she would stand below and cry,

"Rapunzel, Rapunzel! let down your hair!"

Rapunzel had beautiful long hair that shone like gold. When she heard the voice of the witch she would undo the fastening of the upper window, unbind the plaits of her hair, and let it down twenty ells below, and the witch would climb up by it.

After they had lived thus a few years it happened that as the King's son was riding through the wood, he came to the tower; and as he drew near he heard a voice singing so sweetly that he stood still and listened. It was Rapunzel in her loneliness trying to pass away the time with sweet songs. The King's son wished to go in to her, and sought to find a door in the tower, but there was none. So he rode home, but the song had entered into his heart, and every day he went into the wood and listened to it. Once as he was standing there under a tree, he saw the witch come up, and listened while she called out,

"O Rapunzel, Rapunzel! let down your hair."

Then he saw how Rapunzel let down her long tresses, and how the witch climbed up by it and went in to her, and he said to himself,

"Since that is the ladder I will climb it, and seek my fortune." And the next day, as soon as it began to grow dusk, he went to the tower and cried,

"O Rapunzel, Rapunzel! let down your hair."

And she let down her hair, and the King's son climbed up by it.

Rapunzel was greatly terrified when she saw that a man had come in to her, for she had never seen one before; but the King's son began speaking so kindly to her, and told how her singing had entered into his heart, so that he could have no peace until he had seen her himself. Then Rapunzel forgot her terror, and when he asked her to take him for her husband, and she saw that he was young and beautiful, she thought to herself,

"I certainly like him much better than old mother Gothel," and she put her hand into his hand, saying,

"I would willingly go with thee, but I do not know how I shall get out. When thou comest, bring each time a silken rope, and I will make a ladder, and when it is quite ready I will get down by it out of the tower, and thou shalt take me away on thy horse." They agreed that he should come to her every evening, as the old woman came in the daytime. So the witch knew nothing of all this until once Rapunzel said to her unwittingly,

"Mother Gothel, how is it that you climb up here so slowly, and the King's son is with me in a moment?"

"O wicked child," cried the witch, "what is this I hear! I thought I had hidden thee from all the world, and thou hast betrayed me!"

In her anger she seized Rapunzel by her beautiful hair, struck her several times with her left hand, and then grasping a pair of shears in her right—snip, snap—the beautiful locks lay on the ground. And she was so hard-hearted that she took Rapunzel and put her in a waste and desert place, where she lived in great woe and misery.

The same day on which she took Rapunzel away she went back to the tower in the evening and made fast the severed locks of hair to the window-hasp, and the King's son came and cried,

"Rapunzel, Rapunzel! let down your hair."

Then she let the hair down, and the King's son climbed up, but instead of his dearest Rapunzel he found the witch looking at him with wicked glittering eyes.

"Aha!" cried she, mocking him, "you came for your darling, but the sweet bird sits no longer in the nest, and sings no more; the cat has got her, and will scratch out your eyes as well! Rapunzel is lost to you; you will see her no more."

The King's son was beside himself with grief, and in his agony he sprang from the tower: he escaped with life, but the thorns on which he fell put out his eyes. Then he wandered blind through the wood, eating nothing but roots and berries, and doing nothing but lament and weep for the loss of his dearest wife.

So he wandered several years in misery until at last he came to the desert place where Rapunzel lived with her twin-children that she had borne, a boy and a girl. At first he heard a voice that he thought he knew, and when he reached the place from which it seemed to come Rapunzel knew him, and fell on his neck and wept. And when her tears touched his eyes they became clear again, and he could see with them as well as ever.

Then he took her to his kingdom, where he was received with great joy, and there they lived long and happily.

WHY THE SEA
IS SALT

ONCE on a time, but it was a long, long time ago, there were two brothers, one rich and one poor. Now, one Christmas eve, the poor one hadn't so much as a crumb in the house, either of meat or bread, so he went to his brother to ask him for something to keep Christmas with, in God's name. It was not the first time his brother had been forced to help him, and you may fancy he wasn't very glad to see his face, but he said—

"If you will do what I ask you to do, I'll give you a whole flitch of bacon."

So the poor brother said he would do anything, and was full of thanks.

"Well, here is the flitch," said the rich brother, "and now go straight to Hell."

"What I have given my word to do, I must stick to," said the other; so he took the flitch and set off. He walked the whole day, and at dusk he came to a place where he saw a very bright light.

"Maybe this is the place," said the man to himself. So he turned aside, and the first thing he saw was an old, old man, with a long white beard, who stood in an outhouse, hewing wood for the Christmas fire.

"Good evening," said the man with the flitch.

"The same to you; whither are you going so late?" said the man.

"Oh! I'm going to Hell, if I only knew the right way," answered the poor man.

"Well, you're not far wrong, for this is Hell," said the old man; "when you get inside they will be all for buying your flitch, for meat is scarce in Hell; but mind you don't sell it unless you get the hand-quern which stands behind the door for it. When you come out, I'll teach you how to handle the quern, for it's good to grind almost anything."

So the man with the flitch thanked the other for his good advice, and gave a great knock at the Devil's door.

When he got in, everything went just as the old man had said. All the devils, great and small, came swarming up to him like ants round an anthill, and each tried to outbid the other for the flitch.

"Well!" said the man, "by rights my old dame and I ought to have this flitch for our Christmas dinner; but since you have all set your hearts on it, I suppose I must give it up to you; but if I sell it at all, I'll have for it that quern behind the door yonder."

At first the Devil wouldn't hear of such a bargain, and chaffered and haggled with the man; but he stuck to what he said, and at last the Devil had to part with his quern. When the man got out into the yard, he asked the old woodcutter how he was to handle the quern; and after he had learned how to

371

use it, he thanked the old man and went off home as fast as he could, but still the clock had struck twelve on Christmas eve before he reached his own door.

"Wherever in the world have you been?" said his old dame; "here have I sat hour after hour waiting and watching, without so much as two sticks to lay together under the Christmas brose."

"Oh!" said the man, "I couldn't get back before, for I had to go a long way first for one thing, and then for another; but now you shall see what you shall sèe."

So he put the quern on the table, and bade it first of all grind lights, then a tablecloth, then meat, then ale, and so on till they had got everything that was nice for Christmas fare. He had only to speak the word, and the quern ground out what he wanted. The old dame stood by blessing her stars, and kept on asking where he had got this wonderful quern, but he wouldn't tell her.

"It's all one where I got it from; you see the quern is a good one, and the millstream never freezes, that's enough.

So he ground meat and drink and dainties enough to last out till Twelfth Day, and on the third day he asked all his friends and kin to his house, and gave a great feast. Now, when his rich brother saw all that was on the table, and all that was behind in the larder, he grew quite spiteful and wild, for he couldn't bear that his brother should have anything.

"Twas only on Christmas eve," he said to the rest, "he was in such straits that he came and asked for a morsel of food in God's name, and now he gives a feast as if he were count or king," and he turned to his brother and said—

"But whence, in Hell's name, have you got all this wealth?"

"From behind the door," answered the owner of the quern, for he didn't care to let the cat out of the bag. But later in the evening when he had got a drop too much, he could keep his secret no longer, and brought out the quern and said—

"There, you see what has gotten me all this wealth," and so he made the quern grind all kind of things. When his brother saw it, he set his heart on having the quern, and, after a deal of coaxing, he got it; but he had to pay three hundred dollars for it, and his brother bargained to keep it till hay harvest, for he thought, if I keep it till then, I can make it grind meat and drink that will last for years. So you may fancy the quern didn't grow rusty for want of work, and when hay harvest came, the rich brother got it, but the other took care not to teach him how to handle it.

It was evening when the rich brother got the quern home, and next morning he told his wife to go out into the hayfield and toss, while the mowers cut the grass, and he would stay at home and get dinner ready. So, when dinner time drew near, he put the quern on the kitchen table and said—

"Grind herrings and broth, and grind them good and fast."

So the quern began to grind herrings and broth; first of all, all the dishes full, then all the tubs full, and so on till the kitchen floor was quite covered. Then the man twisted and twirled at the quern to get it to stop, but for all his twisting and fingering the quern went on grinding, and in a little while the broth rose so high that the man was like to drown. So he threw open the kitchen door and ran into the parlor, but it wasn't long before the quern had ground the parlor full too, and it was only at the risk of his life that the man could get hold of the latch of the house door through the stream of broth. When he got the door open, he ran out and set off down the road, with the stream of herrings and broth at his heels, roaring like a waterfall over the whole farm.

Now, his old dame, who was in the field tossing hay, thought it a long time to dinner, and at last she said—

"Well! though the master doesn't call us home, we may as well go. Maybe he finds it hard work to boil the broth, and will be glad of my help."

The men were willing enough, so they sauntered homewards; but just as they had got a little way up the hill, what should they meet but herrings, and broth, and bread, all running and dashing, and splashing together in a stream, and the master himself running before them for his life, and as he passed them he bawled out —"Would to heaven each of you had a hundred throats! but take care you're not drowned in the broth."

Away he went, as though the Evil One were at his heels, to his brother's house, and begged him for God's sake to take back the quern that instant; for, said he—

"If it grind only one hour more, the whole parish will be swallowed up by herrings and broth."

But his brother wouldn't hear of taking it back till the other paid him down three hundred dollars more.

So the poor brother got both the money and the quern, and it wasn't long before he set up a farmhouse far finer than the one in which his brother lived, and with the quern he ground so much gold that he covered it with plates of gold; and as the farm lay by the seaside, the golden house gleamed and glistened far away over the sea. All who sailed by put ashore to see the rich man in the golden house, and to see the wonderful quern, the fame of which spread far and wide, till there was nobody who hadn't heard tell of it.

So one day there came a skipper who wanted to see the quern; and the first thing he asked was if it could grind salt.

"Grind salt!" said the owner; "I should just think it could. It can grind anything."

375

When the skipper heard that, he said he must have the quern, cost what it would; for if he only had it, he thought he should be rid of his long voyage across stormy seas for a lading of salt. Well, at first the man wouldn't hear of parting with the quern; but the skipper begged and prayed so hard, that at last he let him have it, but he had to pay many, many thousand dollars for it. Now, when the skipper had got the quern on his back, he soon made off with it, for he was afraid lest the man should change his mind; so he had no time to ask how to handle the quern, but got on board his ship as fast as he could, and set sail. When he had sailed a good way off, he brought the quern on deck and said—

"Grind salt, and grind both good and fast."

Well, the quern began to grind salt so that it poured out like water; and when the skipper had got the ship full, he wished to stop the quern, but whichever way he turned it, and however much he tried, it was no good; the quern kept grinding on, and the heap of salt grew higher and higher, and at last down sunk the ship.

There lies the quern at the bottom of the sea, and grinds away at this very day, and that's why the sea is salt.

377

THE ALLIGATOR

AND THE JACKAL

A HUNGRY Jackal once went down to the river-side in search of little crabs, bits of fish and whatever else he could find for his dinner. Now it chanced that in this river there lived a great big Alligator, who, being also very hungry, would have been extremely glad to eat the Jackal.

The Jackal ran up and down, here and there, but for a long time could find nothing to eat. At last, close to where the Alligator was lying among some tall bulrushes under the clear, shallow water, he saw a little crab sidling along as fast as his legs could carry him. The Jackal was so hungry that when he saw this he poked his paw into the water to try and catch the crab, when snap! the old Alligator caught hold of him. "Oh dear!" thought the Jackal to himself, "what can I do? This great big Alligator has caught my paw in his mouth, and in another minute he will drag me down by it under the water and kill me. My only chance is to make him think he has made a mistake." So he called out in a cheerful voice, "Clever Alligator, clever Alligator, to catch hold of a bulrush root instead of my paw! I hope you find it very tender." The Alligator, who was so buried among the bulrushes that he could hardly see, thought, on hearing this, "Dear me, how tiresome! I fancied I had caught hold of the Jackal's paw; but there he is, calling out in a cheerful voice. I suppose I must have seized a bulrush root instead, as he says," and he let the Jackal go.

The Jackal ran away as fast as he could, crying, "O wise Alligator, wise Alligator! So you let me go again!" Then the Alligator was very much vexed, but the Jackal had run away too far to be caught. Next day the Jackal returned to the riverside to get his dinner, as before; but because he was very much afraid of the Alligator he called out, "Whenever I go to look for my dinner, I see the nice little crabs peeping up through the mud; then I catch them and eat them. I wish I could see one now."

The Alligator, who was buried in the mud at the bottom of the river, heard every word. So he popped the little point of his snout above it, thinking, "If I do but just show the tip of

my nose, the Jackal will take me for a crab and put in his paw to catch me, and as soon as ever he does I'll gobble him up."

But no sooner did the Jackal see the little tip of the Alligator's nose than he called out, "Aha, my friend! there you are. No dinner for me in this part of the river, then, I think." And so saying he ran farther on and fished for his dinner a long way from that place. The Alligator was very angry at missing his prey a second time, and determined not to let him escape again.

So on the following day, when his little tormentor returned to the water-side, the Alligator hid himself close to the bank, in order to catch him if he could. Now the Jackal was rather afraid going near the river for he thought, "Perhaps this Alligator will catch me today." But yet, being hungry, he did not wish to go without his dinner; so to make all as safe as he could, he cried, "Where are all the little crabs gone? There is not one here and I am so hungry; and generally, even when they are under water, one can see them going bubble, bubble, bubble, and all the little bubbles go pop! pop! pop!" On hearing this the Alligator, who was buried in the mud under the river-bank, thought, "I will pretend to be a little crab." And he began to blow, "Puff, puff, puff! Bubble, bubble, bubble!" and all the great big bubbles rushed to the surface of the river and burst there, and the waters eddied round and round like a whirlpool; and there was such a commotion when the huge monster began to blow bubbles in this way that the Jackal saw very well who must be there, and he ran away as fast as he could, saying, "Thank you, kind Alligator, thank you; thank

you! Indeed I would not have come here had I known you were so close."

This enraged the Alligator extremely; it made him quite cross to think of being so often deceived by a little Jackal, and he said to himself, "I will be taken in no more. Next time I will be very cunning." So for a long time he waited and waited for the Jackal to return to the river-side; but the Jackal did not come, for he had thought to himself, "If matters go on in this way, I shall some day be caught and eaten by the wicked old Alligator. I had better content myself with living on wild figs," and he went no more near the river, but stayed in the jungles and ate wild figs, and roots which he dug up with his paws.

When the Alligator found this out, he determined to try and catch the Jackal on land; so, going under the largest of wild fig trees, where the ground was covered with the fallen fruit, he collected a quantity of it together, and, burying himself under the great heap, waited for the Jackal to appear. But no sooner did the cunning little animal see this great heap of wild figs all collected together, than he thought, "That looks very like my friend the Alligator." And to discover if it was so or not, he called out, "The juicy little wild figs I love to eat always tumble down from the tree, and roll here and there as the wind drives them; but this great heap of figs is quite still; these cannot be good figs; I will not eat any of them." "Ho, ho!" thought the Alligator, "is that all? How suspicious this Jackal is! I will make the figs roll about a little then, and when he sees that he will doubtless come and eat them."

So the great beast shook himself, and all the heap of little figs went roll, roll, roll—some a mile this way, some a mile that, farther than they had ever rolled before or than the most blustering wind could have driven them.

Seeing this, the Jackal scampered away, saying, "I am so much obliged to you, Alligator, for letting me know you are there, for indeed I should hardly have guessed it. You were so buried under that heap of figs." The Alligator, hearing this, was so angry that he ran after the Jackal, but the latter ran very, very fast away, too quickly to be caught.

Then the Alligator said to himself, "I will not allow that little wretch to make fun of me another time and then run away out of reach; I will show him that I can be more cunning than he fancies." And early the next morning he crawled as fast as he could to the Jackal's den (which was a hole in the side of a hill) and crept into it, and hid himself, waiting for the Jackal, who was out, to return home. But when the Jackal got near the place, he looked about him and thought, "Dear me! the ground looks as if some heavy creature had been walking over it, and here are great clods of earth knocked down from each side of the door of my den, as if a very big animal had been trying to squeeze himself through it. I certainly will not go inside until I know that all is safe there." So he called out, "Little house, pretty house, my sweet little house, why do you not give an answer when I call? If I come, and all is safe and right, you always call out to me. Is anything wrong, that you do not speak?"

Then the Alligator, who was inside, thought, "If that is the case I had better call out, that he may fancy all is right in his house." And in as gentle a voice as he could, he said, "Sweet little Jackal."

At hearing these words the Jackal felt quite frightened, and thought to himself, "So the dreadful old Alligator is there. I must try to kill him if I can, for if I do not he will certainly catch and kill me some day." He therefore answered, "Thank you, my dear little house. I like to hear your pretty voice. I am coming in in a minute, but first I must collect firewood to cook my dinner." And he ran as fast as he could, and dragged all the dry branches and bits of stick he could find close up to the mouth of the den. Meantime, the Alligator inside kept as quiet as a mouse, but he could not help laughing a little to himself, as he thought, "So I have deceived this tiresome little Jackal at last. In a few minutes he will run in here, and then won't I snap him up!" When the Jackal had gathered together all the sticks he could find and put them round the mouth of his den, he set them on fire and pushed them as far into it as possible. There was such a quantity of them that they soon blazed up into a great fire, and the smoke and flames filled the den and smothered the wicked old Alligator and burnt him to death, while the little Jackal ran up and down outside, dancing for joy and singing—

"How do you like my house, my friend?" Is it nice and warm? Ding-dong! ding-dong! The Alligator is dying! ding-dong, ding-dong! He will trouble me no more. I have defeated my enemy! Ring-a-ting! ding-a-ting! ding-ding-dong!"

HOW THE RAVEN
HELPED MAN

THE raven and the eagle were cousins, and they were almost always friendly, but whenever they talked together about men, they quarreled.

"Men are lazy," declared the eagle. "There is no use in trying to help them. The more one does for them, the less they do for themselves."

"You fly so high," said the raven, "that you cannot see how hard men work. I think that we birds, who know so much more than they, ought to help them."

"They do not work," cried the eagle. "What have they to do, I should like to know? They walk about on the ground, and their food grows close by their nests. If they had to fly through the air as we do, and get their food wherever they could, they might talk about working hard."

"That is just why we ought to help them," replied the raven. "They cannot mount up into the air as we do. They cannot see anything very well unless it is near them, and if they had to run and catch their food, they would surely die of hunger. They are poor, weak creatures, and there is not a humming-bird that does not know many things that they never heard of."

"You are a poor, weak bird, if you think you can teach men. When they feel hunger, they will eat, and they do not know how to do anything else. Just look at them! They ought to be going to sleep, and they do not know enough to do even that."

"How can they know that it is night, when they have no sun and no moon to tell them when it is day and when it is night?"

"They would not go to sleep even if they had two moons," said the eagle; "and you are no true cousin of mine if you do not let them alone."

So the two birds quarreled. Almost every time they met, they quarreled about men, and at last, whenever the eagle began to mount into the air, the raven went near the earth.

Now the eagle had a pretty daughter. She and the raven were good friends, and they never quarreled about men. One day the pretty daughter said, "Cousin Raven, are you too weak to fly as high as you used to do?"

"I never was less weak," declared the raven.

"Almost every day you keep on the ground. Can you not mount into the air?"

"Of course I can," answered the raven.

"There are some strange things in my father's lodge," said the pretty daughter, "and I do not know what they are. They are not good to eat, and I do not see what else they are good for. Will you come and see them?"

"I will go wherever you ask me," declared the raven.

The eagle's lodge was far up on the top of a high mountain, but the two birds were soon there, and the pretty daughter showed the raven the strange things. He knew what they were, and he said to himself, "Men shall have them, and by and by they will be no less wise than the birds." Then he asked, "Has your father a magic cloak?"

"Yes," answered the pretty daughter.

"May I put it on?"

"Yes, surely."

When the raven had once put on the magic cloak, he seized the strange things and put them under it. Then he called, "I will come again soon, my pretty little cousin, and tell you all about the people on the earth."

The things under his cloak were strange indeed, for one was the sun, and one was the moon. There were hundreds of bright stars, and there were brooks and rivers and waterfalls. Best of all, there was the precious gift of fire. The raven put the sun high up in the heavens, and fastened the moon and stars in their places. He let the brooks run down the sides of the mountains, and he hid the fire away in the rocks.

After a while men found all these precious gifts. They knew when it was night and when it was day, and they learned how to use fire. They cannot mount into the air like the eagle, but in some things they are almost as wise as the birds.

THE FROG PRINCE

IN the olden time, when wishing was having, there lived a
King, whose daughters were all beautiful; but the youngest
was so exceedingly beautiful that the Sun himself, although
he saw her very often, was enchanted every time she came out
into the sunshine.

Near the castle of this King was a large and gloomy forest,

and in the midst stood an old lime-tree, beneath whose branches splashed a little fountain; so, whenever it was very hot, the King's youngest daughter ran off into this wood, and sat down by the side of this fountain; and, when she felt dull, would often divert herself by throwing a golden ball up in the air and catching it. And this was her favorite amusement.

Now, one day it happened that this golden ball, when the King's daughter threw it into the air, did not fall down into her hand, but on the grass; and then it rolled past her into the fountain. The King's daughter followed the ball with her eyes, but it disappeared beneath the water, which was so deep that no one could see to the bottom. Then she began to lament, and to cry louder and louder; and, as she cried, a voice called out, "Why weepest thou, O King's daughter? Thy tears would melt even a stone to pity." And she looked around to the spot whence the voice came, and saw a Frog stretching his thick ugly head out of the water. "Ah! you old water-paddler," said she, "was it you that spoke? I am weeping for my golden ball, which has slipped away from me into the water."

"Be quiet, and do not cry," answered the Frog; "I can give thee good advice. But what wilt thou give me if I fetch thy plaything up again?"

"What will you have, dear Frog?" said she. "My dresses, my pearls and jewels, or the golden crown which I wear?"

The Frog answered, "Dresses, or jewels, or golden crowns, are not for me; but if thou wilt love me, and let me be thy companion and playfellow, and sit at thy table, and eat from thy little golden plate, and drink out of thy cup, and sleep in thy little bed — if thou wilt promise me all these, then will I dive down and fetch up thy golden ball."

"Oh, I will promise you all," said she, "if you will only get me my ball." But she thought to herself, "What is the silly Frog chattering about? Let him remain in the water with his equals; he cannot mix in society." But the Frog, as soon as he had received her promise, drew his head under the water and dived down. Presently he swam up again with the ball in his mouth, and threw it on the grass. The King's daughter was full of joy when she again saw her beautiful plaything; and, taking it up, she ran off immediately. "Stop! stop!" cried the

Frog; "take me with thee. I cannot run as thou canst." But all his croaking was useless; although it was loud enough, the King's daughter did not hear it, but, hastening home, soon forgot the poor Frog, who was obliged to leap back into the fountain.

The next day, when the King's daughter was sitting at table with her father and all his courtiers, and was eating from her own little golden plate, something was heard coming up the marble stairs, splish-splash, splish-splash; and when it arrived at the top, it knocked at the door, and a voice said,

"Open the door, thou youngest daughter of the King!" So she rose and went to see who it was that called her; but when she opened the door and caught sight of the Frog, she shut it again with great vehemence, and sat down at the table, looking very pale. But the King perceived that her heart was beating violently, and asked her whether it were a giant who had come to fetch her away who stood at the door. "Oh, no!" answered she; "it is no giant, but an ugly Frog."

"What does the Frog want with you?" said the King.

"Oh, dear father, when I was sitting yesterday playing by the fountain, my golden ball fell into the water, and this Frog fetched it up again because I cried so much: but first, I must tell you, he pressed me so much, that I promised him he should be my companion. I never thought that he could come out of the water, but somehow he has jumped out, and now he wants to come in here."

At that moment there was another knock, and a voice said:

"King's daughter, youngest,
    Open the door.
Hast thou forgotten
Thy promises made
At the fountain so clear
'Neath the lime-tree's shade?
King's daughter, youngest
    Open the door."

Then the King said, "What you have promised, that you must perform; go and let him in." So the King's daughter went and opened the door, and the Frog hopped in after her right up to her chair: and as soon as she was seated, the Frog said, "Take me up," but she hesitated so long that at last the King ordered her to obey. And as soon as the Frog sat on the chair, he jumped on to the table, and said, "Now push thy plate near me, that we may eat together." And she did so, but as everyone saw, very unwillingly. The Frog seemed to relish his dinner much, but every bit that the King's daughter ate nearly choked her, till at last the Frog said, "I have satisfied my hunger and feel very tired; wilt thou carry me up-

stairs now into thy chamber, and make thy bed ready that we may sleep together?" At this speech the King's daughter began to cry, for she was afraid of the cold Frog, and dared not touch him; and besides, he actually wanted to sleep in her own beautiful, clean bed.

But her tears only made the King very angry, and he said, "He who helped you in the time of your trouble, must not now be despised!" So she took the Frog up with two fingers, and put him in a corner of her chamber. But as she

lay in her bed, he crept up to it, and said, "I am so very tired that I shall sleep well; do take me up or I will tell thy father." This speech put the King's daughter in a terrible passion, and catching the Frog up, she threw him with all her strength against the wall, saying, "Now, will you be quiet, you ugly Frog?"

But as he fell he was changed from a frog into a handsome Prince with beautiful eyes, who, after a little while became, with her father's consent, her dear companion and betrothed. Then he told her how he had been transformed by an evil witch, and that no one but herself could have had the power to take him out of the fountain; and that on the morrow they would go together into his own kingdom.

The next morning, as soon as the sun rose, a carriage drawn by eight white horses, with ostrich feathers on their heads, and golden bridles, drove up to the door of the palace, and behind the carriage stood the trusty Henry, the servant of the young

Prince. When his master was changed into a frog, trusty Henry had grieved so much that he had bound three iron bands round his heart, for fear it should break with grief and sorrow. But now that the carriage was ready to carry the young Prince to his own country, the faithful Henry helped in the bride and bridegroom, and placed himself in the seat behind, full of joy at his master's release. They had not proceeded far when the Prince heard a crack as if something had broken behind the carriage; so he put his head out of the window and asked Henry what was broken, and Henry answered, "It was not the carriage, my master, but a band which I bound round my heart when it was in such grief because you were changed into a frog."

Twice afterwards on the journey there was the same noise, and each time the Prince thought that it was some part of the carriage that had given way; but it was only the breaking of the bands which bound the heart of the trusty Henry, who was thence-forward free and happy.

PINOCCHIO'S FIRST ADVENTURES

by CARLO LORENZINI

*How it came to pass that Master Cherry the carpenter
found a piece of wood that laughed and cried like
a child.*

THERE was once upon a time . . .

"A king!" my little readers will instantly exclaim.

No, children, you are wrong. There was once upon a
time a piece of wood.

This wood was not valuable: it was only a common log
like those that are burnt in winter in the stoves and fireplaces
to make a cheerful blaze and warm the rooms.

I cannot say how it came about, but the fact is, that one fine day this piece of wood was lying in the shop of an old carpenter of the name of Master Antonio. He was, however, called by everybody Master Cherry, on account of the end of his nose, which was always as red and polished as a ripe cherry.

No sooner had Master Cherry set eyes on the piece of wood than his face beamed with delight; and, rubbing his hands together with satisfaction, he said softly to himself:

"This wood has come at the right moment; it will just do to make the leg of a little table."

Having said this he immediately took a sharp axe with which to remove the bark and the rough surface. Just, however, as he was going to give the first stroke he remained with his arm suspended in the air, for he heard a very small voice saying imploringly, "Do not strike me so hard!"

Picture to yourselves the astonishment of good old Master Cherry!

He turned his terrified eyes all round the room to try and discover where the little voice could possibly have come from, but he saw nobody! He looked under the bench—nobody; he looked into a cupboard that was always shut—nobody; he looked into a basket of shavings and sawdust—nobody; he even opened the door of the shop and gave a glance into the street— and still nobody. Who, then, could it be?

"I see how it is," he said, laughing and scratching his wig; "evidently that little voice was all my imagination. Let us set to work again."

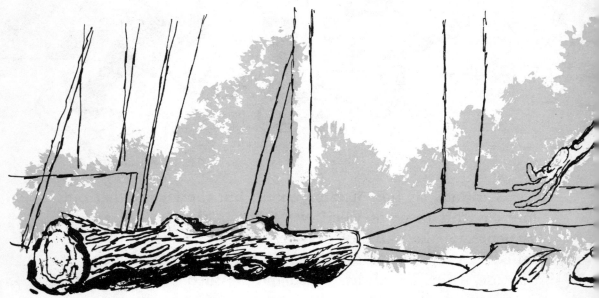

And taking up the axe he struck a tremendous blow on the piece of wood.

"Oh! oh! you have hurt me!" cried the same little voice dolefully.

This time Master Cherry was petrified. His eyes started out of his head with fright, his mouth remained open, and his tongue hung out almost to the end of his chin, like a mask on a fountain. As soon as he had recovered the use of his speech, he began to say, stuttering and trembling with fear:

"But where on earth can that little voice have come from that said Oh! oh! . . . Here there is certainly not a living soul.

Is it possible that this piece of wood can have learnt to cry and to lament like a child? I cannot believe it. This piece of wood, here it is; a log for fuel like all the others, and thrown on the fire it would about suffice to boil a saucepan of beans. . . . How then? Can anyone be hidden inside it? If anyone is hidden inside, so much the worse for him. I will settle him at once."

So saying, he seized the poor piece of wood and commenced beating it without mercy against the walls of the room.

Then he stopped to listen if he could hear any little voice lamenting. He waited two minutes—nothing; five minutes—

nothing; ten minutes—still nothing!

"I see how it is," he then said, forcing himself to laugh and pushing up his wig; "evidently the little voice that said Oh! oh! was all my imagination! Let us set to work again."

But as all the same he was in a great fright, he tried to sing to give himself a little courage.

Putting the axe aside he took his plane, to plane and polish the bit of wood; but whilst he was running it up and down he heard the same little voice say, laughing:

"Have done! you are tickling me all over!"

This time poor Master Cherry fell down as if he had been struck by lightning. When he at last opened his eyes he found himself seated on the floor.

His face was quite changed, even the end of his nose, instead of being crimson, as it was nearly always, had become blue from fright.

Master Cherry makes a present of the piece of wood to his friend Geppetto, who takes it to make for himself a wonderful puppet, that shall know how to dance, and to fence, and to leap like an acrobat.

At that moment some one knocked at the door.

"Come in," said the carpenter, without having the strength to rise to his feet.

A lively little old man immediately walked into the shop. His name was Geppetto.

"Good day, Master Antonio," said Geppetto; "what are you doing there on the floor?"

"I am teaching the alphabet to the ants."

"Much good may that do you."

"What has brought you to me, neighbor Geppetto?"

"My legs. But to say the truth, Master Antonio, I am come to ask a favor of you."

"Here I am, ready to serve you," replied the carpenter,

getting on to his knees.

"This morning an idea came into my head."

"Let us hear it."

"I thought I would make a beautiful wooden puppet; but a wonderful puppet that should know how to dance, to fence, and to leap like an acrobat. With this puppet I would travel about the world to earn a piece of bread and a glass of wine. What do you think of it?"

"Well neighbor Geppetto," said the carpenter, "what is it that you wish of me?"

"I want a little wood to make my puppet; will you give me some?"

Master Antonio was delighted, and he immediately went to the bench and fetched the piece of wood that had caused him so much fear. But just as he was going to give it to his friend the piece of wood gave a shake, and wriggling violently out of his hands struck with all its force against the dried-up shins of poor Geppetto.

"Ah! is that the courteous way in which you make your presents, Master Antonio? You have almost lamed me! . . ."

"I swear to you that it was not I! . . ."

"Then you would have it that it was I? . . ."

"The wood is entirely to blame! . . ."

"I know that it was the wood; but it was you that hit my legs with it! . . ."

"I did not hit you with it! . . ."

"Liar!"

"Geppetto, don't insult me or I will call you Polendina! . . ."

"Ass!"

"Polendina!"

"Donkey!"

"Polendina!"

"Baboon!"

"Polendina!"

On hearing himself called Polendina for the third time Geppetto, blind with rage, fell upon the carpenter and they fought desperately.

When the battle was over, Master Antonio had two more scratches on his nose, and his adversary had two buttons too little on his waistcoat. Their accounts being thus squared they shook hands, and swore to remain good friends for the rest of their lives.

Geppetto carried off his fine piece of wood and, thanking Master Antonio, returned limping to his house.

Geppetto having returned home begins at once to make
a puppet, to which he gives the name of Pinocchio.
The first tricks played by the puppet.

Geppetto lived in a small ground-floor room that was only lighted from the staircase. The furniture could not have been simpler — a bad chair, a poor bed, and a broken-down table. At the end of the room there was a fireplace with a lighted fire; but the fire was painted, and by the fire was a painted saucepan that was boiling cheerfully, and sending out a cloud of smoke that looked exactly like real smoke.

As soon as he reached home Geppetto took his tools and set to work to cut out and model his puppet.

"What name shall I give him?" he said to himself; "I think I will call him Pinocchio. It is a name that will bring him luck. I once knew a whole family so called. There was Pinocchio the father, Pinocchia the mother, and Pinocchi the children, and all of them did well. The richest of them was a beggar."

Having found a name for his puppet he began to work in good earnest, and he first made his hair, then his forehead, and then his eyes.

The eyes being finished, imagine his astonishment when he perceived that they moved and looked fixedly at him.

Geppetto seeing himself stared at by those two wooden eyes took it almost in bad part, and said in an angry voice:

"Wicked wooden eyes, why do you look at me?"

No one answered.

He then proceeded to carve the nose; but no sooner had he made it than it began to grow. And it grew, and grew, and grew, until in a few minutes it had become an immense nose that seemed as if it would never end.

Poor Geppetto tired himself out with cutting it off; but the more he cut and shortened it, the longer did that impertinent nose become!

The mouth was not even completed when it began to laugh and deride him.

"Stop laughing!" said Geppetto, provoked; but he might as well have spoken to the wall.

"Stop laughing, I say!" he roared in a threatening tone.

The mouth then ceased laughing, but put out its tongue as far as it would go.

Geppetto, not to spoil his handiwork, pretended not to see, and continued his labors. After the mouth he fashioned the chin, then the throat, then the shoulders, the stomach, the arms and the hands.

The hands were scarcely finished when Geppetto felt his wig snatched from his head. He turned round, and what did he see? He saw his yellow wig in the puppet's hand.

"Pinocchio! . . . Give me back my wig instantly!"

But Pinocchio, instead of returning it, put it on his own head, and was in consequence nearly smothered.

Geppetto at this insolent and derisive behaviour felt sadder and more melancholy than he had ever been in his life before; and turning to Pinocchio he said to him:

"You young rascal! You are not yet completed, and you are already beginning to show want of respect to your father! That is bad, my boy, very bad!"

And he dried a tear.

The legs and the feet remained to be done.

When Geppetto had finished the feet he received a kick on the point of his nose.

"I deserve it!" he said to himself; "I should have thought of it sooner! Now it is too late!"

He then took the puppet under the arms and placed him on the floor to teach him to walk.

Pinocchio's legs were stiff and he could not move, but Geppetto led him by the hand and showed him how to put one foot before the other.

When his legs became flexible Pinocchio began to walk by himself and to run about the room; until, having gone out of the house door, he jumped into the street and escaped.

Poor Geppetto rushed after him but was not able to overtake him, for that rascal Pinocchio leapt in front of him like a hare, and knocking his wooden feet together against the pavement made as much clatter as twenty pairs of peasants' clogs.

"Stop him! stop him!" shouted Geppetto; but the people in the street, seeing a wooden puppet running like a race-horse, stood still in astonishment to look at it, and laughed, and laughed, and laughed, until it beats description.

At last, as good luck would have it, a carabineer arrived who, hearing the uproar, imagined that a colt had escaped from his master. Planting himself courageously with his legs apart in the middle of the road, he waited with the determined purpose of stopping him, and thus preventing the chance of worse disasters.

When Pinocchio, still at some distance, saw the carabineer barricading the whole street, he endeavoured to take him by surprise and to pass between his legs. But he failed signally.

The carabineer without disturbing himself in the least caught him cleverly by the nose—it was an immense nose of ridiculous proportions that seemed made on purpose to be laid hold of by carabineers—and consigned him to Geppetto.

Wishing to punish him, Geppetto intended to pull his ears at once. But imagine his feelings when he could not succeed in finding them. And do you know the reason? It was that, in his hurry to model him, he had forgotten to make them.

He then took him by the collar, and as he was leading him away he said to him, shaking his head threateningly:

"We will go home at once, and as soon as we arrive we will regulate our accounts, never doubt it."

At this announcement Pinocchio threw himself on the ground and would not take another step. In the meanwhile a crowd of idlers and inquisitive people began to assemble and to make a ring round them.

Some of them said one thing, some another.

"Poor puppet!" said several, "he is right not to wish to return home! Who knows how Geppetto, that bad old man, will beat him! . . ."

And the others added maliciously:

"Geppetto seems a good man! but with boys he is a regular tyrant! If that poor puppet is left in his hands he is quite capable of tearing him in pieces! . . ."

It ended in so much being said and done that the carabineer at last set Pinocchio at liberty and conducted Geppetto to prison. The poor man, not being ready with words to defend himself, cried like a calf, and as he was being led away to

prison sobbed out:

"Wretched boy! And to think how I have labored to make him a well-conducted puppet! But it serves me right! I should have thought of it sooner! . . ."

The story of Pinocchio and the Talking-cricket, from which we see that naughty boys cannot endure to be corrected by those who know more than they do.

Well then, children, I must tell you that whilst poor

Geppetto was being taken to prison for no fault of his, that imp Pinocchio, finding himself free from the clutches of the carabineer, ran off as fast as his legs could carry him. That he might reach home the quicker he rushed across the fields, and in his mad hurry he jumped high banks, thorn hedges, and ditches full of water, exactly as a kid or a rabbit would have

done if pursued by hunters.

Having arrived at the house he found the street door ajar. He pushed it open, went in, and having secured the latch threw himself seated on the ground and gave a great sigh of satisfaction.

But his satisfaction did not last long, for he heard some

one in the room who was saying:

"Cri-cri-cri!"

"Who calls me?" said Pinocchio in a fright.

"It is I!"

Pinocchio turned round and saw a big cricket crawling slowly up the wall.

"Tell me, Cricket, who may you be?"

"I am the Talking-cricket, and I have lived in this room a hundred years and more."

"Now, however, this room is mine," said the puppet, "and if you would do me a pleasure go away at once, without even turning round."

"I will not go," answered the Cricket, "until I have told you a great truth."

"Tell it me, then, and be quick about it."

"Woe to those boys who rebel against their parents, and run away capriciously from home. They will never come to any good in the world, and sooner or later they will repent bitterly."

"Sing away, Cricket, as you please, and as long as you please. For me, I have made up my mind to run away tomorrow at daybreak, because if I remain I shall not escape the fate of all other boys; I shall be sent to school and shall be made to study either by love or by force. To tell you in confidence, I have no wish to learn; it is much more amusing to run after butterflies, or to climb trees and to take the young birds out of their nests."

"Poor little goose! But do you not know that in that way you will grow up a perfect donkey, and that every one will make game of you?"

"Hold your tongue, you wicked ill-omened croaker!" shouted Pinocchio.

But the Cricket, who was patient and philosophical, instead of becoming angry at this impertinence, continued in the same tone:

"But if you do not wish to go to school why not at least learn a trade, if only to enable you to earn honestly a piece of bread!"

"Do you want me to tell you?" replied Pinocchio, who was beginning to lose patience. "Amongst all the trades in the world there is only one that really takes my fancy."

"And that trade—what is it?"

"It is to eat, drink, sleep, and amuse myself, and to lead a vagabond life from morning to night."

"As a rule," said the Talking-cricket with the same composure, "all those who follow that trade end almost always either in a hospital or in prison."

"Take care, you wicked ill-omened croaker! . . . Woe to you if I fly into a passion! . . ."

"Poor Pinocchio! I really pity you! . . ."

"Why do you pity me?"

"Because you are a puppet and, what is worse, because you have a wooden head."

A

MAD

TEA-PARTY

By LEWIS CARROLL

THERE was a table set out under a tree in front of the house, and the March Hare and the Hatter were having tea at it: a Dormouse was sitting between them, fast asleep, and the other two were using it as a cushion, resting their elbows on it, and talking over its head. "Very uncomfortable for the Dormouse," thought Alice; "only as it's asleep, I suppose it doesn't mind."

The table was a large one, but the three were all crowded together at one corner of it. "No room! No room!" they cried out when they saw Alice coming. "There's *plenty* of room!" said Alice indignantly, and she sat down in a large armchair at one end of the table.

"Have some wine," the March Hare said in an encouraging tone.

Alice looked all round the table, but there was nothing on it but tea. "I don't see any wine," she remarked.

"There isn't any," said the March Hare.

"Then it wasn't very civil of you to offer it," said Alice angrily.

"It wasn't very civil of you to sit down without being invited," said the March Hare.

"I didn't know it was *your* table," said Alice: "it's laid for a great many more than three."

"Your hair wants cutting," said the Hatter. He had been looking at Alice for some time with great curiosity, and this was his first speech.

"You should learn not to make personal remarks," Alice said with some severity: "it's very rude."

The Hatter opened his eyes very wide on hearing this; but all he *said* was, "Why is a raven like a writing-desk?"

"Come, we shall have some fun now!" thought Alice. "I'm glad they've begun asking riddles—I believe I can guess that," she added aloud.

"Do you mean that you think you can find out the answer to it?" said the March Hare.

"Exactly so," said Alice.

"Then you should say what you mean," the March Hare went on.

"I do," Alice hastily replied; "at least—at least I mean what I say—that's the same thing, you know."

"Not the same thing a bit!" said the Hatter. "Why, you might just as well say that 'I see what I eat' is the same thing as 'I eat what I see'!"

"You might just as well say," added the March Hare, "that 'I like what I get' is the same thing as 'I get what I like'!"

"You might just as well say," added the Dormouse, which seemed to be talking in its sleep, "that 'I breathe when I sleep' is the same thing as 'I sleep when I breathe'!"

"It *is* the same thing with you," said the Hatter, and here the conversation dropped, and the party sat silent for a minute, while Alice thought over all she could remember about ravens and writing-desks, which wasn't much.

The Hatter was the first to break the silence. "What day of the month is it?" he said, turning to Alice: he had taken his watch out of his pocket, and was looking at it uneasily, shaking it every now and then, and holding it to his ear.

Alice considered a little, and then said, "The fourth."

"Two days wrong!" sighed the Hatter. "I told you butter wouldn't suit the works!" he added, looking angrily at the March Hare.

"It was the *best* butter," the March Hare meekly replied.

"Yes, but some crumbs must have got in as well," the Hatter grumbled: "you shouldn't have put it in with the breadknife."

The March Hare took the watch and looked at it gloomily: then he dipped it into his cup of tea, and looked at it again: but he could think of nothing better to say than his first remark, "It was the *best* butter, you know."

Alice had been looking over his shoulder with some curiosity. "What a funny watch!" she remarked. "It tells the day of the month, and doesn't tell what o'clock it is!"

"Why should it?" muttered the Hatter. "Does *your* watch tell you what year it is?"

"Of course not," Alice replied very readily: "but that's

because it stays the same year for such a long time together."

"Which is just the case with *mine*," said the Hatter.

Alice felt dreadfully puzzled. The Hatter's remark seemed to her to have no sort of meaning in it, and yet it was certainly English. "I don't quite understand you," she said, as politely as she could.

"The Dormouse is asleep again," said the Hatter, and he poured a little hot tea upon its nose.

The Dormouse shook its head impatiently, and said, without opening its eyes, "Of course, of course: just what I was going to remark myself."

"Have you guessed the riddle yet?" the Hatter said, turning to Alice again.

"No, I give it up," Alice replied. "What's the answer?"

"I haven't the slightest idea," said the Hatter.

"Nor I," said the March Hare.

Alice sighed wearily. "I think you might do something better with the time," she said, "than wasting it in asking riddles that have no answers."

"If you knew Time as well as I do," said the Hatter, "you wouldn't talk about wasting *it*. It's *him*."

"I don't know what you mean," said Alice.

"Of course you don't!" the Hatter said, tossing his head contemptuously. "I dare say you never even spoke to Time!"

"Perhaps not," Alice cautiously replied; "but I know I have to beat time when I learn music."

"Ah! That accounts for it," said the Hatter. "He won't stand beating. Now, if you only kept on good terms with him, he'd do almost anything you liked with the clock. For instance, suppose it were nine o'clock in the morning, just time to begin lessons: you'd only have to whisper a hint to Time, and round goes the clock in a twinkling! Half-past one, time for dinner!"

("I only wish it was," the March Hare said to itself in a whisper.)

"That would be grand, certainly," said Alice thoughtfully; "but then—I shouldn't be hungry for it, you know."

"Not at first, perhaps," said the Hatter: "but you could keep it to half-past one as long as you liked."

"Is that the way *you* manage?" Alice asked.

The Hatter shook his head mournfully. "Not I!" he replied. "We quarreled last March—just before *he* went mad, you know—" (pointing with his teaspoon at the March Hare), "—it was at the great concert given by the Queen of Hearts, and I had to sing:

   'Twinkle, twinkle, little bat!
  How I wonder what you're at!'

You know the song, perhaps?"

"I've heard something like it," said Alice.

"It goes on, you know," the Hatter continued, "in this way:

   'Up above the world you fly,
   Like a tea-tray in the sky.
    Twinkle, twinkle—' "

Here the Dormouse shook itself, and began singing in its sleep, *"Twinkle, twinkle, twinkle, twinkle—"* and went on so long that they had to pinch it to make it stop.

"Well, I'd hardly finished the first verse," said the Hatter, "when the Queen bawled out, 'He's murdering the time! Off with his head'!"

"How dreadfully savage!" exclaimed Alice.

"And ever since that," the Hatter went on in a mournful tone, "he won't do a thing I ask! It's always six o'clock now."

A bright idea came into Alice's head. "Is that the reason so many tea-things are put out here?" she asked.

"Yes, that's it," said the Hatter with a sigh: "it's always tea-time, and we've no time to wash the things between whiles."

"Then you keep moving round, I suppose?" said Alice.

"Exactly so," said the Hatter: "as the things get used up."

"But what happens when you come to the beginning again?" Alice ventured to ask.

"Suppose we change the subject," the March Hare interrupted, yawning. "I'm getting tired of this. I vote the young lady tells us a story."

"I'm afraid I don't know one," said Alice, rather alarmed at the proposal.

"Then the Dormouse shall!" they both cried. "Wake up, Dormouse!" And they pinched it on both sides at once.

The Dormouse slowly opened its eyes. "I wasn't asleep,"

it said in a hoarse, feeble voice, "I heard every word you fellows were saying."

"Tell us a story!" said the March Hare.

"Yes, please do!" pleaded Alice.

"And be quick about it," added the Hatter, "or you'll be asleep again before it's done."

"Once upon a time there were three little sisters," the Dormouse began in a great hurry; "and their names were Elsie, Lacie, and Tillie; and they lived at the bottom of a well—"

"What did they live on?" said Alice, who always took a great interest in questions of eating and drinking.

"They lived on treacle," said the Dormouse, after thinking a minute or two.

"They couldn't have done that, you know," Alice gently remarked. "They'd have been ill."

"So they were," said the Dormouse; "very ill."

Alice tried to fancy to herself what such an extraordinary way of living would be like, but it puzzled her too much: so she went on: "But why did they live at the bottom of a well?"

"Take some more tea," the March Hare said to Alice, very earnestly.

"I've had nothing yet," Alice replied in an offended tone: "so I can't take more."

"You mean you can't take *less*," said the Hatter: "it's very easy to take *more* than nothing."

"Nobody asked *your* opinion," said Alice.

"Who's making personal remarks now?" the Hatter asked triumphantly.

Alice did not quite know what to say to this: so she helped herself to some tea and bread-and-butter, and then turned to the Dormouse, and repeated her question. "Why did they live at the bottom of a well?"

The Dormouse again took a minute or two to think about it, and then said, "It was a treacle-well."

"There's no such thing!" Alice was beginning very angrily, but the Hatter and the March Hare went "Sh! Sh!" and the Dormouse sulkily remarked, "If you can't be civil. you'd better finish the story for yourself."

"No, please go on!" Alice said very humbly. 'I won't interrupt you again. I dare say there may be *one*."

"One, indeed!" said the Dormouse indignantly. However, he consented to go on. "And so these three little sisters— they were learning to draw, you know—"

"What did they draw?" said Alice. quite forgetting her promise.

"Treacle," said the Dormouse, without considering at all, this time.

"I want a clean cup," interrupted the Hatter: "Let's all move one place on."

He moved on as he spoke, and the Dormouse followed him: the March Hare moved into the Dormouse's place, and

Alice rather unwillingly took the place of the March Hare. The Hatter was the only one who got any advantage from the change; and Alice was a good deal worse off than before, as the March Hare had just upset the milk-jug into his plate.

Alice did not wish to offend the Dormouse again, so she began very cautiously: "But I don't understand. Where did they draw the treacle from?"

"You can draw water out of a water-well," said the Hatter; "so I should think you could draw treacle out of a treacle-well —eh, stupid?"

"But they were *in* the well," Alice said to the Dormouse, not choosing to notice this last remark.

"Of course they were," said the Dormouse: "well in."

This answer so confused poor Alice, that she let the Dormouse go on for some time without interrupting it.

"They were learning to draw," the Dormouse went on, yawning and rubbing its eyes, for it was getting very sleepy; "and they drew all manner of things—everything that begins with an M—"

"Why with an M?" said Alice.

"Why not?" said the March Hare.

Alice was silent.

The Dormouse had closed its eyes by this time, and was going off into a doze; but, on being pinched by the Hatter, it woke up again with a little shriek, and went on: "—that begins with an M, such as mouse-traps, and the moon, and memory, and muchness—you know you say things are 'much of a muchness'—did you ever see such a thing as a drawing of a muchness!"

"Really, now you ask me," said Alice, very much confused, "I don't think—"

"Then you shouldn't talk," said the Hatter.

This piece of rudeness was more than Alice could bear: she got up in great disgust, and walked off: the Dormouse fell asleep instantly, and neither of the others took the least notice of her going, though she looked back once or twice, half hoping that they would call after her: the last time she saw them, they were trying to put the Dormouse into the teapot.

"At any rate I'll never go *there* again!" said Alice, as she picked her way through the wood. "It's the stupidest tea-party I ever was at in all my life!"

Just as she said this, she noticed that one of the trees had a door leading right into it. "That's very curious!" she thought. "But everything's curious today. I think I may as well go in at once." And in she went.

Once more she found herself in the long hall, and close to the little glass table. "Now, I'll manage better this time," she said to herself, and began by taking the little golden key, and unlocking the door that led into the garden. Then she set to work nibbling at the mushroom (she had kept a piece of it in her pocket) till she was about a foot high: then she walked down the little passage: and *then*—she found herself at last in the beautiful garden, among the bright flower-beds and the cool fountains.

THE LITTLE

ONCE there lived a little gnome,
Who had made his little home
    Right down in the middle of
        the earth, earth, earth.
He was full of fun and frolic,
But his wife was melancholic,
And he never could divert
    her into mirth, mirth,
    mirth.

GNOME

He had tried her with a
   monkey,
And a parrot and a donkey,
And a pig that squealed
   whene'er he pulled its
   tail, tail, tail.
But though he laughed himself
Into fits, the jolly elf,
Still his wifey's melancholy
   did not fail, fail, fail.

"I will hie me," said the
   gnome,
"From my worthy earthy
   home,
I will go among the dwellings
   of the men, men, men.
Something funny there must
   be, that will make her
   say 'He! he!'
I will find it, and will bring
   it her again, 'gain, 'gain.''

The
Blinking Bear

So he traveled here and there,
And he saw the Blinking
    Bear,
And the Pattypol whose eyes
    are in his tail, tail, tail.
And he saw the Linking
    Gloon,

Who was playing the bas-
    soon,
And the Octopus a-waltzing
    with the whale, whale,
    whale.

The Pattypol

The Linking Gloon

The Octopus
and Whale

He saw the Chingo Chee,
And a lovely sight was he,
With a ringlet, and a ribbon
    on his nose, nose, nose.
And the Baggle, and the
    Wogg,
And the Cantilunar Dog,
Who was throwing cotton
    flannel at his foes, foes,
    foes.

All these the little gnome
Transported to his home,
And set them down before
    his weeping wife, wife,
    wife.
But she only cried and cried,
And she sobbywobbed and
    sighed,
Till she really was in danger
    of her life, life, life.

425

The Chingo Chee

The Baggle

The Wogg

Then the gnome was in des-
    pair,
And he tore his purple hair,
And he sat him down in sor-
    row on a stone, stone,
    stone.
"I, too," he said, "will cry,
Till I tumble down and die,
For I've had enough of
    laughing all alone, 'lone,
    'lone."

426

His tears they flowed away
Like a rivulet at play,
With a bubble, gubble, rub-
    ble, o'er the ground,
    ground, ground.
But when this his wifey saw,
She loudly cried, "Haw! haw!
Here, at last, is something
    funny you have found,
    found, found."

She laughed, "Ho! ho! he!
    he!"
And she chuckled loud with
    glee,
And she wiped away her lit-
    tle husband's tears,
    tears, tears.
And since then, through
    wind and weather,
They have said "He! he!" to-
    gether,
For several hundred thou-
    sand merry years, years,
    years.

—Laura E. Richards

The Cantilunar Dog

427

CALICO PIE

I

Calico pie,
The little birds fly
Down to the calico-tree:
Their wings were blue,
And they sang "Tilly-loo!"
Till away they flew;

And they never came back to me!
They never came back,
They never came back,
They never came back to me!

II

Calico jam,
The little Fish swam
Over the Syllabub Sea.
He took off his hat
To the Sole and the Sprat,
And the Willeby-wat:

But he never came back to me;
He never came back,
He never came back,
He never came back to me.

III

Calico ban,
The little Mice ran
To be ready in time for tea;
Flippity flup,
They drank it all up,

And danced in the cup:
But they never came back to me;
They never came back,
They never came back,
They never came back to me.

IV

Calico drum,
The Grasshoppers come,
The Butterfly, Beetle, and Bee,
    Over the ground,
    Around and round,
    With a hop and a bound;

But they never came back,
    They never came back,
    They never came back,
They never came back to me.

Edward Lear

OVER IN
THE MEADOW

Over in the meadow,
    In the sand, in the sun,
Lived an old mother toad
    And her little toadie one.
"Wink!" said the mother;
    "I wink," said the one:
So she winked and she blinked
    In the sand, in the sun.

Over in the meadow,
	Where the stream runs blue,
Lived an old mother fish
	And her little fishes two.
"Swim!" said the mother;
	"We swim," said the two.
So they swam and they leaped
	Where the stream runs blue.

Over in the meadow,
    In a hole in a tree,
Lived a mother bluebird
    And her little birdies three;
"Sing!" said the mother;
    "We sing," said the three:
So they sang, and were glad,
    In the hole in the tree.

Olive A. Wadsworth

I HARDLY EVER CRY

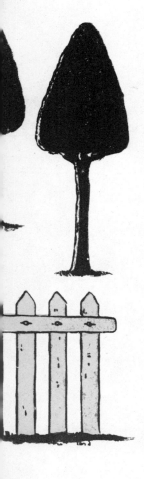

My house is red—a little house,
 A happy child am I,
I laugh and play the livelong day,
 I hardly ever cry.

I have a tree, a green, green tree,
 To shade me from the sun;
And under it I often sit,
 When all my work is done.

My little basket I will take,
 And trip into the town;
When next I'm there I'll buy some cake,
 And spend my bright half-crown.

Kate Greenaway

TIME TO RISE

A birdie with a yellow bill
   Hopped upon my windowsill,
Cocked his shining eye and said:
   "Ain't you 'shamed, you sleepy-head!"

Robert Louis Stevenson

SUSAN BLUE

Oh, Susan Blue,
How do you do?
Please may I go a walk with you?
Where shall we go?
Oh, I know—
Down in the meadow where the
cowslips grow!

Kate Greenaway

RAIN

The rain is raining all around,
It falls on field and tree,
It rains on the umbrellas here,
And on the ships at sea.

Robert Louis Stevenson

MARY'S LAMB

Mary had a little lamb,
    Its fleece was white as snow;
And everywhere that Mary went,
    The lamb was sure to go.

He followed her to school one day,
    Which was against the rule;
It made the children laugh and play
    To see a lamb at school.

And so the teacher turned him out,
    But still he lingered near,
And waited patiently about
    Till Mary did appear.

Then he ran to her, and laid
    His head upon her arm,
As if he said, "I'm not afraid—
    You'll keep me from all harm."

"What makes the lamb love Mary so?"
    The eager children cried,
"Oh, Mary loves the lamb, you know,"
    The teacher quick replied.

And you each gentle animal
    In confidence may bind,
And make them follow at your will,
    If you are only kind.

Sara Josepha Hale

I LOVE
LITTLE PUSSY

I love little Pussy.
　　Her coat is so warm,
And if I don't hurt her,
　　She'll do me no harm.
So I'll not pull her tail,
　　Or drive her away,
But Pussy and I
　　Very gently will play.
She will sit by my side,
　　And I'll give her her food,
And she'll like me because
　　I am gentle and good.

I'll pat little Pussy,
    And then she will purr,
And thus show her thanks
    For my kindness to her;
I'll not pinch her ears,
    Nor tread on her paw,
Lest I should provoke her
    To use her sharp claw;
I never will vex her,
    Nor make her displeased,
For Pussy can't bear
    To be worried or teased.

Jane Taylor

TWINKLE, TWINKLE,
LITTLE STAR

Twinkle, twinkle, little star,
How I wonder what you are;
Up above the world, so bright,
Like a diamond in the night.

When the blazing sun is gone,
When he nothing shines upon,
Then you show your little light,
Twinkle, twinkle, all the night.

Then the traveller in the dark,
Thanks you for your tiny spark;
He could not tell which way to go
If you did not twinkle so.

In the dark blue sky you keep,
And often through my curtains peep;
For you never shut your eye
Till the sun is in the sky.

As your bright and tiny spark
Lights the traveller in the dark,
Though I know not what you are,
Twinkle, twinkle, little star.

Jane Taylor

MIX
A PANCAKE

Mix a pancake,
Stir a pancake,
  Pop it in the pan.

Fry a pancake,
Toss a pancake,
  Catch it if you can.

Christina Rossetti

THE CITY MOUSE
AND THE
GARDEN MOUSE

The city mouse lives in a
    house;—
  The garden mouse lives in
    a bower,
He's friendly with the frogs and
    toads,
  And sees the pretty plants
    in flower.

The city mouse eats bread and
    cheese;—
  The garden mouse eats
    what he can;
We will not grudge him seeds
    and stocks,
  Poor little timid furry
    man.

Christina Rossetti

WHO HAS
SEEN THE WIND?

Who has seen the wind?
    Neither I nor you:
But when the leaves hang trembling
    The wind is passing thro'.

Who has seen the wind?
    Neither you nor I:
But when the trees bow down their heads
    The wind is passing by.

Christina Rossetti

THE COW

Thank you, pretty cow, that made
Pleasant milk to soak my bread,
Every day, and every night,
Warm, and fresh, and sweet, and white.

Do not chew the hemlock rank,
Growing on the weedy bank;
But the yellow cowslip eat,
That will make it very sweet.

Where the purple violet grows,
Where the bubbling water flows,
Where the grass is fresh and fine,
Pretty cow, go there and dine.

Jane Taylor

WHEN
THE COWS COME HOME

When the cows come home the milk
    is coming,
Honey's made while the bees are
    humming;
Duck and drake on the rushy lake,
And the deer live safe in the breezy
    brake;
And timid, funny, brisk little bunny
Winks his nose and sits all sunny.

Christina Rossetti

WHERE
THE BEE SUCKS

Where the bee sucks, there
    suck I;
In a cowslip's bell I lie;
There I couch, when owls do
    cry.
On the bat's back I do fly,
After summer, merrily;
Merrily, merrily, shall I live
    now
Under the blossom that hangs
    on the bough.

William Shakespeare

BOATS SAIL
ON THE RIVERS

Boats sail on the rivers,
    And ships sail on the seas;
But clouds that sail across the sky
    Are prettier far than these.

There are bridges on the rivers,
    As pretty as you please;
But the bow that bridges heaven,
    And overtops the trees,
And builds a road from earth to sky,
    Is prettier far than these.

Christina Rossetti

A BOY'S SONG

Where the pools are bright and deep,
Where the gray trout lies asleep,
Up the river and o'er the lea,
That's the way for Billy and me.

Where the blackbird sings the latest,
Where the hawthorn blooms the sweetest,
Where the nestlings chirp and flee,
That's the way for Billy and me.

Where the mowers mow the cleanest,
Where the hay lies thick and greenest,
There to trace the homeward bee,
That's the way for Billy and me.

Where the hazel bank is steepest,
Where the shadow falls the deepest,
Where the clustering nuts fall free,
That's the way for Billy and me.

Why the boys should drive away
Little sweet maidens from the play,
Or love to banter and fight so well,
That's the thing I never could tell.

But this I know, I love to play,
Through the meadow, among the hay;
Up the water and o'er the lea,
That's the way for Billy and me.

James Hogg

TABLE MANNERS

I

The Goops they lick their fingers,
    And the Goops they lick their knives;
They spill their broth on the tablecloth—
    Oh, they lead disgusting lives!
The Goops they talk while eating,
    And loud and fast they chew;
And that is why I'm glad that I
    Am not a Goop—are you?

II

The Goops are gluttonous and rude,
They gug and gumble with their food;
They throw their crumbs upon the floor,
And at dessert they tease for more;
They will not eat their soup and bread
But like to gobble sweets, instead,
And this is why I oft decline,
When I am asked to stay and dine!

THE

January brings the snow,
Makes our feet and fingers glow.

February brings the rain,
Thaws the frozen lake again.

March brings breezes sharp and chill,
Shakes the dancing daffodil.

April brings the primrose sweet
Scatters daisies at our feet.

May brings flocks of pretty lambs
Sporting round their fleecy dams.

June brings tulips, lilies, roses,
Fills the children's hands with posies.

MONTHS

Hot July brings thunder-showers,
Apricots, and gilly-flowers.

August brings the sheaves of corn;
Then the harvest home is borne.

Warm September brings the fruit;
Sportsmen then begin to shoot.

Brown October brings the pheasant;
Then to gather nuts is pleasant.

Dull November brings the blast—
Hark! the leaves are whirling fast.

Cold December brings the sleet,
Blazing fire, and Christmas treat.

Sara Coleridge

HAPPY THOUGHT

The world is so full of a number
    of things,
I'm sure we should all be as happy
    as kings.

Robert Louis Stevenson

COLOR

What is pink? A rose is pink
By a fountain's brink.

What is red? A poppy's red
In its barley bed.

What is blue? The sky is blue
Where the clouds float through.

What is white? A swan is white
Sailing in the light.

What is yellow? Pears are yellow,
Rich and ripe and mellow.

What is green? The grass is green,
With small flowers between.

What is violet? Clouds are violet
In the summer twilight.

What is orange? Why, an orange,
Just an orange!

Christina Rossetti

LAUGHING SONG

When the green woods laugh with
    the voice of joy,
And the dimpling stream runs
    laughing by,
When the air does laugh with our
    merry wit,
And the green hill laughs with the
    noise of it;
When the meadows laugh with lively
    green,
And the grasshopper laughs in the
    merry scene,
When Mary and Susan and Emily
With their sweet round mouths sing
    Ha, ha, he!
When the painted birds laugh in
    the shade,
When our table with cherries and nuts
    is spread,
Come live and be happy and join
    with me
To sing the sweet chorus of Ha, ha,
    he!

William Blake

458

THE LAMB

Little lamb, who made thee?
Dost thou know who made thee?
Gave thee life and bid thee feed
By the stream and o'er the mead;
Gave thee clothing of delight,
Softest clothing, woolly, bright;
Gave thee such a tender voice,
Making all the vales rejoice;
     Little lamb, who made thee?
     Dost thou know who made thee?

Little lamb, I'll tell thee,
Little lamb, I'll tell thee.
He is called by thy name,
For He calls Himself a Lamb;
He is meek and He is mild,
He became a little child.
I a child, and thou a lamb,
We are called by His Name.
     Little lamb, God bless thee,
     Little lamb, God bless thee.

William Blake

LULLABY OF AN
INFANT CHIEF

Oh, hush thee, my baby! thy sire
    was a knight,
Thy mother a lady, both lovely
    and bright;
The woods and the glens, from
    the towers which we see,
They all are belonging, dear
    baby, to thee.

Oh, fear not the bugle, though
    loudly it blows!
It calls but the warders that guard
    thy repose;
Their bows would be bended,
    their blades would be red,
Ere the step of a foeman draws
    near to thy bed.

Oh, hush thee, my baby! the
    time will soon come
When thy sleep shall be broken
    by trumpet and drum;
Then hush thee, my darling! take
    rest while you may;
For strife comes with manhood,
    and waking with day.

Walter Scott

460

THE PIPER

Piping down the valleys wild,
    Piping songs of pleasant glee,
On a cloud I saw a child,
    And he laughing said to me:

"Pipe a song about a lamb."
    So I piped with merry cheer.
"Piper, pipe that song again;"
    So I piped; he wept to hear.

"Drop thy pipe, thy happy pipe,
    Sing thy songs of happy cheer:"
So I sang the same again,
    While he wept with joy to hear.

"Piper, sit thee down and write
    In a book that all may read—"
So he vanished from my sight;
    And I plucked a hollow reed,

And I made a rural pen,
    And I stain'd the water clear,
And I wrote my happy songs,
    Every child may joy to hear.

William Blake

HIAWATHA'S CHILDHOOD

By the shores of Gitche Gumee,
By the shining Big-Sea-Water,
Stood the wigwam of Nokomis,
Daughter of the Moon, Nokomis.
Dark behind it rose the forest,
Rose the black and gloomy pine-trees,

Rose the firs with cones upon them;
Bright before it beat the water,
Beat the clear and sunny water,
Beat the shining Big-Sea-Water.

    At the door on summer evenings
Sat the little Hiawatha;
Heard the whispering of the pine-trees,
Heard the lapping of the waters,
Sounds of music, words of wonder;
"Minne-wawa!" said the pine-trees,
"Mudway-aushka!" said the water.
Saw the firefly, Wah-wah-taysee,
Flitting through the dusk of evening,
With the twinkle of its candle
Lighting up the brakes and bushes,
And he sang the song of children,
Sang the song Nokomis taught him:
"Wah-wah-taysee, little firefly,
Little, flitting, white-fire insect,
Little, dancing, white-fire creature,
Light me with your little candle,
Ere upon my bed I lay me,
Ere in sleep I close my eyelids!"

    Then the little Hiawatha
Learned of every bird its language,
Learned their names and all their secrets,
How they built their nests in Summer,
Where they hid themselves in Winter,
Talked with them whene'er he met them,
Called them "Hiawatha's Chickens."

Of all beasts he learned the language,
Learned their names and all their secrets,
How the beavers built their lodges,
Where the squirrels hid their acorns,
How the reindeer ran so swiftly,
Why the rabbit was so timid,
Talked with them whene'er he met them,
Called them "Hiawatha's Brothers."

Henry Wadsworth Longfellow

464

FOREIGN LANDS

Up into the cherry tree
Who should climb but little me?
I held the trunk with both my hands
And looked abroad on foreign lands.

I saw the next door garden lie,
Adorned with flowers, before my eye,
And many pleasant places more
That I had never seen before.

I saw the dimpling river pass
And be the sky's blue looking-glass;
The dusty roads go up and down
With people tramping in to town.

If I could find a higher tree
Farther and farther I should see,
To where the grown-up river slips
Into the sea among the ships.

To where the roads on either hand
Lead onward into fairy land,
Where all the children dine at five,
And all the playthings come alive.

Robert Louis Stevenson

MY SHADOW

I have a little shadow that goes in
      and out with me,
And what can be the use of him is
      more than I can see.
He is very, very like me from the
      heels up to the head;
And I see him jump before me, when
      I jump into my bed.

The funniest thing about him is the
      way he likes to grow—
Not at all like proper children, which
      is always very slow;
For he sometimes shoots up taller like
      an India-rubber ball,
And he sometimes gets so little that
      there's none of him at all.

He hasn't got a notion of how children
           ought to play,
And can only make a fool of me in
           every sort of way.
He stays so close beside me, he's a
           coward you can see;
I'd think shame to stick to nursie as
           that shadow sticks to me!

One morning very early, before the sun
           was up,
I rose and found the shining dew on
           every buttercup;
But my lazy little shadow, like an
           arrant sleepy-head,
Had stayed at home behind me and was
           fast asleep in bed.

Robert Louis Stevenson

THE COW

The friendly cow all red and white,
 I love her with all my heart:
She gives me cream with all her might,
 To eat with apple-tart.

She wanders lowing here and there,
 And yet she cannot stray,
All in the pleasant open air,
 The pleasant light of day.

And blown by all the winds that pass
 And wet with all the showers,
She walks among the meadow grass
 And eats the meadow flowers.

Robert Louis Stevenson

ESCAPE AT BEDTIME

The lights from the
   parlor and kitchen
   shone out
Through the blinds and
   the windows and bars;
And high overhead and
   all moving about,
There were thousands of
   millions of stars.
There ne'er were such
   thousands of leaves on
   a tree,
Nor of people in church
   or the Park,
As the crowds of the stars
   that looked down
   upon me,
And that glittered and
   winked in the dark.
The Dog, and the
Plough, and the
   Hunter, and all
And the Star of the
   Sailor, and Mars,
These shone in the sky,
   and the pail by the
   wall
Would be half full of
   water and stars.
They saw me at last, and
   they chased me with
   cries,
And they soon had me
   packed into bed;
But the glory kept
   shining and bright in
   my eyes,
And the stars going
   round in my head.

Robert Louis Stevenson

469

THE LAND OF STORY-BOOKS

At evening when the lamp is lit,
Around the fire my parents sit;
They sit at home and talk and sing,
And do not play at anything.

Now, with my little gun, I crawl
All in the dark along the wall,
And follow round the forest track
Away behind the sofa back.

There, in the night, where none can spy,
All in my hunter's camp I lie,
And play at books that I have read
Till it is time to go to bed.

These are the hills, these are the woods,
These are my starry solitudes;
And there the river by whose brink
The roaring lions come to drink.

I see the others far away
As if in firelit camp they lay,
And I, like to an Indian scout,
Around their party prowled about.

So, when my nurse comes in for me,
Home I return across the sea,
And go to bed with backward looks
At my dear land of Story-books.

Robert Louis Stevenson

WHOLE DUTY OF
CHILDREN

A child should always say what's true
And speak when he is spoken to,
And behave mannerly at table;
At least as far as he is able.

Robert Louis Stevenson

THE LAND
OF COUNTERPANE

When I was sick and lay a-bed,
I had two pillows at my head,
And all my toys beside me lay
To keep me happy all the day.

And sometimes for an hour or so
I watched my leaden soldiers go,
With different uniforms and drills,
Among the bed-clothes, through the hills.

And sometimes sent my ships in fleets
All up and down among the sheets;
Or brought my trees and houses out,
And planted cities all about.

I was the giant great and still
That sits upon the pillow-hill,
And sees before him, dale and plain,
The pleasant land of counterpane.

Robert Louis Stevenson

BED IN SUMMER

In winter I get up
  at night
And dress by yellow
  candle-light.
In summer, quite the
  other way,
I have to go to bed
  by day.

I have to go to bed
  and see
The birds still hopping
  on the tree.
Or hear the grown-up
  people's feet
Still going past me in
  the street.
And does it not seem
  hard to you,
When all the sky is
  clear and blue,
And I should like so
  much to play,
To have to go to bed
  by day?

Robert Louis Stevenson

SWEET AND LOW

Sweet and low, sweet and low,
    Wind of the western sea,
Low, low, breathe and blow,
    Wind of the western sea!
Over the rolling waters go,
Come from the dropping moon
    and blow,
Blow him again to me,
While my little one, while my
    pretty one sleeps.

Sleep and rest, sleep and rest,
    Father will come to thee
    soon;
Rest, rest, on Mother's breast,
    Father will come to thee
    soon;
Father will come to his babe in
    the nest,
Silver sails all out of the west
    Under the silver moon:
Sleep, my little one, sleep, my
    pretty one, sleep.

Alfred Lord Tennyson

LADY MOON

Lady Moon, Lady Moon, where are you roving?
    "Over the sea."
Lady Moon, Lady Moon, whom are you loving?
    "All that love me."

Are you not tired with rolling, and never
    Resting to sleep?
Why look so pale and so sad, as forever
    Wishing to weep?

"Ask me not this, little child, if you love me:
    You are too bold:
I must obey my dear Father above me,
    And do as I'm told."

Lady Moon, Lady Moon, where are you roving?
    "Over the sea."
Lady Moon, Lady Moon, whom are you loving?
    "All that love me."

Lord Houghton

THE WORLD

Great, wide, beautiful, wonderful world,
With the wonderful water round you
      curled,
And the wonderful grass upon your
      breast —
World, you are beautifully drest.

The wonderful air is over me,
And the wonderful wind is shaking the
      tree,
It walks on the water and whirls the mills,
And talks to itself on the tops of the hills.

You friendly Earth! how far you go,
With the wheat-fields that nod and the
      rivers that flow,
With cities and gardens, and cliffs and
      isles,
And people upon you for thousands of
      miles?

Ah! you are so great, and I am so small,
I tremble to think of you, World, at all;
And yet when I said my prayers today,
A whisper inside me seemed to say,
"You are more than the Earth,
      though you are such a dot:
You can love and think, and the
      Earth cannot!"

William Brighty Rands

HORSES OF THE SEA

The horses of the sea
  Rear a foaming crest,
But the horses of the land
  Serve us the best.

The horses of the land
  Munch corn and clover,
While the foaming sea-horses
  Toss and turn over.

Christina Rossetti

THE FAIRIES

Up the airy mountain,
    Down the rushy glen,
We daren't go a-hunting,
    For fear of little men;
Wee folk, good folk,
    Trooping all together;
Green jacket, red cap,
    And white owl's feather!

Down along the rocky shore
    Some make their home,
They live on crispy pancakes
    Of yellow tide-foam;
Some in the reeds

Of the black mountain-lake,
With frogs for their watch-dogs
    All night awake.

High on the hill-top
    The old King sits;
He is now so old and gray,
    He's nigh lost his wits.
With a bridge of white mist
    Columbkill he crosses,
On his stately journeys
    From Slieveleague to Rosses;
Or going up with music
    On cold starry nights,
To sup with the Queen
    Of the gay Northern Lights.

They stole little Bridget
    For seven years long;
When she came down again,
    Her friends were all gone.
They took her lightly back,
    Between the night and morrow;
They thought that she was fast asleep,
    But she was dead with sorrow.
They have kept her ever since
    Deep within the lake,
On a bed of flag-leaves,
    Watching till she wake.

By the craggy hill-side,
        Through the mosses bare,
They have planted thorn-trees
        For pleasure here and there.
Is any man so daring
        As dig them up in spite,
He shall find their sharpest thorns
        In his bed at night.

Up the airy mountain,
        Down the rushy glen,
We daren't go a-hunting,
        For fear of little men;
Wee folk, good folk,
        Trooping all together;
Green jacket, red cap,
        And white owl's feather!

William Allingham

WISHING

Ring—ting! I wish I were a Primrose,
A bright yellow Primrose blowing in the Spring!
  The stooping boughs above me,
  The wandering bee to love me,
The fern and moss to keep across,
  And the Elm tree, for our King!

Nay—nay! I wish I were an Elm tree,
A great lofty Elm tree, with green leaves gay!
  The winds would set them dancing,
  The sun and moonshine glance in,
The Birds would house among the boughs,
  And sweetly sing!

O—no! I wish I were a Robin,
A Robin or a little Wren, everywhere to go;

Through forest, field or garden,
And ask no leave or pardon,
Till Winter comes with icy thumbs
    To ruffle up our wing.

Well—tell! Where should I fly to,
Where go to sleep in the dark wood or dell?
    Before a day was over,
    Home comes the rover,
For Mother's kiss—sweeter this
    Than any other thing!

William Allingham

485

WYNKEN,

BLYNKEN AND NOD

Wynken, Blynken, and Nod
    one night
    Sailed off in a wooden shoe,
Sailed on a river of crystal light
    Into a sea of dew.
"Where are you going, and what do
      you wish?"
    The old moon asked the three.
"We have come to fish for the
      herring fish
    That live in this beautiful sea,
Nets of silver and gold have we!"
    Said Wynken,
    Blynken,
    And Nod.

The old moon laughed and sang
        a song,
    As they rocked in the wooden shoe;
And the wind that sped them all
        night long
    Ruffled the waves of dew.
The little stars were the herring fish
    That lived in that beautiful sea;
"Now cast your nets wherever you wish —
    Never afeard are we!"
So cried the stars to the fishermen three:
    Wynken,
    Blynken,
    And Nod.

All night long their nets they threw
    To the stars in the twinkling foam —
Then down from the skies came
        the wooden shoe,
    Bringing the fishermen home;
'Twas all so pretty a sail, it seemed
    As if it could not be;
And some folk thought 'twas a dream
        they'd dreamed
    Of sailing that beautiful sea —
But I shall name you the fishermen three:
    Wynken,
    Blynken,
    And Nod.

487

Wynken and Blynken are two little eyes,
    And Nod is a little head,
And the wooden shoe that sailed the skies
    Is a wee one's trundle-bed;
So shut your eyes while Mother sings
    Of wonderful sights that be,
And you shall see the beautiful things
    As you rock in the misty sea
Where the old shoe rocked the fishermen three:
    Wynken,
    Blynken,
    And Nod.

Eugene Field

THE CATS
HAVE COME TO TEA

What did she see—oh, what did she see,
As she stood leaning against the tree?
Why, all the cats had come to tea.

What a fine turn-out from round about!
All the houses had let them out,
And here they were with scamper and shout.

"Mew, mew, mew!" was all they could say,
And, "We hope we find you well today."

Oh, what would she do—oh, what should she do?
What a lot of milk they would get through;
For here they were with, "Mew, mew, mew!"

She did not know—oh, she did not know,
If bread and butter they'd like or no;
They might want little mice, oh! oh! oh!

Dear me—oh, dear me,
All the cats had come to tea.

Kate Greenaway

THE DUEL

The gingham dog and the calico cat
Side by side on the table sat;
'Twas half-past twelve, and (what do you think!)
Nor one nor t' other had slept a wink!
    The old Dutch clock and the Chinese plate
    Appeared to know as sure as fate
There was going to be a terrible spat.
    (I wasn't there; I simply state
    What was told to me by the Chinese plate!)

The gingham dog went, "bow-wow-wow!"
And the calico cat replied "mee-ow!"
The air was littered, an hour or so,
With bits of gingham and calico,
    While the old Dutch clock in the chimney-place
    Up with its hands before its face,
For it always dreaded a family row.

(*Now mind: I'm only telling you*
What the old Dutch clock declares is true!)

The Chinese plate looked very blue,
And wailed, "Oh, dear! what shall we do!"
But the gingham dog and the calico cat
Wallowed this way and tumbled that,
    Employing every tooth and claw
    In the awfullest way you ever saw—
And, oh! how the gingham and calico flew!
    (*Don't fancy I exaggerate—*
    I got my news from the Chinese plate!)

Next morning, where the two had sat
They found no trace of dog or cat;
And some folks think unto this day
That burglars stole that pair away!
    But the truth about the cat and pup
    Is this: they ate each other up!
Now what do you really think of that!
    (*The old Dutch clock it told me so,*
    And that is how I came to know.)

Eugene Field

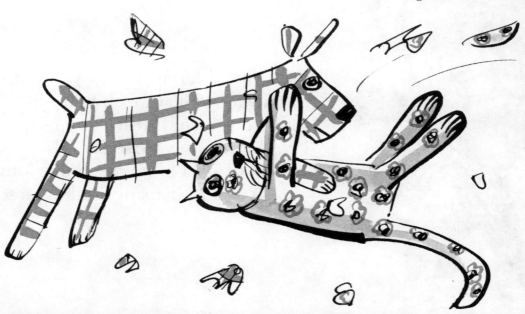

THE WIND

I saw you toss the kites on high
And blow the birds about the sky;
And all around I heard you pass,
Like ladies' skirts across the grass—
    O wind, a-blowing all day long,
    O wind, that sings so loud a song!

I saw the different things you did,
But always you yourself you hid.
I felt you push, I heard you call,
I could not see yourself at all—
    O wind, a-blowing all day long,
    O wind, that sings so loud a song!

O you that are so strong and cold,
O blower, are you young or old?
Are you a beast of field and tree,
Or just a stronger child than me?
    O wind, a-blowing all day long,
    O wind, that sings so loud a song!

Robert Louis Stevenson

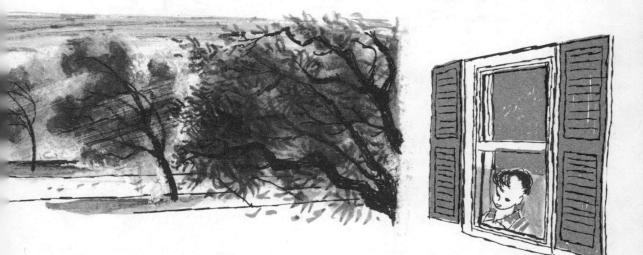

493

THE OWL AND THE PUSSY-CAT

The Owl and the Pussy-Cat went to sea
    In a beautiful pea-green boat:
They took some honey, and plenty of money
    Wrapped up in a five-pound note.
The Owl looked up to the stars above,
    And sang to a small guitar,
    "O lovely Pussy, O Pussy, my love,
    What a beautiful Pussy you are,
            You are,
            You are!
    What a beautiful Pussy you are!"

Pussy said to the Owl, "You elegant fowl,
    How charmingly sweet you sing!
Oh! let us be married; too long we have tarried;
    But what shall we do for a ring?"

They sailed away, for a year and a day,
    To the land where the bong-tree grows;

And there in a wood a Piggy-wig stood,
    With a ring at the end of his nose,
        His nose,
        His nose,
    With a ring at the end of his nose.

"Dear Pig, are you willing to sell for one shilling
    Your ring?" Said the Piggy, "I will."
So they took it away, and were married next day
    By the Turkey who lives on the hill.
They dined on mince and slices of quince,
    Which they ate with a runcible spoon;
And hand in hand, on the edge of the sand,
    They danced by the light of the moon,
        The moon,
        The moon,
    They danced by the light of the moon.

Edward Lear

THANKSGIVING DAY

Over the river and through the wood,
    To grandfather's house we go;
    The horse knows the way
    To carry the sleigh
Through the white and drifted snow.

Over the river and through the wood—
    Oh, how the wind does blow!
    It stings the toes
    And bites the nose,
As over the ground we go.

Over the river and through the wood,
    To have a first-rate play.
    Hear the bells ring,
    "Ting-a-ling-ding!"
Hurrah for Thanksgiving Day!

Over the river and through the wood
        Trot fast, my dapple-gray!
        Spring over the ground,
        Like a hunting-hound!
For this is Thanksgiving Day.

Over the river and through the wood,
        And straight through the barnyard gate.
        We seem to go
        Extremely slow,—
It is so hard to wait!

Over the river and through the wood—
        Now grandmother's cap I spy!
        Hurrah for the fun!
        Is the pudding done?
Hurrah for the pumpkin-pie!

Lydia Maria Child

A VISIT FROM ST. NICHOLAS

'Twas the night before Christmas,
    when all through the house
Not a creature was stirring, not
    even a mouse;
The stockings were hung by the
    chimney with care,
In hopes that St. Nicholas soon
    would be there;
The children were nestled all snug
    in their beds,
While visions of sugar-plums danced
    in their heads;
And mamma in her 'kerchief, and I
    in my cap,
Had just settled our brains for a
    long winter's nap,
When out on the lawn there arose
    such a clatter,
I sprang from the bed to see what
    was the matter.

Away to the window I flew like a
    flash,
Tore open the shutters and threw
    up the sash.
The moon on the breast of the new-
    fallen snow
Gave the lustre of mid-day to objects
    below,
When, what to my wondering eyes
    should appear,
But a miniature sleigh, and eight
    tiny reindeer,
With a little old driver, so lively
    and quick,
I knew in a moment it must be St.
    Nick.
More rapid than eagles his coursers
    they came,
And he whistled, and shouted, and
    called them by name:

"Now, Dasher! now, Dancer! now,
      Prancer and Vixen!
On, Comet! on, Cupid! on, Donder
      and Blitzen!
To the top of the porch! to the top
      of the wall!
Now dash away! dash away! dash
      away all!"
As dry leaves that before the wild
      hurricane fly,
When they meet with an obstacle,
      mount to the sky,
So up to the house-top the coursers
      they flew,
With the sleigh full of toys, and St.
      Nicholas too.
And then, in a twinkling, I heard on
      the roof
The prancing and pawing of each
      little hoof.
As I drew in my head, and was
      turning around,
Down the chimney St. Nicholas
      came with a bound.
He was dressed all in fur, from his
      head to his foot,
And his clothes were all tarnished
      with ashes and soot;
A bundle of toys he had flung on his
      back,
And he looked like a peddler just

opening his pack.
His eyes—how they twinkled! his
   dimples how merry!
His cheeks were like roses, his nose
   like a cherry!
His droll little mouth was drawn up
   like a bow,
And the beard of his chin was as
   white as the snow;
The stump of a pipe he held tight in
   his teeth,
And the smoke,it encircled his head
   like a wreath;
He had a broad face and a little
   round belly,
That shook, when he laughed, like a
   bowlful of jelly.
He was chubby and plump, a right

jolly old elf,
And I laughed when I saw him, in
spite of myself;
A wink of his eye and a twist of his
head,
Soon gave me to know I had nothing
to dread;
He spoke not a word, but went
straight to his work,
And filled all the stockings; then
turned with a jerk,
And laying his finger aside of his
nose,

And giving a nod, up the chimney
he rose;
He sprang to his sleigh, to his team
gave a whistle,
And away they all flew like the down
of a thistle.
But I heard him exclaim, ere he
drove out of sight,
"Happy Christmas to all, and to all
a good-night."

Clement Clarke Moore

Suggested Reading

It should be noted that the ages assigned to these books are only approximations, for reading tastes and abilities of children differ widely.

ABC AND ONE-TWO-THREE

Duvoisin, Roger
Ages 4 to 8
Two Lonely Ducks; A Counting Book. Alfred A. Knopf

Eichenberg, Fritz
Ages 4 to 8
Ape in a Cape, an Alphabet of Odd Animals. Harcourt, Brace

Eichenberg, Fritz
Ages 4 to 8
Dancing in the Moon, Counting Rhymes. Harcourt, Brace

Falls, C. B.
Ages 3 to 6
ABC Book. Doubleday

Francoise
Ages 5 to 7
Jeanne-Marie Counts Her Sheep. Charles Scribner's Sons

Gag, Wanda
Ages 3 to 6
The ABC Bunny. Coward McCann

Ipcar, Dahlov
Ages 4 to 8
Brown Cow Farm. (A Counting Book.) Doubleday

McGinley, Phyllis
Ages 5 to 8
All Around the Town. (ABC.) J. B. Lippincott

NURSERY RHYMES

Bertail, Inez
Ages 4 to 8
Complete Nursery Song Book. (With music.) Lothrop

Brooke, L. Leslie
Ages 2 to 7
Nursery Rhyme Book. Frederick Warne

Brooke, L. Leslie
Ages 2 to 7
Ring o' Roses, a Nursery Rhyme Picture Book. Frederick Warne

Caldecott, Randolph
Ages 3 to 8
Picture Book Number Two. Frederick Warne

Crane, Walter
Ages 4 to 8
The Baby's Bouquet. (With music.) Frederick Warne

Greenaway, Kate
Ages 2 to 7
Mother Goose, or The Old Nursery Rhymes. Frederick Warne

Langstaff, John
Ages 4 to 8
Frog Went a-Courtin'. (With music.) Harcourt, Brace

Lines, Kathleen
Ages 4 to 8
Lavender's Blue; A Book of Nursery Rhymes. Watts

MacKenzie, Garry
Ages 2 to 7
Mother Goose. Crowell

Petersham, Maud and Miska
Ages 5 to 10
The Rooster Crows: American Rhymes for America's Children. MacMillan

Smith, Wilcox Jessie
Ages 2 to 7
Little Mother Goose. Dodd, Mead

ANIMAL FRIENDS

Averill, Esther
Ages 7 to 9

The Cat Club. Harper

Bianco, Margery Williams
Ages 6 to 10

The Velveteen Rabbit. Doubleday

Brown, Margaret Wise
Ages 4 to 8

The Wheel on the Chimney. J. B. Lippincott

Buff, Mary and Conrád
Ages 5 to 9

Dash and Dart. Viking Press

Charles, Robert H.
Ages 6 to 10

A Roundabout Turn. Frederick Warne

Clark, Ann Nolan
Ages 5 to 8

Looking-for-Something. Viking Press

Ets, Marie Hall
Ages 7 to 9

Mister Penny. Viking Press

Fatio, Louise
Ages 4 to 8

The Happy Lion. Whittlesey

Flack, Marjorie
Ages 5 to 7

Angus and the Ducks. Doubleday

Hader, Berta and Elmer
Ages 4 to 8

The Big Snow. MacMillan

Lathrop, Dorothy
Ages 6 to 8

Who Goes There? MacMillan

Mason, Miriam
Ages 6 to 8

Susannah, the Pioneer Cow. MacMillan

Mathiesen, Egon
Ages 6 to 8

The Blue-eyed Pussy. Doubleday

McCloskey, Robert
Ages 5 to 8

Make Way for Ducklings. Viking Press

McGinley, Phyllis
Ages 5 to 8

The Horse Who Lived Upstairs. J. B. Lippincott

Minarik, Else
Ages 5 to 7

Little Bear. Harper

Newberry, Clare Turlay
Ages 5 to 8

Mittens. Harper

Potter, Beatrix
Ages 5 to 8

The Tailor of Gloucester. Frederick Warne

Potter, Beatrix
Ages 3 to 8

The Tale of Benjamin Bunny. Frederick Warne

Robinson, Tom
Ages 5 to 8

Buttons. Viking Press

Sewell, Helen
Ages 4 to 7

Blue Barns, the Story of Two Big Geese and Seven Little Ducks. MacMillan

Ward, Lynd
Ages 5 to 8

The Biggest Bear. Houghton, Mifflin

Will and Nicolas
Ages 5 to 8

Finders Keepers. Harcourt, Brace

BOYS AND GIRLS

Anderson, C. W.
Ages 6 to 8
Billy and Blaze. Macmillan

Aulaire, Ingri and Edgar Parin d'
Ages 6 to 9
Ola. (Norway.) Doubleday

Beatty, Hetty Burlingame
Ages 6 to 9
Bronto. (Cowboys.) Doubleday

Bemelmans, Ludwig
Ages 6 to 8
Madeline. (France.) Simon and Schuster

Beskow, Elsa
Ages 5 to 8
Pelle's New Suit. (Sweden.) Harper

Brown, Marcia
Ages 5 to 8
Henry-Fisherman, a Story of the Virgin Islands. Charles Scribner's Sons

Brown, Marcia
Ages 5 to 7
The Little Carousel. Charles Scribner's Sons

Brown, Margaret Wise
Ages 5 to 7
A Child's Good Night Book. W. R. Scott

Brown, Margaret Wise
Ages 4 to 7
The Dead Bird. W. R. Scott

Clark, Ann Nolan
Ages 5 to 8
In My Mother's House. (Indians of the Southwest.) Viking Press

Clark, Margery
Ages 5 to 7
The Poppy Seed Cakes. Doubleday

Crowley, Maude
Ages 6 to 8
Azor. Oxford

Dalgliesh, Alice
Ages 5 to 8
The Bears on Hemlock Mountain. Charles Scribner's Sons

De Angeli, Marguerite
Ages 6 to 9
Yonie Wondernose. (Pennsylvania Dutch.) Doubleday

Ets, Marie Hall
Ages 3 to 5
Play With Me. Viking Press

Flack, Marjorie
Ages 4 to 7
The Story about Ping. (China.) Viking Press

Garrett, Helen
Ages 5 to 8
Angelo, the Naughty One. Viking Press

Handforth, Thomas
Ages 6 to 8
Mei-Li. (China.) Doubleday

Haywood, Carolyn
Ages 7 to 8
"B" is for Betsy. Harcourt, Brace

McCloskey, Robert
Ages 5 to 8
Blueberries for Sal. Viking Press

McCloskey, Robert
Ages 7 to 9
Lentil. Viking Press

Morrow, Elizabeth
Ages 7 to 9
The Painted Pig. (Mexico.) Alfred A. Knopf

Sayers, Frances Clarke
Ages 6 to 8
Bluebonnets for Lucinda. Viking Press

FUN AND FANCY

Bianco, Pamela
Ages 6 to 8
Little Houses Far Away. Oxford University Press

Bishop, Claire Huchet
Ages 5 to 8
The Five Chinese Brothers. Coward-McCann

Bright, Robert
Ages 5 to 8
Georgie. Doubleday.

Brooke, L. Leslie
Ages 4 to 8
Johnny Crow's Party. Frederick Warne

Brunhoff, Jean de
Ages 5 to 7
The Story of Babar, The Little Elephant. Random House

Burton, Virginia Lee
Ages 5 to 8
The Little House. Houghton Mifflin

Burton, Virginia Lee
Ages 5 to 7
Mike Mulligan and His Steam Shovel. Houghton Mifflin

Daugherty, James
Ages 5 to 10
Andy and the Lion. Viking Press

Du Bois, William Pene
Ages 6 to 9
Lion. Viking Press

Ets, Marie Hall
Ages 4 to 7
In the Forest. Viking Press

Gag, Wanda
Ages 6 to 8
Gone Is Gone. Coward-McCann

Gag, Wanda
Ages 4 to 8
Millions of Cats. Coward-McCann

Gannett , Ruth
Ages 7 to 9
My Father's Dragon. Random House

Gramatky, Hardie
Ages 4 to 7
Little Toot. G. P. Putnam

Grimm, J. L. K. and W. K.
Ages 5 to 8
The Wolf and the Seven Little Kids. Harcourt, Brace

Ivimey, John William
Ages 4 to 7
The Complete Version of Ye Three Blind Mice. Frederick Warne

Krauss, Ruth
Ages 5 to 8
A Hole Is to Dig. Harper

Leaf, Munro
Ages 5 to 9
The Story of Ferdinand. Viking Press

McGinley, Phyllis
Ages 7 to 9
The Plain Princess. J. B. Lippincott

Rey, H. A.
Ages 4 to 7
Curious George. Houghton Mifflin

Seuss, Dr.
Ages 4 to 8
And to Think that I Saw It on Mulberry Street. Vanguard Press

Seuss, Dr.
Ages 5 to 8
Horton Hatches the Egg. Random House

Seuss, Dr.
Ages 6 to 10
The 500 Hats of Bartholomew Cubbins. Vanguard Press

Slobodkin, Louis
   Ages 5 to 7
                               Magic Michael. MacMillan

Slobodkina, Esphyr
   Ages 4 to 8
                               Caps for Sales. Scott, W. R.

TO READ ALOUD

Aesop
   Ages 7 to 10
                               Fables of Aesop. Ed. by Joseph Jacobs.
                                   MacMillan

Anderson, Hans Christian
   Ages 7 to 12
                               Fairy Tales. Oxford University Press

Anderson, Hans Christian
   Ages 7 to 12
                               It's Perfectly True. Harcourt, Brace

Barrie, Sir James M.
   Ages 8 and up
                               Peter Pan. Charles Scribner's Sons

Baum, L. Frank
   Ages 7 to 10
                               The New Wizard of Oz. Grosset & Dunlap
                                   Inc.

Bianco, Margery
   Ages 6 to 10
                               A Street of Little Shops. Doubleday

Carroll, Lewis
   Ages—all
                               Alice's Adventures in Wonderland.
                                   MacMillan

Dickens, Charles
   Ages 8 to 10
                               The Magic Fishbone. Frederick Warne

Grahame, Kenneth
   Ages 8 and up
                               The Wind in the Willows. Charles Scrib-
                                   ner's Sons

Grimm, J. L. K. and W. K.
   Ages 7 to 10
                               Tales from Grimm. tr. and il. by
                                   Wanda Gag. Coward-McCann

Kipling, Rudyard
   Ages 6 to 10
                               Just So Stories. Garden City

Lattimore, Eleanor
   Ages 8 to 10
                               Little Pear. Harcourt, Brace

Lawson, Robert
   Ages 6 to 10
                               Rabbit Hill. Viking Press

Lorenzini, Carlo
   Ages 6 to 10
                               The Adventures of Pinocchio. MacMillan

Milne, A. A.
   Ages 5 to 9
                               Winnie-the-Pooh. E. P. Dutton

Sandburg, Carl
   Ages 7 to 11
                               Rootabaga Stories. Harcourt, Brace

Steel, Flora A.
   Ages 7 to 11
                               English Fairy Tales. MacMillan

Thorne-Thomsen, Gudrun
   Ages 7 to 12
                               East o' the Sun and West o' the Moon.
                                   Row Peterson & Co.

Thurber, James
   Ages 8 to 11
                               Many Moons. Harcourt, Brace

Travers, Pamela
   Ages 8 to 12
                               Mary Poppins. Harcourt, Brace

POETRY

Adshead, Gladys L. and Duff, Annis All ages	*An Inheritance of Poetry.* (Anthology.) Houghton Mifflin
Chute, Marchette Ages 4 to 8	*Around and About.* E. P. Dutton
De la Mare, Walter All ages	*Come Hither.* (Anthology.) Alfred A. Knopf
De la Mare, Walter Ages 7 to 14	*Rhymes and Verses.* Henry Holt
Farjeon, Eleanor Ages 6 to 10	*Poems for Children.* J. B. Lippincott
Field, Eugene Ages 7 to 10	*Poems of Childhood.* Charles Scribner's Sons
Geismer, Barbara, and Suter, Antoinette Ages 5 to 8	*Very Young Verses.* Houghton Mifflin
Greenaway, Kate Ages 5 to 8	*Under the Window.* Frederick Warne & Co.
Lear, Edward Ages—all	*The Complete Nonsense Book.* Ed. by Lady Strachey. Dodd
Love, Katherine Ages 6 to 10	*A Pocketful of Rhymes.* Crowell
Milne, A. A. Ages 5 to 9	*When We Were Very Young.* E. P. Dutton
Richards, Laura E. Ages 7 to 10	*Tirra Lirra.* Little, Brown & Co.
Stevenson, Robert Louis Ages 5 to 9	*A Child's Garden of Verses.* Charles Scribner's Sons

ADULT CHILDREN'S BOOKS

Dolman, John Jr.	*The Art of Reading Aloud.* Harper
Duff, Annis	*"Bequest of Wings."* Viking Press
Eaton, Anne	*Reading with Children.* Viking Press
Fenner, Phyllis	*Something Shared: Children and Books.* John Day
Hazard, Paul	*Books. Children and Men.* Horn Book
Larrick, Nancy	*A Parent's Guide to Children's Reading.* Doubleday (Also Pocket Books, Inc.)
Sawyer, Ruth	*The Way of the Storyteller.* Viking Press

Index of Titles

Index

Index